Dear Readers,

There's nothing like curling up with a good book on a crisp fall evening, and this month we present four new Bouquet romances that are sure to warm your heart.

With Thanksgiving only weeks away, Adrienne Basso's **Sweet Sensations** is a perfect first course in a month full of captivating stories. Adrienne's heroine is a pastry chef who finds that only one man will complete her recipe for love. Next, Zebra and Avon author Jane Kidder serves up a second chance at love in **Heart Song**, when a pianist with a precious secret must face the man she once loved . . . and lost.

Of course, once Thanksgiving draws to a close, Christmas is just around the corner—and this month our authors are inspired by the spirit of the season. Long-time Zebra and Harlequin author Patricia Werner offers the charming tale of a woman in charge of a retirement home who rediscovers her Christmas cheer—with the help of a resident's handsome son—in **Jenny's Star.** And in **A Christmas Bouquet,** three of our favorite authors spread holiday joy. In **"Amy's Gift"** by Suzanne Barrett, a young widow whose children are looking for Santa meets a bachelor who just may fill the bill. Then a Christmas decorating enthusiast and her bah-humbug neighbor clash—passionately—in Kate Holme's **"Merry and her Gentleman."** Last, in Vella Munn's **"Silver Christmas,"** a small-town shopkeeper with contemporary flair meets the handsome, if old-fashioned, man of her dreams.

So build a fire, make a pot of tea, and get ready for the kind of smart, sexy love stories we know you adore.

The Editors

A CHRISTMAS BOUQUET

SUZANNE BARRETT
KATE HOLMES
VELLA MUNN

Zebra Books
Kensington Publishing Corp.
http://www.zebrabooks.com

ZEBRA BOOKS are published by

Kensington Publishing Corp.
850 Third Avenue
New York, NY 10022

First Printing: November, 1999
10 9 8 7 6 5 4 3 2 1

Printed in the United States of America

CONTENTS

AMY'S GIFT

by

Suzanne Barrett

ONE

Amy pressed her foot on the accelerator and a cloud of blue-black smoke spewed from the Jetta's exhaust. Her heart sank. The car had been okay when she and Josh left Park Rapids five days ago, but now, in the middle of California, it was the end of the road for the ten-year-old sedan.

According to the highway sign she'd just passed, Riverton was over the next rise. The engine labored, then coughed. She shifted into low gear and gritted her teeth, willing life into the car. *Please Lord, just a little farther.*

"Mom, I'm hungry. My tummy hurts."

She glanced over at her son. His sky blue eyes, so much like her own, peered out the window and his pale, pinched face made her heart ache. He hunched over in his seat, hands clasped across his belly.

Her heart squeezed. Josh had been so good on the tedious journey out, even though she'd driven ten hours a day since they left Minnesota. He hadn't questioned her decision to leave, even when they'd slept in the car the last two nights and hadn't stopped for lunch today. She'd weighed the pros and cons and decided California had what they both needed—it was as far away from Minnesota as they could get and it held the promise of independence and a job with an old college friend, Clarise.

She crested the hill, and the oil light flashed on. Damn it anyway! They'd never make it to Santa Barbara and Clarise's. She'd have to stop in Riverton and have the car fixed.

She sucked in a breath and let the vehicle coast downhill into the valley. To the right of the road, gentle slopes descended into a grassy meadow where ten or twelve horses grazed. Straight ahead, the little town backed up against the side of the mountain. False-fronted wooden buildings lined the main road through town and a tiny steeple rose amid redwoods. Smoke spiraled up from a dozen chimneys. Amy caught her breath. Riverton looked just like a movie set!

Fifty yards from the town, she crossed a two-lane concrete bridge that spanned the tumbling river. As she approached the traffic signal on the other side, the car belched. The light turned green and she coasted on through, angled right onto a side street, and pulled her car and its small U-Haul trailer off the road.

"Mom, can we please eat now? Please?"

Amy switched off the ignition and closed her eyes. She had exactly thirteen dollars and twenty-seven cents. Not enough to get them a motel room for the night, and not enough to get the car fixed. She stole a glance at her son, noted his wide-eyed gaze, and let out her breath. But she sure had enough for a hamburger!

They'd eaten mostly cold cereal and sandwiches to extend her meager finances on the trip west. Josh had never complained. If the situation in Park Rapids hadn't been so unhealthy for the two of them, she might have delayed leaving. As it was, she had to face facts. If she was going to take charge of her life now that Jonathan was dead, build a life for Josh and herself, then she had to leave the senior Wilsons' household. Josh was her first priority. He didn't deserve to suffer. She flashed him a smile. "What do you say we find a restaurant?"

"I say yes!"

She locked the Jetta and marched down the road to the main street, Josh at her side.

The town nestled among redwoods and pine trees. A block away from the main street, water gurgled over the river's rocks. They passed Doyle's gift shop and the bank, where a round clock hung in the window, its hour hand pointing to three. Next came the hardware store. A red-haired man straightening garbage cans in front of the building stopped and grinned at them. "Afternoon. Nice day."

"Yes, it is," Amy answered. Despite the car problem, it was a beautiful sunny afternoon. Back in Park Rapids they'd be expecting the first snowstorm. Thank God she no longer had to worry about shoveling snow!

A Dalmatian on a red leash tugged an elderly woman along. When the dog paused to sniff Josh's trousers, the woman fell in beside Amy.

"Don't mind Buster, he's just curious," she explained with a smile. "He likes kids."

"We're looking for a restaurant," Amy said.

"You can't do better than Cassidy's. Right here."

"Look!" Josh pointed to the weathered wood building directly in front of them. "Bet they have hamburgers in there!"

Amy studied the place. Lace curtains hung over the lower half of a picture window; across the upper half was emblazoned Cassidy's. Beneath the window sill, crimson chrysanthemums cascaded over a green planter box.

Amy grinned. "Bet they do, too. C'mon." She turned to the older woman. "Thank you."

"Enjoy your lunch." The woman tugged her dog's leash and set off down the street.

Amy watched her disappear around the corner. Friendly sort of place. Small-townish. A real contrast with Park Rapids.

Inside, she steered Josh to a table next to the window. On the wall behind him hung an old bridle and a pitchfork. A nice touch, appropriate for a country cafe. A galvanized milk can propped open the back door.

A harried-looking man wearing a green canvas apron plopped two menus on the table. "Be with you in a minute." A *Help Wanted* sign stuck out from under his arm. He edged around Amy and taped the sign in the window. A moment later, he reappeared with two glasses of water and fumbled for his order book.

"Two hamburgers and two fries," Amy told him. He tramped back to the kitchen and Amy glanced about the room. The spotless cafe appealed to her sense of order.

Eight tables filled the small room; each had fresh flowers in tiny ceramic vases. The wooden plank floors shone with a mellow patina. An elderly man sat at a corner table reading his newspaper, a coffee cup beside him. In another corner, a woman ate alone, gazing idly at a notepad between bites. Amy's throat tightened. *So simple, and so peaceful.*

The waiter brought their hamburgers. Josh tore into his as if it were his last meal. Amy bit into hers more slowly. Delicious. Cooked just right, with tomato, pickle, onion, and lettuce, the fries light and crispy. The Dalmatian lady was right. Food didn't get much better than this.

"Gee, Mom, this place is nice. Why do we have to go to some other town?" From over his half-eaten hamburger, Josh's blue eyes pleaded. "Couldn't we just stay in Riverton? I'm tired of driving."

"I'm tired, too, honey. But we have to go where I can find work. I have a job waiting in Santa Barbara."

He pointed to the window. "That sign says they need someone right here. And besides, you said something's wrong with the car."

Josh was right about the car. The Jetta wasn't going anywhere without an overhaul, but without money, she couldn't afford to have the car repaired. She needed a job *now*. She hadn't waited tables since college, but so what? The place was inviting, the food good.

Maybe Riverton was a fortuitous stop. It certainly beat living with Jonathan's parents. His death had made them even more demanding. For three years, she'd tried to build a life for herself and Josh, but her in-laws made it impossible. They tried to make all the decisions, even what school was best for her son.

She looked over the cafe once more and her tension eased. The homey atmosphere exuded a warmth she hadn't felt in months. Here in tiny Riverton she might find a new start.

An instant later, she found herself stepping toward the cash register, where their waiter shuffled through receipts. "I'd like to speak to the owner, please."

The fiftyish man gave her a tired sigh and shoved a wisp of silver hair off his forehead. "You're looking at him."

Amy's heart thumped. Out of the corner of her eye, she saw the old man look up from his newspaper. The woman in the corner stared at her with interest.

She took a fortifying breath. "I'd like to apply for the waitress job."

The owner adjusted gold wire-framed glasses a fraction higher on his nose and peered at her. "You new in town?"

"We arrived today."

The cafe owner rolled his eyes. "Had any experience?"

Amy paused. "When I was in school."

"Watcha been doing since?"

Goodness, but he was direct! She clasped and unclasped her hands. "I worked in an office."

"Kinda odd, you wanting a waitress job, isn't it?"

Desperation made her pulse pound. Suddenly she wanted this job. Wanted it very much.

She squared her shoulders. "I'm dependable and trustworthy. And I need a job." She swallowed. She needed *this* job.

"That your boy?" the man asked, directing his gaze at Josh.

Amy nodded. A band tightened around her heart. Josh needed a safe nest as much as she did.

He thought for a minute. "Sure don't look like transients," he muttered under his breath. "When can you start?"

Amy's gaze darted to her son and back. "Tomorrow." If she could find a place to spend the night.

"The shift's ten till four. You get lunch and a salary." Again he peered across the room at Josh, who was sopping the last of his French fries in a pool of ketchup. "Got a place to stay?"

Amy gave him a tight smile. "I'll find one."

"Try the Shady Nook. Cottages by the river . . . 'bout three blocks down. Owner's Ed Merton. Tell him Dave sent you."

Fifteen minutes later, Amy picked her way along redwood round steps leading to the Shady Nook office, one of a half-dozen tiny cottages set back from the road. The door stood ajar. A rusty screen, loose on its hinges, shielded a cluttered office. She knocked.

"You the lady Dave sent?" a tenor voice called from inside. A second later, a ruddy-cheeked man of uncertain age appeared. "He called," he explained. "Said you needed a place to stay."

He grabbed a ring of keys from the wall and pushed

the screen door open, then offered a chubby hand. "I'm Dave's brother-in-law, Ed Merton. I'll show you what I have."

He took her to the last cottage in the lane. It stood in a thick grove of redwoods, and tree needles and debris covered the yard. Wood shingles hung loose from the siding and rats had gnawed the door frame. Amy's heart sank. After the comfort of Cassidy's, the Shady Nook was downright grim.

Inside, though, was a cozy bedroom and an alcove off the breakfast area for Josh. An apartment-sized propane stove filled the dingy kitchen, and a stone fireplace covered one wall in the tiny living room.

"It's been vacant for six months," Ed explained. "But I'd let you have it cheap if you cleaned it up." He named a price.

She barely hid her dismay. The cottage was reasonable enough, but filthy. It would take weeks of work to make it livable. But she'd run out of options. She had no money, but she did have plenty of time.

She took a deep breath and faced the owner. "I'll take it, Mr. Merton. But I can't pay you until next week."

"I can live with that." He plodded over to the stove, struck a match and lit the pilot light. "Propane tank's full."

Thank God for little miracles. At least she could cook.

An hour later, Amy and Josh unloaded the small U-Haul. By nightfall she had swept out the mouse droppings, set a trap under the kitchen sink, scrubbed the porcelain, and moved their suitcases inside. Her back ached like a knife was wedged between the vertebrae.

After Josh fell asleep, she hung two sheets over the bare windows and pulled on her long flannel nightgown. Then she rummaged in a box of kitchenware for her electric teakettle, filled it, and brewed herself a cup of Earl Grey. She never dreamed she'd end up in a rat-infested hovel without decent heat.

Lowering herself onto a wooden crate in the living room, she inspected the drab walls. The room smelled like it needed a good scrubbing. A fire in the fireplace would help, too. Moonlight filtered through a hole in the roof. She let out a sigh. That would need fixing soon. When it rained. . . .

Hell's bells! She couldn't think about it now. For three years she had struggled to be free, to break away from her overprotective parents and her disapproving in-laws. She stared at the gap in the roof, the bleak, unadorned walls. *And now that I have, my real struggle is just beginning.*

"Damn you, Jonathan." She swallowed over the lump in her throat. "Damn you for dying!"

Outside the November wind howled. She rubbed her cold arms, took a swallow of hot tea, and straightened her spine. It could be worse, she thought. She should count her blessings. In one afternoon she'd found a job and a place to stay.

She felt like a fish out of water. A strange town, new job, people she didn't know, and a run-down summer cottage to fix up. She was scared to death. But she had to make it work.

TWO

"More coffee?" Amy poured a stream of fragrant liquid into Ben Peterson's cup. In the two weeks Amy had worked at Cassidy's, she'd gotten to know the regulars. Old Ben tottered in each day at one and read his newspaper until four. Sometimes he ordered a slice of apple pie, but mostly he just read and listened to the banter around him. He was lonely.

Dolly Samuels worked for Myra Templeton and had a weakness for fudge brownies. Geno, who owned the Riverton garage, liked his chili extra hot. Myra herself dropped in every noon and ordered a chef's salad with bleu cheese dressing—and two peanut butter cookies, which she wrapped in a napkin and carried back to her accounting office. Amy listened to each of them and remembered some detail for the next time they stopped in.

Then there was that McHugh fellow. Something about the man gave her butterflies each time she saw him. Dave said he managed the ValuKing where she shopped. He was tall, with reddish-brown hair, the greenest eyes she'd ever seen, and a grin that slammed into her middle.

She bit back a laugh. The first time she'd seen him, she slopped chili over the rim of the bowl and nearly scalded Geno's shoulder with the fiery concoction. The tall man definitely had a face one would remember, if one were inclined—which she certainly was not. Right now, a man was the last thing she needed, even one as good-looking as what's-his-name McHugh.

She spent every spare minute fixing up the cottage. Ed Merton cleaned the chimney and brought over a box of scrap lumber so she and Josh could have a fire at night. She taped a sheet of plastic over the hole in the roof and scrubbed every trace of dirt from the walls and floors. Then she and Josh jockeyed the blue denim-covered sofa she'd brought with her into the tiny living room. The unbleached muslin curtains from her bedroom in Park Rapids now hung over the narrow living room windows, shielding her from the street.

Monday she enrolled Josh in second grade at Riverton Elementary. The small one-story school sat on a corner, facing a sleepy side street. A large supervised playground stood between the concrete block structure and the ValuKing supermarket. Josh could play there until she got off work.

Ben stood up and folded his paper under his arm. "Guess I'll mosey on down the road."

The clock on the wall read one-thirty. "You're leaving early."

"Got to. The Grey Bears are meeting at the town hall today. Gonna make plans for the annual Christmas dinner." He puffed out his thin chest. "Shay's been elected to the town council, and since he's chairin' the food drive, we're bound to be busy."

"Shay?" Amy repeated. Whoever the guy was, he'd better not ask too much of Ben. The frail old man had more grit than strength. A thread of apprehension snaked through her.

"Yep. Wouldja look?" Ben swung around to the cafe door. "That's 'im now."

The door opened and Mr. McHugh strode in. "Ben. How's it going?"

"Can't complain. Nossir. Just now headin' over to the hall."

"See you there," Shay called to the old man's retreating figure. He looked at Amy and gave her a grin. "Where's Dave keeping himself?"

Amy stomach lurched. "He's back in the kitchen. Can I get you something?"

He looked her over her with a gaze that stopped her heartbeat. A long moment passed between them.

"Another time. I'll find him myself." He brushed past her and strode into the kitchen.

Amy stared after him. Good looking didn't come close to describing the store manager. What was his name—Shay? Heat crawled up her neck, and she let out her breath in a slow stream.

Tight-lipped, she snatched up Ben's cup and saucer and clattered them into the dirty dish tray, then wiped the Formica table. If McHugh turned up the sex appeal another notch, she'd have to splash cold water over her face.

She tossed the sponge into a basin of sudsy water. She didn't need that kind of complication in her life— didn't need *any* man in her life, good-looking or not.

So why was she thinking about him?

Because she was lonely. But, she reminded herself, she was also leery of involvement. She knew love led to heartbreak.

At five till four, she walked over to the playground to meet Josh, and the two of them walked home through a wooded area, collecting pieces of downed limbs to burn in the fireplace.

She made potato soup and cornbread for dinner, then curled up on the sofa with Josh and read him the tale of Peter Rabbit. Embers glowed in the fireplace. If it wasn't for her desperate financial situation, she'd feel almost content.

When Josh went to bed, Amy pried the lid off the gallon can of paint Ed had dropped off and stirred it with a stick. *A man like Shay McHugh probably has a wife and four children.* She dipped her paintbrush into the can and spread Sunny Yellow over the wall above the sink in short, even strokes. *Men like him don't stay single.*

Stop thinking about him, she ordered herself. Her own marriage had taught her a lot of things, mainly that she wasn't going to repeat the experience.

"What's the verdict?" Amy faced Geno over the grease-blackened counter in his small auto shop office, waiting while he tallied a column of numbers. A Willie Nelson song pulsed from a CD player; the sound of a pneumatic drill droned above the music.

The burly mechanic ran his fingers through his thinning hair. "Engine's got a lot of miles on her. Lessee, if we just do rings and valves . . . be a lot cheaper."

The sum he mentioned made her stop and think. Anything was too much at the moment, but she didn't relish the thought of Josh tramping through the rain and mud to get to school each day. She glanced down at her sludge-spattered brown oxfords. It had sprinkled last night and left dozens of puddles. "I can't pay for the work right away. Maybe the week after next."

"No problem. I've got the valve cover off—we'll leave it until I get some time."

As usual, Amy set aside half her tips for the car repair and used the rest to buy groceries.

"Mom," Josh pleaded in the supermarket that afternoon. "I'm tired of potato soup. Can't we have stew or something with meat in it?"

Amy examined the contents of her shopping cart—a

bag of russet potatoes, half a dozen carrots, three yellow onions, eggs, bread, leaf lettuce, and a head of cabbage. She had splurged on two cubes of butter and a jar of strawberry jam for Josh's morning toast. Could she afford another extra? Josh was growing and he needed more nourishment. She wheeled the cart to the meat case and picked up a one-pound package of beef stew meat. She'd make it last for three meals.

"Don't forget cat food," Josh reminded.

How could she forget? Yesterday Josh had found a little ball of gray fur hunkered under the ValuKing dumpster. "Please, can we take it home?" he had asked. She'd refused at first, but when he'd looked up at her with round eyes and told her the lost kitten story they'd heard at school that day, she hadn't the heart to refuse.

She tousled his hair. "There are three cans of liver and chicken just for Sam."

"What if Sam turns out to be Samantha?" Josh asked.

We'll cross that bridge when we come to it. "I hope to God it's a Sam."

She reached down to the bottom shelf and hefted a two-pound box of powdered milk into her cart. "I think we're done. Let's check out and go home."

A smiling black-haired young man stood at the cash register. Pete Alfonso, his name tag read. He'd checked the other day when she'd shopped for household cleaners. Josh had taken to him right away, blurting out his name and where they lived. He'd even told the man his father was dead.

"Getting settled, M-Mrs. Wilson?" Pete slipped a second bag inside the first and began placing her purchases inside.

"Still fixing it up, but yes, we're getting settled." She counted out her change and dropped the exact amount in his hand.

"Need some help out to your car?"

"Our car's broken," Josh supplied. "We have to walk."

Pete's eyes flashed. "I'm sorry to hear that."

"It's no problem," Amy said quickly, giving Josh a prod beneath the counter. "Josh and I enjoy the exercise." She looked hard at her son. "Don't we?"

Josh scraped the floor with one foot. "Guess so."

Amy shouldered her shopping bag and pushed Josh along ahead of her. She'd have a word with her son. He couldn't keep telling everyone about their difficulties. Nice as Pete Alfonso might be, she didn't want the world to know she was widowed and struggling. It was her business and hers alone.

The next week flew by. Amy finished painting the kitchen and above the tiny window she hung a yellow checked valance she found at the Goodwill. It matched the checked gingham tablecloth she'd brought from Minnesota. For Thanksgiving, she roasted a hen and made Josh's favorite sage stuffing. This morning she had tucked the last of the slices of meat into a sandwich for his lunch.

Now, as she slipped into the nearly empty cafe, Dave eyed her curiously.

Her chest tightened. On Tuesday, Josh had told her he couldn't stay on the playground until four o'clock, so she'd left work early to meet him at the supermarket. Twice Dave had seen her leave, and she guessed what was on his mind.

"Got a minute?" he asked. He pursed his lips and looked at a spot beyond her. "You've been leaving early."

"I have to meet my son at school."

"I appreciate that," Dave said evenly, "but I have a business to run. I need help that sticks around until closing." He fidgeted with his hands. "I'm gonna have to hire someone else."

Amy's breath caught. What on earth was she to do? She needed this job! "I—I could . . ." She closed her mouth. She couldn't think of a thing she could do.

"Sorry," Dave said. "I've got to let you go."

Amy's stomach churned. She poured coffee for Ben Peterson and dished up an extra hot portion of chili for Geno, all the while considering her options. At the moment, it didn't look like she had any.

THREE

When Myra Templeton sat down for lunch, Amy hadn't the heart to even try to be merry. Two more days and she'd be out of a job.

"Chef's salad with bleu?" She knew the answer, just didn't know what else to say.

"Not today," Myra said. "This isn't one of my better days. I think I'll have something different." She took the menu Amy handed her, scanned it, and slapped it down on the table. "The New York steak, medium rare. Bad news deserves a steak."

She glanced up at Amy. "You look as though you need a steak, too."

Amy flinched. "Steak would be nice, but what I really need is a job."

"What's the matter with this one?"

She explained about Josh and Dave's letting her go.

Myra peered intently over the rim of her glasses. "There are restaurants in Beechwood advertising in the paper."

"Beechwood is ten miles away and I have no car. I'll have to find something in Riverton." The no-nonsense accountant didn't need to hear about the Jetta's rings and valves.

Myra harrumphed. "This is the only place in town."

"I'll find something." She stepped to the kitchen and

called in the order. Myra was right. What else could she do in Riverton?

Ten minutes later, she set Myra's steak on the table. "Would you like steak sauce?"

Myra sat with her knife and fork poised in the air. "Do you type?"

"I was an office administrator back in Minnesota."

"Glory be. I knew it! Pardon me for saying it, but you don't look like a waitress any more than I do." She patted the chair beside her. "Sit down."

Amy glanced around the room. Dave was in the kitchen.

"Conscientious type. That's good." Myra leaned closer. "Fact is, Dolly quit today. That's why you haven't seen her. She walked in, bold as you please, said she'd decided to move to San Jose, and then walked out just like that. Left me with five clients waiting in the office."

Myra folded her hands on the table. "I can offer you a part-time job as office manager. You could leave in time to pick up your son." She named a salary twice what she was making at the cafe.

Amy struggled to hide her elation. *God's in His heaven, and all's right with the world.*

Myra tented her long fingers and fixed Amy with a direct look. "What do you think?"

Her heart pounding, she squared her gaze with the older woman's. "I think you just hired yourself an office manager."

"Shay McHugh, you're too soft by far!" Prudence Packwith's iron gray curls bobbed on her head like tiny springs.

Shay stared at his sharp-nosed store detective. On most days, Pru maintained peace and order in his grocery store, but whenever she got on his case, it meant trouble. Like now. He flinched as Pru's eyes snapped.

"The primary cause for loss in a store like ValuKing is shoplifting."

"Calm down, Pru. You know we don't get much of that in Riverton."

"Not much of it?" Her voice ratcheted up a notch. "We don't want *any* of it." She steepled her hands under her pinched face, her black eyes fixed on him with particular brilliance.

In the six years he'd been manager at ValuKing, Shay had made an honest effort to be attentive to the concerns of his staff. But Prudence Packwith, the chain's newly appointed loss prevention officer, was fiercely determined to stamp out even the hint of crime. He'd listened to her rant for the past fifteen minutes about every transgression possible in a store like his. Now he found his attention wandering.

"It's happening right under your nose," Pru said in a waspish tone. "What are you going to do about it?"

Shay took a deep breath. "What do you want me to do?" He turned his gaze to the video monitor focused on the variety aisle, where a tow-headed boy gazed with unusual intensity at gold-foil-wrapped boxes of chocolates. The boy looked to be seven or eight, small, with metal-framed glasses and a shock of wheat-colored hair that fell over his forehead. Shay had seen him there the day before, alone, and staring with particular fascination at that same two-pound gold foil box of assorted chocolates. "So he's been in twice before. All he does is look."

"I saw him pick up one of the boxes and shake it."

No doubt Pru meant well, but she tackled her task too aggressively to suit him. Thank God she only worked his store on Tuesdays and Fridays. He shrugged his watch from under his shirtsleeve. Two forty-five. He had just enough time to make his rounds, then join the meeting at the town hall.

His heart warmed at the thought. As chairman of this year's community food drive, he'd already managed to surpass all previous years' canned good donations. Soon his committee would pack the baskets for needy families in the Valley. That was the part he enjoyed most.

Miss Packwith cleared her throat.

"Look, I'd rather not jump to conclusions," he told the middle-aged spinster. "I'll just keep an eye on the boy."

Miss Packwith huffed. "It's your store. Don't say you weren't warned." She snatched up her handbag and stalked out of the office, her brown oxfords clumping noisily down the stairs.

Shay let out a pent-up breath. Most days he enjoyed his job. Running a grocery store took thought and perseverance, and he liked the chances it gave him to help people. His own frugal upbringing made him all the more determined to support the food banks. That's why he'd run for a seat on the town council.

He focused on the three wooden plaques hanging on the wall above his desk. Public service commendations. That was the way it should be in a small town like Riverton. People helping each other. He remembered the glow in old Ben Peterson's eyes at last year's annual Grey Bears Christmas dinner. The old man had said it was the best Christmas he'd had in years. That's what Shay worked hard for. He loved Riverton, loved its small town atmosphere. Helping its citizens made him feel satisfied.

He was eternally grateful the district office hadn't stuck him in a big city like Sacramento or San Jose. Now that he'd finished remodeling his riverfront house, he was anxious to rebuild the dock and get his powerboat ready for launch next summer. These projects and his civic duties made him a busy man. In fact, they filled his life.

Filled it, but did not make him completely happy. Something was missing.

He glanced once more at the video monitor. The boy had gone. Cute little kid. Odd that he'd come in three times in as many days alone, but he seemed well-mannered. Shay smiled. A man would be proud to have a son like that. The truth was, he wished he had a family of his own.

Not much chance of that here in Riverton. He knew all the young women. Nice, but no sparks—except for the new waitress he'd seen a couple of times at Dave Cassidy's. She'd been something.

He sifted through the papers on his desk until he found his employee evaluation sheets and scribbled a name in the block. Maybe he'd take that cruise Dave mentioned the other day—do him good to get away for a couple of weeks. Who knows, a Caribbean vacation, maybe a shipboard romance. . . .

He shelved the idea as soon as he thought of it. He didn't want to leave Riverton at Christmastime. Riverton surpassed all the Valley towns when it came to decorations, and he enjoyed being a part of it. Now that he was on the town council, he had a say in what they did. In fact . . . his thoughts trailed off as he tried to concentrate on the evaluation.

"Hey, Shay." Pete Alfonso poked his head inside the office doorway. "Wouldja take a look at the produce display?"

"Be right there." Shay scrawled a note on the form, then flashed a grin at his assistant. He glanced again at his watch. He'd better get off his duff and finish checking the end caps in each department while he was at it, or he'd have to come back after the council meeting.

He shoved the evaluation folder in a drawer, straightened his tie, and strode down the stairs.

At the end of the produce aisle, Pete had made an eye-catching pyramid of avocados. Nearby sat a clear plastic holder with free recipe cards for guacamole dip. Avocado prices were up, and they hadn't sold well. He reached over and fingered two on the top of the stack. In their softened state, they wouldn't keep long, either. A reduced price and a free recipe. Quick thinking on Pete's part. He'd bet they'd sell out by tomorrow.

Pete stood by, waiting for him to comment. "Looks good to me," Shay said after he scanned neatly stacked tables of apples, oranges, and grapefruit. "You've done a great job, as usual." He shifted his gaze to his assistant. Pete Alfonso was twenty-eight, five years younger than he. But Pete had four kids and another one on the way. He worked hard and deserved the praise he got.

"How's Monica?"

Pete laughed. "Big as a house. If we didn't know better, we'd say it was twins." He ran his fingers over his olive-skinned chin and the stubble of new beard. "You coming to the party? Monica'd be real disappointed if she didn't have you to rave over her lasagne."

Shay chuckled. "I'd be disappointed if I couldn't be there to rave. Week from Saturday, right?"

Pete nodded. "I've been meaning to tell you we got shorted again—an entire board of paper. Must be a run on at the warehouse. Here," he handed a clipboard to Shay. "I highlighted the code numbers on the invoice for you."

Shay scanned the printout. It wasn't unusual, especially at holiday time, for the warehouse to send fewer pallets than ordered. He thrust the clipboard back into Pete's hand and gave him a friendly jab on the shoulder. "You know what to do. Call Bill and tell him we'd better have a full shipment next week or heads will roll. You done with the load?"

"Yeah. Santos is throwing the last board of water now."

Shay gazed around the aisles and started toward the dairy section. "Good. I'll go check out the rest of the displays."

"See ya, boss." Pete positioned another avocado on top of the pyramid.

Amy shoved the last file into the steel drawer beside her desk. Everything up to date until tomorrow. She glanced at the closed door leading into Myra's office, where the older woman conferred with the owner of the bookshop two doors down. It was only December tenth, and already she'd booked appointments for Myra through March. If the upcoming tax season proved as demanding as the current business, she'd be hard-pressed to finish her office work and still collect Josh on time when he got out of school.

She glanced at the clock above the file cabinets. Two-forty-eight. Time to go.

She ran a comb through her short-cropped hair and threw on her worn but serviceable blue corduroy jacket. "I'm leaving now," she called to Myra.

Amy stepped outside. A pale sun shone through the stalwart row of Douglas firs that lined Riverton's main street. One block away, taller redwoods and a few sparse-needled knobcone pines marched up the mountainside. It was the scene she looked forward to each day as she made her way to the school. The crisp pine-scented air added to the small town's charm.

Amy drew a deep, exhilarating breath and set a brisk pace toward the corner crosswalk and Josh. They'd lived here only a month and already she loved the place, so different from Park Rapids and the flat Minnesota plain.

Last week, all the shops had begun decorating their windows. Mr. Brody's toy store, next door to Myra's small accounting office, featured a display of Steiff bears seated around a green tree with miniature candlelights and a blanket of cotton snow. Clusters of red and green glass ornaments in random trios decorated the "snow."

At Johnny's Java House, a string of tiny white lights outlined the picture window. Each pane had mounds of fake snow sprayed in its lower corner, and mistletoe tied with bright red ribbon streamers hung in the doorway. A squishy stuffed Santa sprawled in a bistro chair next to the tiny round table in the window, enjoying a latte with an enormous black and white panda. Amy smiled in spite of herself. Santa had arrived while she'd been at work.

She crossed the street and headed toward the supermarket. She didn't like to leave Josh waiting too long. Riverton seemed safe, but Josh was only seven and small for his age. Thank goodness she'd found Myra Templeton! Not many employers would allow her flexible hours, and she certainly couldn't afford child care.

A gust of wind lifted her hair as she rounded the corner. Shivering, she turned up her collar.

Josh sat on the bus bench in front of the market, a denim backpack at his side. "Hi, Mom."

Amy caught herself just as she was about to hug Josh. Last week he'd informed her guys didn't hug their mothers in public. She suppressed a smile at his grown-up demeanor.

"How was lunch?" Tuesdays and Fridays were hamburger days at the cafeteria. She'd managed to budget her extra change so he could buy his lunch those two days.

An odd expression crossed his face. "Okay, I guess."
He gave her a grin. "But you make better ones."

"Do you want me to pack a lunch on Friday?"

"Nope," Josh answered determinedly. "I need to eat
a hamburger."

Amy stared at her son. That was an odd way to put
it, but she let it pass. They strolled along the sidewalk
toward the town square. Two workmen in a cherry
picker strung colored lights in the branches of the
Nordmann fir in the town square, while two others anchored bright red bows around each of the twelve
streetlights.

"Know what?" Josh tugged on Amy's sleeve. "I wish
we could have a tree this year."

A band tightened around Amy's heart. Her finances
were stretched to the limit, and just yesterday Geno had
found a burned valve. "I wish we could, too, honey.
Maybe next year."

Josh kicked at a stone and focused on the sidewalk.
"You said that last week."

Amy clamped her mouth shut and allowed herself a
moment before answering.

"Sometimes life doesn't seem fair, does it?" She
paused where the pavement ended, and they waited for
the cross traffic before continuing along the roadside.
"I know it's hard for you to understand, but I have to
pay for the car repair before we can spend money on
extras."

Josh darted a backward glance, then slipped his hand
in Amy's. "I know, Mom. It's just . . ." His voice trailed
off, and he gave her a smile that cut deeper than if he'd
burst into tears. He was so brave, so accepting. Jonathan
had been like that, too, but his needless heroics had
cost him his life.

"Know what, Mom?" Josh said as they came to the
dirt lane that led to their cottage. "My friend Tony is

having a Christmas party at his house. Least his parents are. He said I could come."

Amy stopped at the mailbox and retrieved three envelopes. Two bills and a letter from Jonathan's parents, who no doubt wanted Josh to spend next summer with them. She shoved them into her shoulder bag to be read with a fortifying cup of tea.

"Could I go to Tony's for the party? Huh?"

"I'll see, honey. I'll have to talk to his mother first."

They made their way to the cottage set among the redwoods. Cool in the summer, no doubt, but downright cold in winter. But the price had been right, And when she built a fire and dished up bowls of vegetable soup from the crockpot, it seemed quite cozy.

Amy unlocked the front door and they stepped inside. Josh dropped his book bag on his bed in the alcove off the kitchen. "Can I have a bowl of soup now?" he asked. "I'm kinda hungry."

Goodness, but Josh's appetite had picked up of late. Amy stared at the boy. His pant legs barely met his socks. His jeans couldn't have shrunk; she'd bought them at the Goodwill, and they'd no doubt seen many washings. He'd grown two inches since last summer.

She dished up a bowl of vegetable soup for him and buttered a slice of day-old whole wheat bread. While he ate, she switched on the electric kettle, settled herself in the straight-backed kitchen chair Ed Merton had given her, and opened the letter.

We assume Josh will come for the summer as usual. Impossible. She knew what they wanted. They'd take over, just as they had ever since she'd married Jonathan. They hadn't thought Josh measured up then, and they wouldn't approve of him now.

With a hand that shook, she poured boiling water over a peppermint teabag. He wasn't going, and that was that. For one thing, she couldn't afford it. For another, Josh didn't need their veiled hostility or their criticism, and she didn't want their charity any longer. She'd manage somehow.

The second envelope was a bill from Bauman's Racing Motors in Duluth. They had not received the December payment on the new engine Jonathan had bought before he was killed.

She took a sip of the hot tea and sighed. At this rate, she would never catch up. The engine work on the Jetta would have to wait.

FOUR

Shay shoved the last of the employee reviews into an envelope and sealed it, then dropped it in the canvas mail pouch. As he straightened, he looked down at the candy aisle. The tow-headed boy was back again.

He checked his watch and smiled. Yep, two-forty-five. Same time as yesterday and the day before. Out of the corner of his eye, he spotted Miss Packwith bearing down on the lad. Her look spelled trouble.

He raced down the stairs toward the candy aisle seconds ahead of her.

The boy picked up the foil box and examined the coins in his hand. "Hey, you!" Prudence shouted from behind a candied fruit display.

The boy whipped around, his face white. Like lightning, he stuffed the box inside his windbreaker. For a split second, Shay hesitated, then made his way down the aisle.

At that moment, a petite blond woman headed down the aisle on the other side, followed by Miss Packwith. The ferocity on his store detective's face sent a shiver down Shay's back.

He elbowed his way among the shoppers and reached the boy just ahead of Miss Packwith. His gaze fell on the shelf where the chocolates had been. In the empty space lay four crumpled bills and some change.

Shay scooped it up. He had to think quickly. Pru would not accept that the boy had left the money as payment. In her opinion, there was no such thing as a purchase without a receipt.

The boy spun toward the blond woman. "Mom!" Then he pivoted and flashed Shay a stricken look.

Shay's heart twisted. He clapped his hand on the boy's shoulder. "Young man, I'd like you and your mother to come to my office." He tried to ignore the startled expression in the young woman's eyes.

Miss Packwith pulled up short, bewilderment written on her pinched face. Shay tried not to smile. He'd snatched her suspect from right under her nose.

Inside his office, he closed the door and pulled out chairs for the boy and his mother. "Don't worry, things aren't as bad as they seem." He turned to the boy. "What's your name, son?"

"His name is Josh," the woman said. "Please tell me what is going on." She thrust out her chin and raised her gaze to his.

Shay made a lengthy perusal of the young woman.

Wait a minute! She was the waitress from Dave's. And stunning, even in her confusion. He allowed himself a good look at her short, silvery-blond hair. Below her jacket, navy leggings outlined slim, sexy legs. Her wide-set gray-blue eyes looked frosty enough to put icicles on the office heater. Her lips were generous, but not too full, and except for lipstick, she wore no makeup, as far as he could tell. His stomach did a queer little flip-flop.

He tore his gaze away from her long enough to gather his thoughts. "It's not what you think, Mrs.—"

She didn't offer her name, so he went on. "That's why I rescued him from Miss Packwith."

The woman looked uncomprehending. "Our loss

prevention officer," he added. "She's a bit of a dragon." He turned to Josh and grinned.

"The chocolates were for Mom's Christmas present," Josh murmured in a somber voice. He pulled the box out from his windbreaker and thrust them into Shay's hand. "Only—only now it's not a surprise."

"Josh!" exclaimed his mother. A shadow passed over her perfect features. "It was a nice thought, honey. But you can't just take things."

"It's all right," Shay broke in. He drew out the money Josh had left and laid it and the chocolates on his desk. "His intentions were honest." He gave the woman a reassuring smile. "No harm done. He paid for his purchase, after all."

"But—" the woman spluttered.

He tore his gaze away from her long enough to look at Josh. "He's been choosing that present for days, haven't you, son?"

The woman eyed the coins on his desk. "But how—where did you get the money?"

Josh scraped the floor with one shoe. "I—I saved my lunch money."

The color drained from her face. "So that's why you've been so hungry at night! Oh, Josh." She closed her eyes for a long moment, then stared at the floor. Finally, her gaze met Shay's. "We always meet here after school. I work part-time and the ValuKing is near Riverton Elementary. But I never thought—"

"Mom," Josh said, "I—I just wanted you to have a *real* present. Other moms get presents, but now that I don't have a daddy any more, there's only me." His voice quavered.

Color flamed in the woman's cheeks. "Josh!" She turned to Shay. "I'm sorry. My husband died three years ago. I'm afraid Christmas hasn't been very special for Josh since then."

Shay's chest tightened. He found himself wanting to protect this vulnerable young woman and her son. He handed the chocolates to Josh. "Here, son. They're yours."

The boy's mother rose from the chair. "Thank you for helping my son, Mister"—she eyed the brass name tag on Shay's shirt pocket—"McHugh. We'll be going now." She grabbed her son's hand and drew him toward the door. "Come along, Josh. We've taken up enough of this man's time."

"Mom, I've got a rock in my shoe, and it's a long walk home. Can I take it out first?"

The woman nodded, and the boy slipped off his sneaker. Shay noted the sole was worn through.

"Look, Mrs. . . ." When she did not supply a name, he plunged on. "I was just leaving myself," he lied hastily. "Let me drop the two of you off at your house."

"No, thank you. We're used to walking."

From his office doorway, Shay watched the two of them head down the stairs. At the bottom stood Prudence Packwith, who flashed him a dark look. Shay waited until Josh and his mother slipped out the front entrance door and turned left on River Road. Then he turned his gaze to his store detective.

Prudence glared up at him. "You should have let me talk to that boy."

"No problem. He'd paid for the candy." He stepped back inside his office and shut the door.

Long after the woman and her son had gone, Shay found himself thinking about them. That boy had skipped his school lunches so he could buy his mother a gift. Shay's throat closed. Remembering how it had been in his own poverty-stricken childhood, it took him a moment to regain his composure.

The woman had seemed defensive. Prickly. But in his six years in Riverton, she was the most beautiful creature he'd seen. Where had she come from? Intrigued, he headed down the stairs to find Pete building a holiday display in the beverage section.

"Hey, Pete. Got a minute?"

The dark curly head turned. "Yeah, boss? What's up?"

Shay glanced around to make sure they were alone. "Did you notice that blond woman with the little boy who just left my office?"

Pete grinned. "Sure did. She's a looker, that one." He bent to his display and started stacking jars of Tom and Jerry mix.

"Well?"

"Well, what?" Pete focused on Shay.

"Who is she? What do you know about her?"

"Name's Amy Wilson. She's been in town 'bout a month. She lives in one of Merton's dilapidated summer cottages on Acorn Road. I suspect she's pretty hard up."

"How's that?"

"Well, she only buys basics and stuff that's on sale." He leaned toward Shay, and his voice lowered. "I cashed a payroll check for her once. Signed by Myra Templeton. I guess she must be the new gal Myra hired to take Dolly's place. You'd think she'd be able to afford decent groceries."

Shay stepped back and eyed Pete's display. A plan began to take shape in his mind, one he chose to keep to himself.

"Yeah, well, thanks. I was just . . . curious." He circled to the right and viewed the end cap from a different angle. "Nice work here."

Shay set off down the canned goods aisle, spot-checking the shelves of soups and sauces. Amy Wilson, he thought. Nice name. Even nicer face and figure, definitely worth a second look. On the short side, though.

At five-eleven, he was no giant, and her head came up only to his chin.

He righted an overturned can of tomato sauce, turned down the end aisle, and cast a look at the deli. Potato salad, coleslaw, and tortellini salad with fresh basil sat in shiny stainless bowls. Evening shoppers on their way home from work would deplete the offerings in no time.

Fran, his deli clerk, set a platter of freshly sliced roast turkey breast beside a tray of pepper-topped sirloin slices, temptingly moist and pink. "Hi, boss."

Shay nodded. The deli was known throughout the valley for quality food. He rubbed his chin with one forefinger. Something in that woman's proud eyes tugged at him. Something elemental. He wasn't sure why, but he knew he needed to see her again. He cast another look at the food in the deli case.

Does Amy Wilson like roast beef or turkey?

"Mom," Josh yelled into the bedroom. "Someone's here."

Amy switched off the vacuum cleaner and followed her son to the front door. Probably Jenny from across the road, wanting another cup of sugar.

She opened the screen and stopped dead in her tracks. Good heavens! It was the ValuKing manager who'd rescued Josh this afternoon. Shay McHugh, that was his name. Her heart thumped. What on earth was he doing here?

"Hello, Mr. McHugh. Is something wrong? I thought we'd cleared things up earlier." Goodness, but his eyes were gorgeous. Up close he was truly handsome. He stared at her in a way she found disconcerting. She swallowed and felt herself growing warm under his perusal.

His arms clasped around a brown paper shopping

bag, the manager gave her a sheepish smile and kept on looking. "Don't worry. I, uh, happened to be in the neighborhood and thought you'd like some items from the deli." He shifted the bag toward her.

Amy stiffened and jerked her gaze from his mesmerizing eyes. A tight band coiled around her chest. He *just happened* to be in the neighborhood? Ha! "I don't believe you for one minute. We're not that easy to find."

He clamped his lips together and looked away for a second. "You're right. I drove out specifically to see you and Josh. I'm sorry about today, really sorry. I wanted to make amends, so I brought some things from the deli."

He held out the bag, but she kept her hand on the door frame. *Why is he doing this?*

"I came because I wanted to see you again," he said. He blew at a shock of red-brown hair that flopped down on his forehead, then returned his gaze to hers.

Amy's pulse pounded. "So you brought food? You needn't concern yourself over our welfare."

"I wanted—want to see you."

"I'm afraid I don't understand."

"Do you not accept visits from men, either?"

Amy felt herself flush. "Is that what this is?'

"Yeah, that's what this is."

"Oh. I—well, I . . ." Tongue-tied, Amy let her voice trail off. She didn't know what to say. It had been so long since she'd even thought about a man she'd forgotten the conversational buzzwords. She'd even forgotten to be polite! Inside she felt warm and fuzzy; outside she felt threatened and short-tempered—like a bear coming out of hibernation.

FIVE

Amy's breath caught. He had the sexiest voice, a warm baritone that rolled over her like honey on a June day. He seemed honest and sincere, and she respected that. If she were truthful, she'd admit she rather liked him. More than a boy-next-door type, this man seemed the genuine article in a world of fakes, and she'd seen plenty of those. His approach was a bit unorthodox, but . . . despite her attempt at suppression, a smile escaped.

"This bag is getting heavy," he said finally. "Could I set it down somewhere?"

"I guess so, sure." She opened the screen door and led the way to the round oak table between the living area and the kitchen. "I'm sorry, Mr. McHugh. I . . . we don't often get visitors, and I—"

She stopped mid sentence as she glanced at the contents of the bag. "Oh, my! So much food. Way too much food for just two of us." Heat crept into her cheeks, but she forced herself to look him square in the eye. "Mr. McHugh, thank you for your kindness, but I will only accept this if you share it with us."

What made me say that? The idea of sitting across from this man with the fascinating green eyes set her pulse hammering. He made her think about candlelight, mulled wine by the fireside . . . romance.

As quickly as the thought surfaced, she pushed it aside. She had no interest in romance.

A dazed expression spread over Mr. McHugh's handsome face.

"Of course, you probably have a million things to do—"

"Actually," he broke in, his voice low, "I'm free tonight." He shut his mouth suddenly, as if he'd said too much, and focused on Josh.

Her son tugged on his sleeve. In a barely audible voice, Josh whispered, "Please, oh, please?"

Crinkles formed at the corners of the store manager's green eyes. He flashed her a crooked smile. "If that's an invitation, I'd like very much to stay."

Amy studied her visitor. Deep red highlights glinted in the thick hair curling over his collar. He had an eagle-beak nose that must have been broken at one time, and a golden tan.

He gestured toward the bag. "I wasn't sure what you liked, so I got a little of this and a little of that."

Amy lifted a bottle of California Riesling out of the bag, then a square, foil-covered aluminum container. She peeked inside at slices of roast beef and turkey. Tortellini salad filled one plastic container, another held coleslaw, a third roasted vegetables. At the bottom of the bag nestled a flat box. Four pieces of apple strudel!

Amy took a deep breath. "I don't know what to say, Mr. McHugh."

"Shay."

Josh danced a little jig around the table. "Say, 'thank you,' Mom! That's what you always tell me to say." He lifted the foil, his gaze riveted on the sliced meat. "Can we eat now?"

Amy had to laugh. There was nothing subtle about Josh. "In a bit. Go feed the cat, then wash up."

He skipped toward the kitchen, and Amy pulled her attention back to Shay. "Have a seat while I set things up. Would you like some wine?"

"Why don't we both have a glass? And I could help— if you'd let me."

"Mister, you just found yourself a job." She eyed him once more, drawn to his affable nature in spite of her resolve. But, she reminded herself in the next moment, she wasn't in the market. She wouldn't be interested in a man ever again, and that was that.

Amy whisked the deli containers off the table and set them on the cracked tile counter in her small kitchen. Then she pulled three printed cloth napkins from one drawer and pointed to the one above it. "Silverware's in there. So's the corkscrew."

Good Lord! She hardly knew the man, and not only had she invited him to dinner, she'd ordered him to set the table! With shaking fingers, she lifted three plates down from the cupboard. *Get a grip on yourself, girl. He's only a man, a nice guy.*

When she reached for the wineglasses, they clinked together dangerously. She placed them on the counter without mishap and poured apple juice into one for Josh. *Jonathan had been easygoing and likable, too. Once.* She leaned against the edge of the sink. Perhaps if she counted to ten . . . She took a deep breath, spun around, and bumped into Shay's hard chest.

"Easy, now." He grasped her shoulders to steady her.

Heat from his hands radiated through her blue knit sweater clear up to the crown of her head. "Sorry. This kitchen is impossible." Her voice sounded odd.

He gave her a probing look and very slowly removed his hands. "Cozy's a nicer word," he responded in a low tone.

He curled his fingers around the bottle of Riesling and splashed the pale gold wine in the glasses. "How about a toast?" His fingers brushed hers, and a warmth spread into her belly.

"To new friendships."

She sipped her wine, then spooned the salads into serving dishes, her mind racing. *I can't believe I'm doing this. We've barely met and I'm acting like a giddy teenager.*

By the time she slid the meat slices onto an oval platter and the vegetables into a dish, Shay had set the table and topped their glasses. He moved about her kitchen with ease.

She took a steadying breath, called Josh from his room, and they sat down to eat.

Shay took a helping of everything and waited until she had served herself. Josh dug right in, but she ate little, aware of Shay's watchful expression. He was so handsome he made her heart flutter. She found herself staring at his mouth, the lower lip a bit fuller than the upper. A sensual mouth, she decided.

Then there were his hands—the way his long, tapering fingers curved around his fork. Sensitive hands. Her pulse quickened.

Dancing with him, being held by those purposeful hands . . . *Stop thinking about it!*

In less than ten minutes, Josh had cleaned his plate. He stood up, sheer contentment written all over his face. "Thank you for bringing the yummy food."

Amy's heart sang. Count on Josh to say the right words.

Shay forked a bite of turkey and paused with it halfway to his lip. "I think it's the company that makes the meal." He slid his gaze to Amy.

A weightless feeling enveloped her that had nothing to do with the glass of wine she'd drunk. She got to her feet, then reached for Josh's plate. "Would you like coffee with the strudel?" She didn't trust herself to look directly at him. All through dinner he'd made her think things she had no business thinking—for instance, how nice having dinner with a man could be.

"Sure, if it's no trouble."

"No trouble." She stacked the plates and made her way to the sink. "Have a seat in the living room and I'll make the coffee. Josh, you may have your dessert at the table." Without waiting for his answer, she switched on the electric kettle.

Shay eased himself onto the denim-covered sofa. A fringed burgundy throw lay across one rounded arm, and a pair of soft printed pillows invited him to settle deeper. He studied the room. The cottage itself was a tumbledown affair, but the furnishings spoke of a different lifestyle in a different place. For the second time that day, he wondered where she had come from.

She'd cobbled together bricks and boards to make bookshelves along one wall. Above them hung a still life in oils, its heavy gold-leafed frame contrasting with the unfinished pine boards. He glanced at the books. *Les Miserables, The Count of Monte Cristo, Ulysses, Dr. Zhivago, Breathing Lessons,* and a few Ellis Peters mysteries. Skewed on the end of the top shelf lay *The Horse Whisperer.* Quite a mix.

A dark red wing chair sat at right angles to the sofa. A distressed pine chest that served as a coffee table, a floor lamp, an artist's easel, and a Persian rug comprised the rest of the room, which wasn't much bigger than the entry at his home. Despite the cheap pine paneling and worn wood floor, she'd achieved a simple but homey look. Judging by some of the furniture and the dinnerware, though, she was used to nicer. He found himself more intrigued than ever. What was she doing in a small, out-of-the way place like Riverton?

She brought in the coffee and strudel and set the dishes down on the chest. While she poured the coffee, he stood and walked over to the easel. The watercolor

was only half finished, but he recognized Loch Lomond.

"Did you do this?"

"I dabble. I'm not terribly accomplished."

"I'd say you were *very* accomplished." He reached for
the coffee and took a sip. Strong and black, just right.
She knew how to make coffee. "Very accomplished,"
he repeated. He settled on the sofa and studied her
pale blue eyes, inhaled her fresh lavender scent. She
was not only sexy but wholesome.

"Mom," Josh called from the table. "I'm done. Can
I watch TV?"

Amy sent her son a quick look. "You may watch until
eight o'clock, then time for bed. Keep the volume low."

"Okay. Good night, Mr. McHugh." The boy scampered toward an alcove. A moment later, Shay heard
the familiar theme of "All Creatures Great and Small."

Amy sank into the wing chair. Her gaze flitted from
one object to another before resting on him.

"No coffee for you?" he asked.

"No, it keeps me awake at night. I have one cup in
the morning."

Shay sipped the coffee and again found himself staring at her. He liked the way she curled into the chair,
one foot tucked under her. He just plain liked her. *He'd*
like to be what was keeping her awake at night.

She had on a patchwork pullover sweater in shades
of blue that matched her snug-fitting denims. She wore
no jewelry, and he'd bet money she was a natural
blonde. He liked that, too.

Their gazes locked, and she gave a tense laugh.

"What's funny?"

"You. You seem preoccupied." She tented her fingers
beneath her chin. "I was just thinking about how dull
this must be for you. You've hardly said a word."

But the things I've been thinking! Shay took a healthy swallow of his coffee and nearly choked. "It's anything but dull," he got out at last. "I'd like to ask lots of things, but I wasn't sure you'd—I don't want to seem nosy."

Her eyes darkened. "You can ask," she said, her voice strained. "I might not answer, of course."

Shay's chest tightened. *Careful, buddy, you're treading in deep water.* She seemed strung so tight one wrong word could snap her.

"You're new to Riverton."

"Josh and I came out from Minnesota in October. My parents still live there."

"That explains your coloring. Norwegian?"

"Swedish."

"You sure blow my theory that all Scandinavians are tall."

She stiffened in the chair. "I have five brothers, all over six feet. I'm the runt of the litter, but I'm sure you don't want to hear—"

"But I do! I'm an only child myself," Shay said, desperate to keep the conversation going. "It, uh, must be wonderful to be part of a large family."

Her eyes flashed. "Sometimes. But with five burly brothers, I grew up overprotected."

"Is that why you came to Riverton? To get away from that?"

"Partly." She clung to the arms of the chair, her back rigid. "There were other reasons, too."

Her look told him she didn't want to talk about it. In fact, she didn't seem to want to talk at all.

He tried a new tack. "You were widowed," he said.

Her face became expressionless, and she stared at the wall. "My husband died three years ago this Christmas," she said in a clipped tone. "A car racing accident."

"I'm sorry," Shay murmured, at a loss for words. How did he manage to bring up all the wrong subjects? He hadn't been this tied up in knots since high school!

She moved her gaze to his. Her eyes looked sad. "It wasn't a marriage made in heaven."

Shay set his cup down as a bolt of joy warmed his chest. He should feel sympathy, but the news her marriage was not happy had the opposite effect. He realized he wanted her to be free!

He struggled for something to say. "Josh . . . uh, Josh seems to be a brave little boy."

"Jonathan was . . . gone . . . a lot before the accident. Josh was so young he doesn't remember what it was like to have a dad."

"So after he died you came out here?"

"I came out here," she said simply. She brushed back a strand of hair and stared at the coffeepot.

"I, uh, see you like to read."

A rare smile lit Amy's face. "Oh, yes, I do. Every chance I get. But I'm starting an advanced computer class at Beechwood College and homework takes up my free time."

"Computer class." He pointed to the coffee table. "That your textbook?"

She nodded but said nothing.

"I hear you work for Myra Templeton. Great gal, Myra."

"Isn't she? She lets me schedule my own hours so I can meet Josh after school and get to my morning class." She straightened her leg and moved to the edge of her chair. Shay had the distinct impression she was poised to flee at any moment.

The clock chimed eleven. "Good grief, I didn't mean to stay so late." He shot her what he hoped was a suitably apologetic look. In truth, he'd enjoyed every minute of the evening except for one thing. She was as edgy as a politician under investigation.

Whenever he asked a question, she squirmed like hell or clammed up. She went to school, painted, made do on an obviously limited income. She was a pretty independent lady, and she made sure he knew it. He'd really like to see her again, but her self-sufficient, I-don't-need-you attitude was discouraging.

He rose from the sofa and moved to the door. To hell with her independent streak! He had to see her again. He felt the pull clear through to his bones.

"Every year in Beechwood, there's a Dickens Christmas Faire," he heard himself say. "Would you and Josh like to go? It's great fun for the little kids—for the big ones, too."

She stood beside him, and he saw her catch her lower lip between her teeth. Suddenly, he had an uncontrollable urge to kiss her.

"Please say yes."

Her eyes grew luminous. He sensed a struggle within her, and his throat closed.

Finally, she gave him a tremulous smile. "No, thank you."

Shay tamped down his disappointment and flashed her a brief smile. "Well, anyway, thanks for the evening."

Amy stood at the sink, dishcloth in hand. For Josh's sake, maybe she should have accepted the invitation. Shay McHugh was nice.

Too nice. For some reason, that scared the bejesus out of her.

She'd struggled for three years to gain control over her life, to find peace of mind and independence after Jonathan died. She wasn't about to risk getting knocked off balance by an extremely good-looking man with an attractive face and nice manners.

She let the water drain out of the sink and hung the dishcloth over the rack. But Josh was just a child; he needed a little Christmas spirit in his life. Maybe they *could* go to the fair. Sure, they could take the bus! Yes, she'd pack a lunch and they'd have a day of fun in Beechwood. Her chores could wait.

She eyed two juicy apples in the fruit basket. After all, it was Christmas.

She carted the wooden kitchen chair over to the cupboard. Planting both feet on the rickety seat and steadying herself, she seized her thermos from the top shelf.

She'd manage just fine without Shay McHugh.

SIX

Amy set a bowl of hot oatmeal in front of Josh, then punched down the toaster. "Don't dawdle. We have to catch the bus in forty minutes."

He yawned and finger-combed his tousled hair. "It's Saturday. Where are we going?"

She slathered strawberry jam over the toast, sliced it in two, and slid one half onto the plate beside his cereal bowl. She bit into the other half, washing it down with coffee. "Beechwood."

"Do I have to go?" Josh asked between spoonfuls of cereal.

"There's a fair. I thought you'd like to see it."

"A fair?" His eyes grew round. "With cows and horses?"

Amy drained her cup and began clearing the dishes. "Probably men and women in costumes, maybe a puppet show, Christmas decorations, that sort of thing."

"Like the ones in Mr. Brody's toy store?"

"I suppose so."

Josh loved to moon over that store window. At least twice a week he begged to walk by Brody's so he could see if the good-natured proprietor had changed his window display. Josh grew particularly wistful as he studied each detail of the HO gauge train setup circling the display. He commented on every new boxcar, the trestle, even the miniature water tank.

A lead weight settled in her heart. Her brothers had all had trains when they were growing up. If only she could afford one for Josh.

But it was impossible in her present situation. She might as well wish for the moon. She pressed her lips together.

"Why couldn't we go to the fair with Mr. McHugh? I heard him ask you last night."

Amy groaned. "You were supposed to be asleep."

"I got up to get a drink." He bit into his toast and chewed for a moment. "Mom, don't you like Mr. McHugh?"

"No," Amy said too quickly.

"What's the matter with him?"

"Nothing." *Everything.* "He is . . . very nice." *He is gorgeous.* "I just think we need to go by ourselves, not take up his time."

"Bet Mr. McHugh knows all about fairs." Josh sighed, scraping the last of the cereal onto his spoon.

Amy locked her thoughts away and faced her son. "Get into your clothes."

"Mom." Josh's expression turned thoughtful. "I think Mr. McHugh is really nice."

A knot formed in her chest. Yes, he was. She knew that. She was protecting herself. She had to. "Five minutes and we leave."

Fifteen minutes later, they stood at the River Road bus stop, Josh brightly visible in his yellow slicker. Amy frowned up at the gray cloud cover. A pale sun had shone earlier, but now rain threatened. She adjusted the strap of her shoulder pack. Inside she'd tucked her collapsible umbrella, a thermos of hot chocolate, two apples, and a half-dozen peanut butter cookies. The thing weighed a ton.

A green four-by-four squealed its tires as it rounded the bend in the road. "Watch out," Amy cautioned.

Josh jumped back just in time to miss the shower from a roadside puddle.

She glanced at her watch. *Where is that damned bus?*

Another car, a white Porsche, streaked toward them. The driver glanced their way, then skidded to a stop fifteen yards beyond the bus stop. He backed up slowly until he drew alongside, then leaned over and opened the passenger door.

Josh's eyes lit up and he bounded over. "Mom, it's Mr. McHugh!" He flashed the man an eager smile. "We were just talking about you, weren't we, Mom?"

Amy groaned.

Shay's eyebrows rose. "I'm not sure I was meant to hear that, Josh." He kept his gaze on Amy.

Her pulse raced, and she swiped at a lock of hair. "I was just—"

"Mom's taking me to the fair," Josh blurted before she could finish. "We're waiting for the bus."

Under the heat of his gaze, Amy's tongue seemed welded to the roof of her mouth. "Josh needs . . . that is . . . I felt the experience would be good for him," she managed. Her cheeks flamed, but she refused to turn away.

Shay's eyes darkened. "Get in."

"Wow, really?" Josh's eyes grew as round as saucers. He danced on one foot, then the other.

Before Amy could think of an appropriate refusal, Shay had shoved the bucket seat forward, and Josh was clambering into the impossibly small rear compartment.

Shay flipped the seat back and waited, his eyes never leaving her face.

Amy gritted her teeth and stepped toward the waiting car. She'd been outmaneuvered this time, but she wouldn't let it happen again. She eased herself onto the black leather seat and shut the car door. Turning, she made sure Josh's seat belt was secured.

He flashed her an impish grin.

Shay reached across her lap and snapped her own seat belt in its clasp. His forearm brushed her thigh, and she drew in a sharp breath. Needles danced along her spine.

He shoved the car into gear and peeled away from the curb. His Adam's apple bobbed; she could tell he wanted to say something. She might just as well clear the air before they got too far.

"I thought about the fair last night and decided you were right. Josh needs to be involved in more activities, so I thought . . ." She glanced over at Shay and saw only his profile. She couldn't tell what he was thinking. Probably wondering why she'd refused the invitation. "If you'd rather not have us along—" Her mouth was full of cotton.

"I invited you, didn't I?" He kept his eyes on the road, but his voice sounded amused, and she relaxed a trifle.

"Yes, but—" A thought struck her, and she broke off. "Were you on your way to the fair?"

"I am now." He gave her an appraising look. "Look, there's no need to explain. It doesn't matter how or what. Let's just enjoy the day."

Relief washed over her. If he was angry, he hid it well. "Yes, let's."

The person she least expected to see today was the man beside her. In one way, he was the *last* man she wanted to see. In another way . . . her heartbeat quickened.

She didn't want to think about it. One thing she knew for certain: despite living a solitary life the last three years, she wasn't immune to a man's charms. Especially this man's!

Oh, boy. She'd admitted it. Now she had to make sure he never, never guessed.

Shay parked under a covered enclosure two blocks from the Beechwood downtown area. "Beechwood's got a covered shopping mall, so if it decides to rain, we won't get drenched."

Josh chattered away like there was no tomorrow, but Amy seemed thoughtful. Uneasy. Damned if he could figure her out. Friendly one minute, frozen the next. Last night he'd left her place more disturbed than he cared to admit. He wanted to show them a good time at the faire. Then when he'd seen them at the bus stop, he almost ran off the road.

He turned off the ignition, climbed out, and opened her door. Josh scampered out of the tiny rear seat with the boundless energy of a seven-year-old. He grinned in spite of himself. Gray skies notwithstanding, this looked like the start of a capital "I" interesting day. Prickly or not, he liked Amy Wilson. He also reacted to her in the most elemental physical way. Whether that was wise, he didn't want to think about.

The mall had been transformed into a Victorian village. Booths lined the covered expanse. At one, painted blue with red and gold banners fluttering from its top, two puppets whacked each other to the delight of half a dozen youngsters crowded around.

Josh tugged on her sleeve. "Mom, look. Why are they fighting?"

Shay broke in. "That's a Punch and Judy show. They always argue."

Josh stared a moment longer at the squabbling puppets, then focused his attention on a display of wooden soldiers at another stall.

As they strolled the length of the mall, Josh oohed

and aahed at decorated windows. Amy admired the costumed staff wearing muffs, fur caps, and 1840s dress.

Shay loved watching her face. When she broke into
a smile and dimples formed, he wanted to dip his
tongue into them.

Josh darted ahead, careening in and out of the
throng. "Stay with us," Amy cautioned.

But Josh was off again, looking at everything. At one
window, he stopped and pressed his nose against the
glass.

Shay stepped behind him. "What's so interesting?"

A model train circled the display area, which had
been elaborately crafted to resemble an Old West town.
The sweeper engine belched steam, and miniature people went in and out an electronic station. Tiny stone
boulders had been positioned on either side of the oval
track, and a wooden water tower stood at the approach
of the cardboard town. The pretty little village looked
a lot like Riverton.

"You like that?" Shay asked.

"Man, oh man," Josh murmured against the glass.
"It's the best train I ever saw." He turned to his mother.
"That's what I want. When we get some money, I mean."

A shadow passed over Amy's features. "I'll keep it in
mind."

"That train," Josh went on, "is even better than the
one at Mr. Brody's."

Amy gave the boy a stern look. "We'll talk about it
later."

"Aw, Mom." Josh thrust out his lower lip.

Shay fished in his pocket for a twenty and handed it
to Josh. He pointed to a street vendor standing beside
a bright red wooden cart. "That fellow's selling mince
tarts. Why don't you get us each one?"

Amy jerked to attention. "I packed a thermos of hot
chocolate."

Shay strode over to the vendor. "Add two mulled wines and a hot cider to that order." He carried the steaming cups back to a small round table, and Josh followed with the miniature pies.

"We'll indulge in your mom's hot chocolate after we finish these." He grinned at Amy.

She frowned. "But I brought cookies."

"Save them for another time. At a Dickens Faire, one should have tarts." He settled back and pretended not to see the annoyed look on her face. When she captured a crumb on her lip with the tip of her tongue, it was nearly his undoing. Even eating she looked sexy as hell.

After their snack, Shay ushered them through a maze of revelers. Father Christmas, carolers, Scrooge, and Tiny Tim snaked through the crowd, greeting everyone they met. Laughter and cries of "Merry Christmas" rang over carols sung by a school choir.

"Oh, look!" cried Amy. She stared at a group of hoop-skirted ladies and top-hatted gentlemen. "Fezziwig's Dance Company," she breathed.

Couples began to sway to a waltz. Shay circled Amy's waist and drew her into the crowd of dancers. "Not typically Dickens, but I expect he'd join in if he'd had the chance." He closed his hand over hers, leading her into the steps, but she stiffened.

"No, please. I'd rather not."

"C'mon, Amy. You get to have fun, too." He couldn't strike out three times in a row with this woman. He had to do *something* right.

After a moment, she fell in step with him, then hesitated. "Josh?"

"Is five feet from your backside, taking in the dancers, the costumes, and us." He spun her around. "Looks like he approves."

Her cheeks reddened. Aha! At least she wasn't immune to him. That was good. Or was it? He splayed his fingers across her back, pulling her closer. Her head came just to his chin, but they fit perfectly as they moved around the dance area. God, her hair smelled good. Clean, like rosemary and lavender.

She missed a step, and they collided. For an instant her breasts pressed into his chest, then she backed away.

Heat settled in his groin. He made a conscious effort to concentrate on the music.

When the music ended, they broke apart. Shay felt a queer surge of loneliness. He waited for another tune, but none started.

"Mom!" Josh exclaimed. "You looked real nice out there. Prettier than those other women."

"Josh!"

Shay bit back a laugh. Josh had a candor he found refreshing, if disconcerting. He'd bet money she'd have a word with the boy when she got him home. "Don't be too hard on him," he whispered. "He only said it because it's true."

This time she turned beet red. "The two of you are impossible!" Her smile was quavery, but it gradually warmed until her eyes sparkled. He felt his chest tighten. He liked it when she smiled. "How about that hot chocolate?"

He led them to the mall center, where a circular built-in bench stood. They sat down and Amy rummaged in her pack, then poured out two cupfuls, sharing hers with Josh.

A harlequin-costumed juggler stepped into the center ring, lofting four, then five juggling sticks. As the crowd gathered, Josh moved closer to watch the nimble figure.

Shay sipped his chocolate, watching the boy, then Amy. "He's very inquisitive. Nice kid."

Amy set her cup down beside her. "He's interested in so many things. He keeps me on my toes."

"Must be hard raising him by yourself."

The light in her eyes faded. She screwed the lid back on the thermos. "I'm managing. It's not always easy, but we get by."

"I'd like to get him something as a souvenir of the faire."

A frown creased her forehead. "I'd rather you didn't. I want Josh to understand that gifts have to be earned."

Good Lord. She was as complicated a bundle of opinions as he'd seen. "Where I come from, a gift is a gift. It's not something you earn." He gave her a long, hard look. "What's your objection to my getting him something?"

Her eyes turned a softer shade of blue. "Why would you want to do this?"

He expelled a gust of air. "I never had brothers or sisters to get things for. It's something I'd like to do for Josh. There are no strings attached."

"Look, Shay. I do the providing for Josh and me. It's important to me."

"It's important to me, too. Don't spoil my fun, Amy."

She thrust her hand out in a gesture of acquiescence. "All right. If you want to get him some small token, I won't object. Nothing extravagant, though."

Shay considered her words, then strode over to Josh. "C'mon, guy." They set off toward the toy store. "Wait right here," he called over his shoulder. "We'll only be a minute."

Ten minutes later, they returned, Josh clutching a brown paper bag. "Mom," he chortled. "Mr. McHugh got me a water tower!"

Shay stepped up behind the boy. "For the train."

Amy jumped to her feet. "But Josh doesn't have a train set."

"I know. It'll give him something to work toward."

Her look told him she was thinking of a rebuttal. One he probably wouldn't like. *Hellfire, what am I supposed to say now?*

"Uh, I'm hungry. How about dinner?" he blurted. *Damn it, that wasn't what I wanted to say. I'll scare her off!*

"Both of us," he added. "All of us, I mean."

A long minute passed, and she continued to stare at him.

"Even choosy mothers have to eat," he managed to get out. "And I don't accept refusals."

She stared a moment longer, then the corners of her mouth lifted into the ghost of a smile. "That would be nice."

SEVEN

Shay opened his mouth and abruptly closed it. Just when he thought he had Amy figured out, she turned around and surprised the hell out of him! He wanted to whistle, but settled for a secret smile.

They walked toward the parking lot, Josh skipping ahead. She leaned closer and muttered under her breath, "That water tower is no trinket. You pressed your advantage."

Shay allowed his smile full rein. "Yes, ma'am. 'Tis the season." He ignored her barbed look. The way Josh beamed was worth a dozen barbs. In fact, putting that smile on Josh's face made him feel warm all over.

Dusk had fallen by the time they reached the Riverton road. Amy settled against the seat back and watched the oncoming headlights, an endless line of cars with wreaths and ribbons decorating the grilles. The faire had been a treat for Josh—for her, too, though she hated to admit it. She'd intended to keep her distance from the attractive man beside her, but as the day went on, she'd found it impossible.

When he'd danced with her, held her in his arms, her body had responded with a fire she thought had been quenched years ago—as exhilarating as it was disturbing. She snuggled deeper into the seat, a curious sense of peace battling her nervousness.

Five minutes later, Shay pulled the car up in front of a fancy steakhouse. An elaborate rooftop sign read "DelNorte."

Amy tensed. She'd never been in the place, but it didn't take any brains to see the DelNorte was expensive. If Shay McHugh thought she'd go along with a posh dinner, he was mistaken.

"I said okay to a meal, but I didn't mean anything fancy. Maybe some place that's . . . plainer. She hated to use the term "cheaper."

He lifted one eyebrow. "You don't like steak?"

Amy watched a well-dressed couple alight from a Mercedes and stroll toward the restaurant's carved oak door. "I don't feel comfortable having you spend a lot of money on us. I—we . . . don't know each other that well."

Shay slanted her a smile. "Okay, let's get to know each other better. *Then* we can eat steak." He leaned back in his seat, feigning self-defense. "Sorry, only kidding."

"You know what I mean," Amy said.

"Yeah, but I like to watch the way your mouth curves when you become discombobulated."

She gasped. "I don't!"

"Yes, you do. You look cute."

Warmth spread through her belly. Instinctively, she clasped her arms around her waist.

He made a U-turn in the parking lot and headed back toward Beechwood. Half a mile down the road, he pulled the Porsche up at Monte's Roadside Cafe, a green building with a flat roof. "This plain enough?"

Amy peered through the plate glass window. Formica tables, paper placemats, college students in jeans waiting tables. "It looks perfect."

Shay rolled his eyes. He helped them out of the car

and led them inside. He motioned to a corner booth, then seated himself after Amy and Josh had slid in.

The vinyl was cold, but the place looked cozy and clean. A Carpenters' tune echoed over the clatter of dishes. *He said I look cute.* She shoved the thought to the back of her mind. She wouldn't think about it now. In fact, she wouldn't think about Shay McHugh at all.

A redhead with untidy curls slapped three plastic menus down in front of them. "What'll it be?"

Amy looked at Shay.

He shrugged. "I haven't been in for a while, but the fish and chips used to be good."

"I love fish and chips!" Josh declared.

"That sounds fine for me, too." Amy turned her attention to the decorated Christmas tree in the window.

Shay gave the order.

"Hey, Shay," a voice rang out.

Amy looked up to see Pete from the ValuKing making his way toward them. A pretty, dark-haired, very pregnant woman walked beside him, followed by a boy about Josh's age. They halted in front of the booth.

"Thought you didn't come here any more," Pete joked.

Shay looked nonplussed. "I . . . made an exception."

"Mom!" Josh exclaimed. "This is my friend Tony from school."

The dark-haired woman turned to Amy. "So you're Josh's mother. Tony talks about Josh constantly." She held out a work-reddened hand. "I'm Monica Alfonso."

"Hiya, Amy," Pete said before she could answer. "I see her in the store," he explained to his wife.

He gave Shay a thumbs up and grinned at Josh. "I see you're busy. Guess we'll mosey on over to another booth."

Josh flashed him a smile and turned to Shay. "Could Tony eat with us?"

"Josh!" Amy reddened.

Shay stared at her, then turned to Josh. "I don't see why not. In fact, I don't see why we all can't share this booth. It's plenty big. How about it?"

Pete glanced hesitantly at Amy. "We don't want to horn in."

"Not at all," Amy answered. Perhaps with Pete and Monica here, she could keep her mind off Shay.

As Shay slid closer to make room for Pete, Monica, and Tony, his thigh grazed hers. Butterflies tangoed in the pit of Amy's stomach; she swallowed and inched away.

Shay leaned across her to speak to Monica. "Where are the girls?"

"At Grandma's," Monica answered. "Have to have some time away from the brood." She turned to Amy. "I'm so glad to finally meet you."

Amy's mouth turned to cotton as heat from Shay's thigh spread to hers. She grasped her water glass and took a swallow.

"Amy just moved here from Minnesota," Shay supplied. "She works for Myra Templeton." He caught Amy's eye. "This is Pete, my assistant at ValuKing and a lucky devil, 'cause Monica's the best darned cook in the valley." He gave Pete a playful jab in the shoulder. "She's making that lasagne just for you, buddy, so you'd better bring a healthy appetite. Better yet, why not bring three appetites. Bring Amy and Josh, too."

Monica's eyes sparkled. "Oh, yes, please do come. We'd love to have you!"

Shay grinned at Amy. "Pete and Monica are having their annual Christmas party this Saturday. Good food, lots of music and laughs. I can pick you up at seven."

"No, I don't think—well, I . . ." *Hell's bells, girl! This isn't charity. They're just nice, friendly people.*

"Mom! You told me I could go to Tony's party!"

Amy pressed her lips together. "I said I'd see." She hesitated a moment longer.

"Oh, do come, Amy," Monica urged, shaking back a lock of chestnut hair. "We'd love to have you." Her dark eyes lit up as if she sensed Amy's indecision. "I don't get out much now. I'd really like to get acquainted."

"Please, Mom," Josh coaxed. "Say yes."

Shay nodded and shot her a hopeful look.

Amy glanced at Josh, then back to Monica, and laughed quietly. "I'm outnumbered. All right, we'll come. Is there something I could bring?"

"Amy and I'll bring the wine and a bottle of brandy," Shay interjected.

Amy shot him a measured look. He was doing it again—making decisions for her, just as her brothers had done all her life. "I'll bring some fruit bread."

"You don't need to do that," Shay whispered.

She squared her jaw. "I *want* to do it!"

He looked wounded, and she felt a stab of regret. She knew she was overreacting, but it reminded her of her family, and of Jonathan's parents. All of them had tried to direct her life. She might be struggling financially, but she could certainly contribute something.

On the way home, Shay cleared his throat. "I didn't mean to push you. I thought I'd make it easier for you."

"I know, and I'm sorry. But I need to do it. Besides, I make pretty good fruit bread."

"I'm sure it'll be great. But I'd like it if sometimes you tried to see my point." He broke off as he pulled up in her driveway, switched off the engine, and turned to her. "Look, I respect your need to be independent, but sometimes you go overboard."

He spread his hands in a palms-up gesture and smiled. "I just want you to know I'm trying to help, not hinder. Okay?"

Was that what she did? Go overboard? She bit her lip

and thought about it, then let out her breath slowly. Perhaps he was right.

She smiled in spite of herself. "Okay."

"Okay what?"

"I'll count to three before I answer," Amy said.

He walked them up to the door. She unlocked it and watched Josh as he scooted off to his alcove.

Shay stopped her at the threshold. "I won't stay, just wanted to . . . thanks for coming. I enjoy being with you."

Her heart skipped a beat. She hadn't had this much fun in years. She raised her head and looked steadily into Shay's green eyes. He had made the difference. He'd been nice. A little strong-minded, but nice. She hated to admit it, but she rather liked feeling he was in charge. He wasn't pushy or overbearing like Jonathan's parents, and he certainly seemed to like Josh. Jonathan had cut Josh off when he was displeased. Shay didn't.

They stood on the front step under a low light, the chill of the night air at their backs. Amy watched the cloud of his breath escape from between his lips. He tipped her chin up and ran the tip of his finger across her lower lip. "I like you, Amy Wilson. I like you a lot."

Her breath stopped, and her knees went weak. Shay placed his hand on her shoulder, hesitated a fraction of a second, then turned and strode to his car.

Amy let herself into the house and leaned back against the closed door. Her lip tingled where his finger had been. She touched the spot with her knuckle.

"I like you, too, Shay McHugh," she whispered to the darkened room. "Too much for my own good."

Amy shoved the morning's client files into their respective places in the metal file cabinet. Shay's easy smile and green eyes rose in her memory. All morning, thoughts of him had distracted her, and here she was, thinking of him again.

She reached for the afternoon appointment files. Brody, Cunningham, Thomas, Utman. She set the files in the top basket on her desk and absently rubbed her knuckle over her lip.

Would he have kissed her? Did she want him to? She squeezed her eyes shut. Yes.

No!

She'd felt giddy while dancing with him. She hadn't felt that way in years. If she had any sense, she'd stop thinking about it right now. Shay McHugh was not part of her life, and that was that.

Myra stepped over to the desk and grabbed the appointment files, eyeing them as she slipped back into her office. She returned a moment later with her purse and a wrapped package. "I'm going to the post office to mail this." She reached for the door, but it swung open before she touched the knob.

Shay poked his head inside. "Sorry. Did I startle you?"

"You did. Never mind, I was just leaving."

He eased himself inside and Myra slipped past, closing the door. Amy thought she detected a smile on the older woman's face.

Shay blew on his hands. "Wow, it's cold out there!" Over his blue oxford-cloth shirt and navy trousers, he wore a tan shearling jacket. Two spots of color highlighted his cheeks.

She stared up at him. "What are you doing here?"

He glanced at his watch. "Lunch break. I would have called you this morning, but you don't have a phone." He perched on a corner of her desk. "I want you to help me buy a Christmas tree."

"I can't. The girl next door is watching Josh. I—I have to pick him up."

"The three of us can get the tree. We can put it up at my place and have dinner later." He grinned down at her, his eyes crinkling at the corners. "I make a mean spaghetti sauce—with a little help from Paul Newman."

A momentary thrill raced through her. Dinner with Shay sounded wonderful. But she couldn't.

Couldn't what? Go tree shopping with him? Eat dinner? She'd argued with herself on that point for hours.

"I'm off at three. Meet you at your house at three-fifteen." He hopped off the desk and slipped out the door before she could answer.

Amy sat speechless. How should she deal with a man like Shay? She liked being with him. Little by little he was becoming an important part of her life.

"The tree could have been a little fuller," Shay said as he drove along River Road toward his house. "But I didn't want to spend all afternoon comparison shopping for Douglas firs."

Josh sat between them in the cab of the pickup. "I think it's a bee-yoo-ti-ful tree." He craned his neck for another glimpse of the seven-foot fir lying in the bed of the old truck.

"You're right," Amy agreed. "It is 'bee-yoo-ti-ful.' "

Shay pulled up in a circular driveway, and Amy looked over the sprawling redwood bungalow set back from the road. A neat, low fence divided shrubbery from a long gravel path. In the distance, she made out a wooden dock and the river.

He hopped out and untied the tree. "Want to give me a hand with this?" he asked Josh.

Amy followed the two inside. Usually she could tell the bachelor houses; they were the ones with the unkempt yards and peeling paint. Not this one! The shingle siding gleamed a warm, rich brown, and rhododendrons grew in a well-tended bed along the front of the house.

Shay and Josh wrestled the fir into a stand and anchored it upright while Amy looked around the open-beam living room. She had expected to find a rustic, messy bachelor pad. Instead, the house took her breath away. Wood plank flooring, a tan Berber rug in front of the seating area, a comfortable-looking brown leather chair—a dream house.

Along one wall sat a large woodstove with embers glowing, while one wall held floor to ceiling bookshelves. She'd bet he read nothing but Tom Clancy. But judging by the mix of popular fiction and classics, his reading tastes were similar to hers.

A round oak table held boxes of tree lights and ornaments. Amy gasped. Not messy. Not a bachelor pad. Perspiration broke out on her brow.

A divider with a pass-through separated the living room area from the kitchen. She pressed her lips together and wandered over to take a closer look. Running her fingers over a cool green granite counter, she noted the island work surface and spotless range. A kitchen to die for, everything tidy and in its place.

Shay stepped up behind her. "You like it?"

"It's beautiful," she breathed. She hated it! What right did a good-looking man have to maintain a tastefully attractive house? She didn't want to like either one of them!

"I had the devil of a time getting the counter in. Pete and I could barely lift the granite slab."

"You did this?" She hated him, too! A man who did his own remodeling and kept his rugs vacuumed?

"The kitchen was my last project. I started with the

bathrooms and bedrooms, then worked on the living room."

She pivoted, looking first at a wall of pale oak cabinets, then a walk-in pantry. *Wow. I really like this!* "Yeah, it's okay, I guess."

"Want a tour before we decorate the tree?"

"No. Yes!" She did and she didn't. Part of her wanted to run her fingers over the exquisite cabinetry and share the moment with him. Another part of her wanted to get as far away from this maddeningly capable man as she could.

Her nerves were jangled after the house tour. She'd seen more of the inner, private Shay than she'd wanted revealed in his masculine study and elegantly subdued master suite.

Amy set to work stringing lights and hanging green and gold balls on the scented branches. Shay fed a log into the woodstove, then grabbed a step stool from the pantry and perched a gold star on top of the tree. When he had adjusted it to suit Josh, he climbed down and stood back to admire his handiwork. Reluctantly, Amy admired it, too.

Distracted by Shay's happy whistling, Amy hung tinsel over the branches while he donned a chef's apron and disappeared into the kitchen. Just as she draped the last strands of tinsel on the tree, he carried out steaming plates of garlic bread, spaghetti topped with grated Parmesan, and a wooden salad bowl, and set them on the table.

Oh, God, he can cook, too!

Josh plugged in the lights. "Oooh," he murmured.

Amy shivered. Her thoughts exactly.

EIGHT

Pete Alfonso greeted Amy and Shay at the door, a bottle of chianti in one hand and a Santa cap perched on his head at a rakish angle. "Ho ho ho! *Buon Natale.*" He swung the door wide. "That's Merry Christmas in Italian," he said.

Shay chuckled. "And the season's best to you, *Don Pietro.*"

An air of happiness pervaded the room. A tree festooned with silver tinsel, garlands, and red bows stood in front of a picture window. "What Child Is This" poured from a CD player, punctuated by giggles from the two little girls in red and green party dresses. In spite of her earlier misgivings, Amy found herself instantly at home in the noisy, joyful mélange. She glanced up at Shay, who met her gaze with a mysterious smile. A warm glow flowed through her.

"All right, rug rats, games are in the playroom," Pete said, chucking a dark-haired toddler under her chin. "Keep it down to a low roar," he admonished his son, then grinned as the girls dashed down the hall with Josh and Tony in pursuit.

Shay lowered his body onto a loveseat in the old-fashioned living room and motioned Amy to sit beside him. She settled near him, her leg brushing his. A spark of fire raced up her spine. *Careful, girl.*

She edged away, watching a very pregnant Monica sink onto the sofa and ease her belly into a relaxed position. Amy focused on Monica's composed features. She had to be uncomfortable, and *still* she entertained. How did she have the energy? "When is the baby due?"

"Two weeks," Monica replied. "The last weeks are the hardest. I feel like I've been pregnant my entire marriage." She patted her tummy. "Omega here is the last one, even if it turns out to be another girl."

"You don't know what the baby is?"

Monica smiled. "We want it to be a surprise. Did you know about Josh?"

Amy turned away. Josh had been the biggest surprise of her life. "No." She looked up to meet the warmth in Shay's moss-green eyes. An odd heat settled in her belly. Her reaction to him was a big surprise, too.

Monica's lasagne tasted rich and spicy. After Amy helped stack the dishes in the dishwasher, she and Monica returned to the living room. Pete brought in a decanter of eggnog and filled four cups.

Shay raised his. "A toast to Monica. Great cook, great housekeeper, great mother. The ideal wife."

Amy sipped and set her glass down. Monica Alfonso *was* a great cook, hostess, Mother, and housekeeper. Shay's admiration nettled her. Amy was as different from Monica as night and day. The furniture in her own living room would never pass a white glove test. Her cooking was passable, but she wanted a career, not more children. If he wanted a woman like Monica, why was he interested in her?

After coffee and homemade fruitcake, Monica seated herself at the piano and began to play carols. By the time she launched into "O Come, All Ye Faithful," the four Alfonso children and Josh had joined Pete and Shay. Josh's eyes sparkled as he stood arm in arm with Tony.

A steel band tightened around Amy's heart. Josh came alive in a group of people. Was her solitary lifestyle too lonely for him? She realized suddenly how much he needed things she could not provide—friends, the warmth of family life. And—she stared at the man beside her—a father.

Pete and Monica sang "God Rest Ye, Merry Gentlemen," and the sound of their voices rang through the living room. Shay took his place beside Pete and provided a lusty baritone, while Amy stood in the arched entry and listened. She closed her lids and allowed herself to daydream. How nice it was to be a part of the joy in this house.

Monica and Pete broke into "The Twelve Days of Christmas," and Shay wandered over to where Amy stood. At "five golden rings," he curled his hand over hers, pulling her closer.

Her throat tightened. Being near him tonight, smelling his woodsy scent, feeling his warmth filled her with longing. It seemed right somehow.

Her pulse quickened. Liking him this much was disturbing, but at this instant, she didn't care. She wanted to feel cherished. Loved.

Shay's lips brushed hers. "You're beautiful. I've wanted to do that all evening." He kissed her again.

Her heartbeat quickened, and she stood very still as he deepened the kiss. Lord, he tasted good! Unconsciously, she found herself melting into him, wanting more.

Her lips parted. She raised her head, drinking in his clean, masculine scent. She had wanted this, had unconsciously waited for it. It didn't matter that it was here, in the Alfonsos' living room in front of Josh. The moment was precious.

Breathless, she pulled away. "Why did you do that?" she murmured.

He pointed upward to the arch, where a sprig of mistletoe dangled from a red ribbon. He touched her lips with his forefinger, and fire shimmered down her spine. "But the real reason is I just wanted to, needed to. And I'd like to do a lot more of it."

Her breath caught and her knees turned to jelly, but she remained very still.

He pulled her back into his embrace. "Amy, I think we need to go somewhere and talk. About us."

"Wh-what about us?"

"You, me, Josh. Now that we've found each other, what are we going to do about it?"

An alarm bell clanged in her head. Her mouth went dry. He asked too much. She'd promised herself she would never get involved again. She'd worked too hard to be self-sufficient. She wasn't going to risk loving another charming man who would not want a wife with interests outside the home.

With his likable manner and exciting kisses, Shay was threatening her resolve. She wasn't the kind of wife he wanted. She wasn't about to sacrifice her independence, no matter how wonderful his kisses.

Shay turned the Porsche onto River Road, and Amy's thoughts tumbled. She liked being with him, but he complicated her life, made her long for the things she'd given up—a family, marriage. Lovemaking.

Shay carried a still sleeping Josh inside the door and deposited him on his bed. He closed the front door and turned toward her catching her shoulder. "About tonight. Amy, I—"

She pulled away, and took a deep breath. "Maybe we shouldn't see so much of each other."

Shay's jaw tensed. "Why the hell not?"

"I—I'm not looking for a serious relationship."

Pain slashed across Shay's face. He shoved his hands in his pockets. "So you're going to shut yourself off from life, live like a hermit? Is that it?"

She wouldn't speak. His question cut too close to the truth.

"What are you afraid of?" he continued, staring at her. "Marriage? Life? God knows I'd never hurt you. I just—hell, I'm a normal male, ready to settle down. Ready to love someone for the rest of my—"

"Shay," she whispered. "Shay, stop. I'm not what you want."

"I'll decide that. The question is am *I* what *you* want?"

Oh, yes, she thought. *Yes!* She wanted him, all right. She just couldn't face the thought of another marriage. Again, she left his shattering question unanswered.

"I see," he said. He kissed her hard and turned away.

When she heard his boots echo on the steps, she burst into tears. *What have I done?*

Myra Templeton stepped out of her office and squared her gaze with Amy's. "If that's the best you can do for Christmas spirit, you'd better take the day off. A face that preoccupied turns away clients!" She marched over to Amy's desk and stood with her hands on her lean hips. "What's the trouble, dear?"

"Nothing."

Everything. Shay McHugh was a wonderful man. Amy Wilson had cold, cold feet. She shoved a file into the desk drawer.

"Come on," Myra coaxed. "Out with it. What's eating you?"

Amy sighed. "A complication. A man."

"Men will do that. Anyone I know?"

"Shay McHugh."

Myra let out a whistle. "That's a complication? Girl,

you should consider yourself lucky. Shay is the marrying kind."

"That's the trouble." Amy stared up at the older woman. "I don't want to remarry. Ever. I'll lose everything I've worked so hard for—the freedom to make my own decisions, to raise Josh the way I think best."

Myra leaned against the desk. "I can understand your wanting to be self-sufficient, but some freedom's no freedom, especially if you have to bury yourself to get it. You want more out of life than that."

The older woman circled the small room and returned to the desk, her hazel eyes as animated as her spare form. "For three years you've been alone. Don't you think it's time you came out of your cave and started trusting your heart?"

Myra reached over and covered Amy's hand with hers. "Shay is easygoing, dependable, and as caring a man as you'd hope to find. He has a great future in Riverton." Her gaze softened.

"Oh, Myra. I'm not the kind of woman he wants."

Myra's gaze narrowed. "What type do you think he wants?"

"A homemaker." Amy chewed on her lower lip. "A wife who stays home, cooks, sews, raises children. Shay wouldn't understand my wanting a career, art classes."

"Maybe. Maybe not. Fact is, you might be exactly what Shay McHugh needs." Myra shrugged into her coat and strode out the door.

In the ensuing quiet, Amy struggled to keep her mind on her work. Was Myra right? Was she hiding because she was afraid, using her fear of a second marriage to avoid facing life? Maybe she did need to trust her heart instead of her head for a change.

Yesterday when she'd stopped off for groceries, Shay's face had shown his hurt. His businesslike manner told her he was trying to maintain the distance she wanted.

But instead of feeling relieved, she ached inside. The only thing she was sure of was that she missed Shay, missed their time together, missed the way he took Josh under his wing.

Josh missed him, too. Each day he asked questions about Shay until she wanted to scream. Each night she dreamed about the green-eyed, russet-haired man who had kissed her with such passion under the mistletoe. She yearned to hear his voice, feel his touch. She found herself thinking of him constantly.

She knew without a doubt she wanted him in her life. But she also wanted her independence, an education, a career, things Shay wouldn't value in a wife. Shay wanted a wife like Monica. And yet . . .

Amy needed him. She knew that now, and she wanted to tell him. She clamped her lips together and straightened her spine. Tomorrow was Christmas Eve. She had to talk to Shay.

All of a sudden she had to get out of the office. What she wanted was to see Shay, but she'd bolster her courage first.

She walked next door to Johnny's Java House, ordered a latte, and searched the room for a table. Suddenly she saw Shay seated in the corner, his back to her. Her pulse raced. God and fate had tossed an opportunity right into her lap.

She took a deep breath, forced her feet forward, and made her way over. "May I share your table?"

Startled, he looked up. "Sure. I—"

"I—"

They laughed uncertainly.

Amy looked at him hesitantly. "I was going to stop by the store after work. I wanted to say something to you."

Shay's eyes widened. "I was going to drop in at the office. I wanted to say something, too."

"You first," she said.

He swallowed, searching her face. Finally, in a low voice he said, "For three days I told myself I wouldn't try to see you. But it's no good. I do want to see you, Amy." He reached for her hand, released it, then reached for it again. "I've done a lot of thinking and I'd like to—" He cleared his throat. "If you don't have plans for Christmas Eve—"

"I'm sorry about the other night," Amy broke in. If she didn't tell him now, she never would. "I—I'm still a little gun-shy when it comes to men, I guess." She sipped the latte and focused on his square jaw. A faint shadow outlined the beginning of his beard. "Would you like to spend Christmas Eve with us? We don't have a tree or anything, but I'm going to make our traditional Swedish supper."

Relief flashed across his face. "Why don't you and Josh come over to my place? You could have the kitchen to yourself. Even better, why don't you stay the night?"

Amy opened her mouth, then closed it. An odd flutter moved from her heart to her belly. "Did you say stay the night?"

"Amy," Shay breathed. "Please. We can open gifts in the morning." A look of apology flashed across his face. "I might as well tell you, I got something for Josh."

Amy stared at him. He was incorrigible. Maddening. Wonderful. He shouldn't have bought anything for Josh, at least not without consulting her! He had a tendency to take charge, she acknowledged. Just what she didn't need.

"Yes," she heard herself say. After all, it was Christmas, and she was suddenly filled with warmth. She would give herself and Josh and Shay a gift. They would spend Christmas together. "We'll come."

NINE

Amy locked the office door and marched down the sidewalk to the ValuKing. She filled her cart with fresh halibut, half and half, butter, candied fruit, confectioners' sugar—things she and Josh had done without for the last three months. She gulped when she paid the bill, but thanks to Myra's generous bonus, she would cook the best Christmas Eve dinner Shay McHugh had ever eaten.

When she got home, she stepped into the living room and lifted her completed painting of Loch Lomond off its easel. As soon as she'd finished it, she knew it belonged on the wall above Shay's sofa. She wrapped it with the roll of gold foil paper she'd bought and tied a glittery gold bow in the center. Warmth radiated from a spot deep inside her heart. It would be her special gift to him, a part of herself.

She assembled her recipes and laid them beside her krumkake iron and cookie press, then dug through a box until she located the Lucia crown. She untwisted the crumpled plastic holly leaves and smoothed them until the wreath looked presentable. Maybe Saint Lucia would look favorably on her tomorrow. With a smile, she set it on her head, then peeked at her reflection in the kitchen window.

* * *

At precisely six-fifteen, Shay slid his key in the front door and pushed it open, his pulse quickening at the thought of Amy and Josh there to greet him. The aroma of cinnamon, cardamom, and anise permeated the room, and a carol he'd never heard drifted from the stereo. He gazed around his living room at the lighted tree and the large gold package beneath, at the red-gold embers glowing in the woodstove, at his dining-room table dressed with woven red runners and a centerpiece of holly and ivy.

Amy emerged from the kitchen, dressed in a pine green skirt and matching sweater. Over that she wore his canvas chef's apron.

"Doesn't seem like the same place I left this morning," he said. "And it smells as wonderful as it looks!" He strode over to the counter to inspect a tray of cookies. Some were S-shaped, others looked like thin, crisp creme-filled pancakes.

Amy's eyes brightened. She positioned dessert forks above each plate, then stood back, eyeing him. "Like it?"

"Yeah, I like it." He loosened his tie.

Josh bounded out of the study and stopped short. "Hi, Shay. Mom'n me made cookies and Lucia buns. She's got a wreath to wear'n candles, too! But we have to wait."

"We do?" He stared at Josh, then Amy. "Can I help?"

Amy repositioned a plate. "No. Supper's almost ready. Go watch television or something."

He hesitated, but Josh tugged his hand. "You gotta come with me, else it won't be a surprise." Shay allowed himself to be pulled into his study.

Ten minutes later, Amy called, "You can come in now."

Shay let Josh lead him. The lights had been dimmed except for those on the Christmas tree. Bowls of fragrant soup sat on matching plates. Red cabbage salad and pickled herring formed mounds in hand-painted dishes in the center of the table. A loaf of homemade bread peeked out from under a napkin in a wicker basket. A platter of cheese lay alongside. The food looked delicious.

He waited beside Josh, who darted a look toward the hallway.

Suddenly, lights flickered. "She's coming," Josh whispered.

An instant later, Amy appeared, moving slowly into the darkened room, candlelight dancing along the wall. Over her sweater and skirt, she'd tied a long white embroidered apron. What caught his eye was the wreath of lighted candles on her head. His heart pounded. She looked like an angel.

She sang a carol in a language he didn't understand, and in her hands she carried a tray of oddly shaped rolls and steaming mugs.

Her lips curved into a mysterious smile as she made her way toward him. She was so serene, so beautiful! He was afraid to move, for fear he would break the spell.

She stepped up to him and offered the tray. "You may take it from me and set it on the table."

He reached for the tray, and she looked into his face and said, *"God Jul."* She reached for a roll and held it out to him. "May the spirit of Saint Lucia bless this house and all therein."

Shay took the offering, touched it to his lips. "Thank you."

Carefully, she removed her wreath and blew out each candle. "Let Christmas begin."

They sat down together at the table.

Shay took a bite of herring. "This is fantastic. I had no idea fish could taste so good!"

"It's how we celebrate Christmas in Minnesota. But I haven't played Saint Lucia since . . . in three years."

"I'm glad you saved her for me," Shay murmured.

Amy's voice lowered. "I'm glad I did, too."

After dinner, they savored coffee and cookies by the fire. When Josh went to bed, Amy poured hot mulled wine into two mugs. Shay took his and set it on the coffee table. "Be right back."

He wrestled in two huge boxes from his car and opened one of them. His hands shaking, he lifted out sections of track, then a model train engine, a caboose, and six boxcars. "Want to give me a hand setting this up?"

Amy's eyes widened. "You didn't get that for Josh!"

Shay grinned. "Actually, it's for both of us. I'll have as much fun as he will." He opened the second box and removed a station house, tiny trees, and two additional buildings. "How about it? I need some expert advice."

"But . . . but it's so expensive!"

He clambered over the pieces until he was kneeling beside her. "I hope you won't be upset, Amy. I had to get it. Josh wanted the train and besides . . . well, I . . ." He fumbled in his pocket. "Here. This is for you."

He opened a small green velvet box. Inside rested a carved gold ring. "I want you and Josh to stay in my life."

"Oh, Shay," Amy breathed. "Shay, you shouldn't . . . I mean, I didn't plan to remarry . . ."

"Change your plans," he said.

"I'm not right for you. I'm too independent, for one thing. You deserve a wife like Monica, not someone who wants a career, a job."

He settled down by her side. "Look at me. I love you,

Amy Wilson. I want you, just as you are." He brushed her lips with his fingers. "Career and all."

He took her hand in his. "I understand you need freedom to be yourself. You will have that. I just want us to be together."

He held her eyes a moment longer, then held out the box. "It's called a claddagh." He willed his voice not to break. "If you wear the heart facing out, it means you're available. Facing in, it means you're taken."

He swallowed. "I don't want to rush you, but before I met you I was just marking time, puttering around with boats and cars, wondering what life was all about. You changed all that."

Amy's lower lip trembled. She captured it between her teeth, and Shay's breath stopped. She lifted the ring out of its velvet box and slipped it on her ring finger.

He began to shake. He'd never been so frightened in all his life. He forced his gaze to her finger.

The heart faced in.

Joy surged through him. "I'm not a patient man," he said in a gravelly voice. "I want to hold you, make love to you. But I can wait, if you say so."

Amy's heart squeezed. The golden glow from the embers in the woodstove highlighted Shay's skin, and she brushed a lock of russet hair from his forehead. "After we set up the train," she whispered, kissing the spot her fingers had touched. "And every day after that for the rest of our lives."

MERRY AND HER GENTLEMAN

by

Kate Holmes

ONE

"Merry Christmas?"

The clerk in the Drivers License Bureau slid her glasses down to the tip of her nose and peered at Merry over the rims.

"I can't help it." Merry bristled defensively. "Look at my birth date."

The clerk slid her glasses back up and scowled at the form Merry had set in front of her. "Hmmmm

"My parents thought it was cute."

"Cute?"

"That's right." Merry let her jaw harden and her eyes narrow ever so slightly to show she wasn't someone the clerk could push around, regardless of the name on her license. "Now can we finish here, please? I have some shopping to do."

"Humph." The clerk turned to key the information for a license renewal into the computer. As she worked, her eyes got squintier and her thin lips pinched into a disapproving frown.

Merry's grip on her purse tightened. Twenty-three years of living with her parents' idea of cute hadn't made it any easier to deal with the snickering amusement of people who thought names like Sally and Bill were as daring as anyone ought to get.

Not that Merry didn't agree with them, of course, but

she never would have told her parents that. Other than their regrettable taste in names, they were the kindest, most loving parents a person could want.

The trouble was, her father, John Doe, had grown up with the burden of a name that was a cliché for everything from a nonentity to an unidentified corpse. He'd almost missed enrolling in kindergarten because the principal thought someone was playing a joke on him; the college of his choice had treated his application as a test run for a new admissions system and promptly lost it; and when he'd been arrested for participating in the peace marches in Washington in the early seventies, the police had taken a jaundiced view of what they thought was more political troublemaking.

John's high-school and college sweetheart had happily joined him in the D.C. jail, women's section, but she'd almost refused to marry him on the grounds she couldn't possibly go through life with a name like Jane Doe. Given her political leanings, she would have kept her maiden name, but she'd been hoping marriage would release her from the burden of having been christened plain Jane Smith.

Fortunately for Merry, her mother had eventually given in despite the name. Jane, like John, had been an only child and the only things she wanted more than peace on earth were a loving husband, a rambling old house, and a big family with which to fill it.

Unfortunately, John and Jane's experiences had convinced them their children needed names more memorable than theirs. The first child rash enough to venture into the world had been named Mick Jagger Doe in honor of Jane's youthful infatuation with the Rolling Stones.

Mick, who swore he'd stopped resenting his name when his mother informed him Pink Floyd was her other idol, had been followed by Clarence Darrow

(Dare) Doe, Robert John Kennedy (Ken) Doe, and Martin Luther Doe (who went by King, since John and Jane admitted they would have named him Martin Luther King Doe, to distinguish him from the original Martin Luther, if they hadn't forgotten the religious reformer in all the excitement).

After King, there'd been a break of a few years when Jane began to fear that four children were all she would have. But then Neil Armstrong Doe came along, with Willie Nelson Doe hard on his heels—Jane's taste in music having mellowed somewhat from her hard-rock years—and it began to look as if all Jane's dreams were going to come true after all—except the peace on earth part, which she was beginning to suspect was out of her hands anyway.

By the time Willie entered preschool, John and Jane had settled into a comfortable suburban life spiced with just enough political and social activism to keep them busy and give the boys plenty of time to get into trouble. They picketed for educational reform, helped build houses for Habitat for Humanity, marched to save wetlands, and, over the years, welcomed more than a dozen foster kids into their house and their hearts.

Only one thing marred life's perfection. John and Jane wanted a little girl. With each pregnancy, they sorted through possible names without ever really deciding on one in particular.

"She could be Gertrude Stein Doe." Jane liked obscure literature almost as much as she liked popular music.

"Eleanor Roosevelt Doe," John countered. His own mother had met Mrs. Roosevelt once and had raised her son with a sound respect for the lady's achievements.

"Well," Jane said dubiously, "I suppose that would be all right. Better than Gloria Steinem Doe, anyway. I knew a Gloria in high school. Terrible creature. Always stealing other girls' boyfriends. And her family voted Republican.''

John and Jane shuddered at the thought.

But all the debate went for naught, for one baby after another had popped out male, and Jane finally gave up hope of ever having a daughter.

When she found she was pregnant with a seventh child, she resigned herself to the inevitable and agreed this one would be called Jonas Salk Doe, since both she and John had decided it was time they looked a little farther afield for their sons' role models.

Merry's unexpected arrival on Christmas morning caught everyone by surprise, her mother most of all. Without a girl's name waiting in the wings, so to speak, Jane and John had done the next best thing—they'd named their only daughter after their favorite holiday.

No matter how much she loved her parents, there were times when Merry wished she'd been called Eleanor Roosevelt instead. December was one of those times and renewing her driver's license was another. It was just bad luck that the two always fell at the same time of year. The only consolation was her license didn't have to be renewed every year.

"Look into the camera, please," the clerk said, and snapped Merry's picture before she had a chance to do more than open her mouth and squint at the light.

The computerized machine cranked and whirred and spat out the plasticized license. Still frowning, the clerk studied the result, then slid it across the counter to Merry. "There. And Merry Chris—er, Happy Holidays."

"Thank you," Merry said, taking the license. "The same to you." What else was she supposed to say?

A few choice words occurred to her once she was outside the license bureau's kiosk and had a chance to look at the picture. Silently vowing to drive very carefully for the next five years, Merry tucked the license into the back of her wallet, then pulled out her Christmas gift list.

In an effort to be more "customer friendly"—*yeah, right,* Merry thought grumpily—the license bureau had placed its service kiosk in the area's largest mall. With a little careful planning at the start, she might be able to cross most of the items off her list with one marathon swing through the shops.

She eyed the crowd, then ran one last check. Credit cards? Yup. Checks? Those, too. Canvas totes? Five of them, all large, and all equipped with sturdy shoulder straps. One even had wheels. List? The full three feet of it. She'd used a strip of adding machine paper so she'd have it all in one piece.

As a last precaution, she knelt and tied double knots in the laces of her walking shoes. One quick glance to get her bearings, then Merry took a deep breath and plunged into the crowd, headed for the first stop on her list.

"One of those, I guess, and one of those. And this and this." Geoffrey Winston Hanover III pointed to four bottles among the selection of perfumes the stunning blond behind the counter had showed him, then plucked two more brightly colored boxes off their respective displays and added them to the pile. "Those, too."

The way he figured, there was no sense in shopping at the area's largest and most expensive department store if you couldn't take advantage of the selection as well as the gift-wrap service. He frowned at the jumble of boxes, silently counting. Six. He needed nine.

"What about this?" He pointed to a shiny gold box lying open on the counter. The crystal vial of perfume it held glowed like amber in its satiny nest. "Do women like this, whatever it is?"

The clerk gave him her most fetching smile. "Oh, yes. *Enchantress* is very popular. And *very* sexy," she added, letting her voice drop to a more seductive level as she dabbed a bit of the perfume on her wrist. "Don't you agree?" She leaned over the gleaming glass counter and waved her wrist under his nose.

He pulled back in distaste. "Yes, fine. All right. I'll take two. No, make it three. But wrap them in a different kind of paper so I can tell them from the others."

"Of course." Her pout had the look of having been practiced in a mirror.

If he'd been sixteen, he probably would have embarrassed himself by getting a hard-on right there in the middle of perfumes and cosmetics. But he was thirty-two, not sixteen, and he'd been the recipient of more than his fair share of sexy pouts in the intervening years. The woman's efforts at seduction left him cold.

"Can I offer you anything else?" she asked, discreetly smoothing her sleek black dress over her perfect hips.

"Just the bill and the gift wrap." He pointedly turned away as she gathered up the boxes and wobbled off on heels so high they would have crippled a normal woman.

Letting out a disgusted sigh, he shoved his hands into his trouser pockets and leaned against the counter. Hell of a time for Ms. Gompers to take a vacation.

For years his superefficient secretary had handled all his Christmas shopping, which was just the way he liked it. If he'd had any idea the stores would be this crowded or the noise this bad, he'd have refused to approve her vacation until she'd finished the job.

Well, all right, he wouldn't have gone that far, but he'd have made damned sure she found somebody else for the job first.

Maybe he should have gone skiing in Switzerland after all, as he usually did. After twenty-some consecutive Christmases spent skiing, however—his parents had first packed him off to St. Moritz with a tutor and some of his boarding-school friends when he was nine—he'd decided it was time for a change.

Too bad he hadn't thought about what he'd change to before he'd canceled his reservations and given Ms. Gompers three weeks' vacation. Now here he was, two weeks from Christmas, with no plans, no place to go, and no one to do his Christmas shopping for him.

That's what he got for acting on impulse. He should have known better. Life always went more smoothly when he kept to a routine, when everything was neat, orderly, carefully thought out, and nothing was left to chance.

He pulled his hand out of his pocket and checked his watch. Half an hour wasted, and probably another hour on top of that by the time he got the rest of the gifts and fought his way back to his car. Maybe more.

He groaned and shoved his hand back in his pocket.

The clerk at the Elizabeth Arden display across the aisle—a sleek brunette, but otherwise indistinguishable from the sleek blond who'd waited on him—smiled sympathetically.

Geoff deliberately shifted so he couldn't see her come-hither look and found himself staring straight at another customer who was standing a few feet farther down the counter, studying a crumpled shopping list that spilled over her hands like a battle pennant. Judging from the overstuffed bags that hung from her shoulders or sat on the floor at her feet, she must be almost finished. He wouldn't have thought it was humanly possible for one woman to carry so much . . . stuff.

With her clunky shoes, worn jeans, and battered ski jacket, she was a notable contrast to the elegantly garbed salesclerks behind the cosmetics counters. But her worn jeans couldn't disguise the appealing way she filled them. The shoulders and back of her coat were half buried under a wild mass of red-gold curls, and what woman in her right mind would go shopping in high heels, anyway?

She frowned as she reached the end of her list, then rapidly scrolled back to the top. Still frowning, she eyed the shiny display of cosmetics in front of her, lifted one of the boxes to peer at the sticker on the bottom, then set it back with a sigh.

"Mr. Hanover?" The blond was back, smiling brightly. "Your total came to one thousand four hundred sixteen dollars and seventy-three cents. Would you like me to put that on your company charge for you?"

"No." He pulled out his wallet, selected one of several platinum-colored cards, and tossed it onto the counter. "Put it on this, will you? And make sure the price stickers are off all the boxes. Someone missed one last year."

She dimpled and fluttered her lashes. "I don't know a single woman who would mind seeing *those* stickers!"

He glared.

Her dimple vanished. "I'll be right back with the charge slip."

TWO

The name caught Merry's attention. She glanced up, curious, and for the first time noticed the gorgeous hunk standing at the perfume counter a few feet away.

The amount of the purchase almost made her gasp. She was on the verge of maxing out her single credit card—green, not gold or platinum—and hoping her end-of-the-year bonus would cover it, and she hadn't spent a fourth of what he'd just dropped on a few shiny boxes of perfume.

But the name . . .

She studied him surreptitiously. It might be him. Hard to tell, though. She'd caught only an occasional glimpse of the man who'd moved into the big house next door to her family's, but the names were the same. The height looked about right, six-two or so. Dark brown hair instead of black, but that was an easy enough mistake to make from a distance. Black coat, charcoal gray suit, brilliant white shirt with a neat, dark tie—that all matched, too. Their new neighbor might as well wear a uniform. She'd never seen him in anything except black topcoats, dark suits, white shirts, dark ties.

Those glimpses from a distance hadn't revealed that the topcoat was cashmere, however, or that the suit was hand tailored. She hadn't even guessed at the gold cuff links or shoes that looked Italian and probably couldn't be breathed on for under five hundred a pair.

And nothing, not even her one attempt to get a better look at him by using King's binoculars, had suggested their new neighbor was knock-your-socks-off gorgeous or that an aura of raw, masculine sexuality floated in the air around him like a strong dose of the expensive perfume he'd just bought.

Her stomach, which had been complaining about its empty state for the past hour, suddenly squeezed against her backbone. If she'd guessed he might be this good-looking, she'd never have had the nerve to leave that silly crayon-and-construction-paper Thanksgiving dinner invitation she'd taped to his front door right after he moved in.

Maybe it was just as well he'd never responded to the invitation and never answered the two times she'd actually worked up the courage to knock on his front door. He'd never called, never stopped by to introduce himself, never even so much as bothered to wave hello the few times they'd happened to be getting into their respective cars at the same time.

She *had* noticed he drove a big, black Mercedes, but he didn't get any points for that, not when her parents' driveway was always filled with a miscellaneous collection of vans, sedans, and battered four-by-fours—not to mention her beloved Beetle, Mehetabel, whose better days had come and gone, leaving it with half a front bumper, a bright pink fender that clashed with the rusting orange body, and a radio antenna held on by duct tape and prayer.

He couldn't possibly know about that unfortunate run-in between Mehetabel and his rosebushes. Just a little patch of ice, no damage done. Really.

He was only a few feet from her. All she had to do was go up to him, say hi, introduce herself, talk about the weather, maybe, or the crush of shoppers in the mall—make small talk. She'd done it a million times. But somehow, now that she'd seen him . . .

Merry blinked, startled, as his gaze locked with hers. The blond had walked off with his charge card and she'd never noticed.

No help for it. She crammed her list into her pocket, picked up the bags at her feet, and moved over.

She'd been mistaken. He was six-four if he was an inch. She had to tilt her head back to look into his eyes—gorgeous eyes, a startling blue-gray and shadowed by sinfully thick black lashes.

Her stomach did a flip-flop.

She forced a smile. "Excuse me. Are you Mr. Hanover? Our new neighbor?"

Those gorgeous eyes turned wary. "My name is Hanover. And you are . . . ?"

Merry dropped her bags and stuck out her hand. "Merry. Merry Doe. I live in the green house to the east of you. The one with all the cars." She hoped her smile didn't look as lopsided as it felt.

"Ah." Recognition dawned. It wasn't a good thing. Mr. Hanover might be wearing a wool suit and cashmere overcoat, but he'd suddenly developed a bad case of frost around the edges.

"If you'll just sign here, Mr. Hanover . . ." The blond had reappeared as if by magic. "Then I'll wrap your purchases and—"

"Perhaps you could assist Miss . . . ah, Miss Doe, first." He indicated Merry with a coolly dismissive wave of his hand.

As a brush-off, it was a beaut. Merry stiffened. Her smile vanished as her face got hot. One of the curses of red hair was that she couldn't hide her feelings, no matter how hard she tried.

"That's not necessary," she said, angrily shifting one

of the shopping bags higher on her shoulder. "I'll come back later. I wouldn't want to keep you from personalizing Mr. Hanover's gifts."

She bent to pick up the bags on the floor, hoping he'd attribute the red in her face to the effort of bending over. When she straightened, she found him staring at her with such a comical expression of surprise that she might have laughed out loud if she hadn't been so angry.

"Do have a happy holiday, Mr. Hanover," she said. "There's nothing like a little shopping to put you in the mood for the season, is there?"

Before he had a chance to reply, she turned around and stalked off, head high.

Her departure would have been a little more effective if she hadn't had to stop halfway down the aisle to adjust her load, but it was the best she could manage under the circumstances.

Geoff watched her walk away and realized too late his mouth was hanging open. He snapped it shut, as irritated with himself as with her. If he'd never glanced at the woman, she'd never have approached him in the first place.

He had to admit, though, he hadn't expected she'd flounce off like that, certainly not when he'd been so considerate as to suggest the clerk help her before finishing with his purchases.

He frowned suddenly. Could a woman flounce in jeans and an old ski jacket?

He thought about it, remembering the way she'd moved, the energy that had seemed to radiate from her. He especially remembered the way her hair flared out with each step, as though electrified by her anger.

At the thought of her hair, his fingers curled into involuntary fists. His palms tingled oddly and he realized, suddenly, he'd wanted to run his fingers through that wild, red mane even as he watched her walk away.

Flounce away.

He grimaced at the credit card he held. No doubt about it. She'd definitely flounced.

The nerve of the man! What arrogance! What rudeness! What unmitigated gall!

Merry stopped, blinked, then burst out laughing.

Unmitigated gall? Where had *that* come from?

A harried mother with a fussing child glanced at her, startled, then hurried past.

She was making too much of it, Merry told herself. He didn't know her, after all. A man as good-looking and as well-off as he was probably had a lot of strange women come up to him like that. And he *had* suggested the clerk take care of her before wrapping his purchases.

All the same . . . she thought of the coldness in those gorgeous eyes and the easy way he'd dismissed her.

To heck with him. He wasn't worth wasting Christmas cheer on.

With a sigh, she readjusted her bags, which were making her shoulders ache, and headed toward men's wear. Her father, who normally didn't pay much attention to his clothes, had a passion for funky ties. She'd spotted one here the other day which would be a perfect addition to his collection, and another that would go perfectly with that new pinstriped suit Willie was so proud of.

The ties were perfect. The prices were not.

Once again Merry pulled out her crumpled shopping list and tried to add up the total. It was dangerously close to her credit limit and there was always the chance she'd forgotten a charge or two.

The thought of having her card rejected made her shudder. She had the money in her checking account, but that meant she wouldn't have enough left to pay for the new easel Ken wanted. On the other hand, the owner of Bill's Art Supply would probably let her work a few nights to cover the purchase, so that was all right.

Resigned, she shoved the list back in her pocket, picked out the ties she wanted, and headed toward the big wood- and brass-trimmed display area where the cash register and the really expensive ties were located.

The blonde had wrapped three boxes and still had six to go when Geoff lost all patience with the process.

"Here," he said, pulling out his business card and a twenty. "I'll finish my shopping while you wrap the rest."

He walked away before she finished protesting she was almost done, really! Next year, he'd send Ms. Gompers to do the shopping, then give her the rest of the day off. In fact, he'd give her the rest of the week off. She'd deserve it.

At least men were easy to buy for. They wouldn't care if they all got the same maroon silk tie. They wouldn't even care if by some odd chance they all ended up wearing them at the same time. Only women made life difficult by insisting on having something different from everyone else.

"Twelve of your best silk ties," he told the sleek young man behind the counter. "Mix 'em up, box 'em, then stick a bow on 'em. No wrap. I don't want to wait."

"Yes, sir."

And that was that. Men were much more reasonable than women!

While the clerk, with admirable efficiency, selected the ties and arranged them between tissue in the store's signature gift boxes, Geoff idly studied the display of leather travel kits beside him. Jim might like one of those, he thought. His brother traveled almost as much as he did. Come to think of it, he could use another, himself.

He pulled two from the display at random. "I'll take those, too. But you only need to wrap one."

"Which one, sir?"

Geoff shrugged and tossed a credit card down beside the kits. "Doesn't matter. You choose."

The purchase made him feel virtuous. He couldn't remember the last time he'd given Jim anything other than a tie . . . or gotten anything from him except a tie, for that matter.

Pleased with himself, he strolled down the counter. Nothing else caught his eye on this side. He rounded the corner and stopped dead.

The redhead from the perfume counter was at the other register. She'd evidently paid with a check, because she had her billfold open and was showing something in it to the clerk. A driver's license, he supposed.

The clerk stared at the license, frowned, then glanced up at her, clearly startled.

She glared back. "It's perfectly legal."

The clerk gave up the battle. "Yes, ma'am. Of course." He finished scribbling the information on the check, then ran it through the register, ripped off the receipt, and handed it and two unboxed ties to her. "You sure you don't want a bag for them?"

She rolled the ties together and stuffed them into the already overstuffed bag on the counter. "I'm sure. Plastic bags are bad for the environment."

Geoff grinned. That had to be the first time in the history of Dailey & Sage that someone had refused one of their famous shopping bags.

"Here you are, Mr. Hanover." The clerk who had

waited on him deposited one of Dailey & Sage's larger bags on the counter in front of him. "Total charges came to seven hundred thirty-four dollars and nineteen cents."

At the mention of his name, the redhead looked up, then stiffened angrily.

For some reason, her anger stung. He gave her a curt nod of recognition. Experience had shown it was safer to keep his distance from attractive female neighbors. "Miss Doe."

She eyed the bag disdainfully. "One-stop shopping, Mr. Hanover? Makes things a lot easier if you buy everyone the exact same thing, doesn't it?"

She hoisted her bag onto her shoulder, picked up the rest from the floor, and started to move away. But then she stopped and swung round to face him, her green eyes sparking fire. "By the way, *paper* bags are bad for the environment, too."

She might as well have socked him on the jaw. Before he could think of a suitably sharp reply, she'd marched off, leaving him with no one to growl at except the clerk, who would have gotten by with looking deaf, dumb, and stupid if it weren't for the twinkle of amusement in his eyes.

THREE

Merry shoved her bags on top of the spare in Mehetabel's trunk and slammed the lid. It hit the rusty latch and bounced right back.

She slammed it again, harder.

So she'd been rude. He'd been rude first. Handsome Hanover probably didn't associate with women in blue jeans who couldn't afford to toss platinum credit cards around as if they were playing Old Maid. Not even if they were his next door neighbor.

Mehetabel started with a throaty roar. Neil might not have had time to fix the outside, but he'd done a fantastic job on the old car's innards. He'd overhauled the engine and electrical system, fixed the heater, redone the brakes, and put on new tires before he'd let her take it out of the small specialty garage he owned. Mehetabel might look like she was ready for the junk heap, but she ran like a top.

With a cheery wave for the two steely-eyed drivers who were waiting to claim her parking space, she pulled out into mall traffic. *First guy to think about his paint job loses.*

Left turn at the end of her parking lane, up two lanes, another left, a right, and she ought to be home free. Or in the line waiting to get out, anyway.

She spotted him the instant she made the second left.

How could you miss a guy like Handsome Hanover when he was standing in front of a shiny black Mercedes—especially when the Mercedes' hood was up in the universal sign of a car that adamantly refused to start?

Handsome did not look happy. In fact, he looked downright furious. Like he could chew nails and like it.

Merry almost laughed out loud.

She shifted into second and roared right past him. The quick bleep on the horn was just to let him know she cared.

Halfway down the row, guilt struck.

At the three-quarter mark, she slammed on the brakes. In the rearview mirror, she saw him grab the edge of the hood and slam it shut.

So what? All he had to do was call for help. A man who dropped two thousand dollars in one short shopping spree probably had a dozen cell phones lying around.

She shifted from second to first. Mehetabel chugged patiently, waiting for her to let out the clutch.

He could call, but how long would it take for a tow truck to reach him? It was Friday night, only twelve shopping days left till Christmas. If he was lucky, he might get somebody by Easter.

Not her problem.

She started to let out the clutch, then stopped.

Peace on earth, goodwill to men, remember? Handsome might be an arrogant slime, but he still fell into the category of male. *Very* male—tall, broad shoulders, strong, masculine jaw, eminently kissable lips, and eyes you could drown in. There was something about that starched-shirt polish that made a woman think wild, wicked thoughts.

And just when had she noticed his lips?

With a sigh, Merry put Mehetabel in reverse and

backed up, then rolled down her window. "Need a ride?"

He glared at her and Mehetabel. "No." Then, as a reluctant afterthought, he added, "Thank you. I've already called my office and told them to send someone out."

Even grumpy he looked gorgeous.

Merry sucked in her breath. Maybe this wasn't such a good idea after all. Her. Him. The two of them in Mehetabel.

Jane, her mother, had once admitted to "doing it" in John's old VW—several times. Merry had tried to figure out the gymnastics involved and decided her mother had been suffering from erotic delusions. No one over four-feet-three could have managed the feat, and her father was almost six-feet-two.

She glanced at the backseat and grinned. It was buried under an untidy heap of papers, coats, and discarded Wendy's burger wrappers. In that mess, mice would have problems.

Leaving the engine running, she took Mehetabel out of gear, put on the emergency brake, and climbed out.

"Where are your shopping bags?"

"What?"

Poor fellow. He probably shouldn't be allowed out without a keeper. She was feeling more kindly disposed to him every minute.

His lips were *very* kissable.

"The gifts you bought. You don't want to leave them in the car. They're too much of a temptation to thieves."

"Really, I—"

"The way I see it," she said, trying to be stern, "you have two alternatives. You can come home with me now, or you can wait for someone to show up. The mall won't close for another"—she checked her watch—"four and a half hours. They might make it here by then."

His protest died unspoken.

"Right." While he was trying to get his wits together, she walked around him and opened the driver's side door of his car.

The cell phone—she knew he'd have one—lay on his seat. The shopping bags occupied the passenger seat. Propping one hand on the back of his seat, she leaned across to grab the bags. The fine leather was like silk beneath her hand.

She couldn't help herself. She craned to get a better look at the backseat.

It was huge. Even somebody six-feet-four would have no trouble making love back there. She could think of a half dozen positions—

Get a grip!

Merry gulped and backed out faster than she went in, but not without grabbing his shopping bags and his cell phone first.

"Here." She slapped the phone into his hand. "Call your office and tell whoever to meet you at your house to pick up the keys. You have the keys, right?"

He nodded dumbly.

"Don't forget to lock everything," she added, and dived into Mehetabel. Finding room for his two big bags was going to take a little creative rearranging.

Geoff watched her rough-and-ready effort at house cleaning with stunned amazement. The last woman who'd left him speechless was Mary Lou Pointer, who had unbuttoned her blouse and showed him her breasts. At the time, he'd been eleven and she'd been a mature fourteen, so there'd been some justification for his befuddlement. But nothing had prepared him for this opinionated, redheaded whirlwind. Nothing.

He tried to think of a reasonable objection to her plan, without success. It would take them half an hour, maybe forty-five minutes, to get home, but it would take at least twice that long for someone from his office to reach him—if he was lucky.

He didn't much like the thought of imitating a sardine, especially not when *she* would be packed into the same tin can, but he liked the thought of waiting here even less.

Muttering under his breath, he went to lock up his car and call his office.

Merry eyed the mess in the backseat and the two high-class shopping bags with their load of expensive presents carefully propped in the middle of it. It was a sorry sight, and the frayed strip of cloth that dangled from the ripped liner overhead didn't help any. About the only thing Mehetabel and the Mercedes had in common was they ran on four wheels.

But Mehetabel was still running and the Mercedes wasn't.

She backed out again and found him still standing on the far side of the car, staring at her.

"Did you get hold of your office?"

He nodded and eyed Mehetabel doubtfully. "You sure this thing is safe?"

All her bustling goodwill of a minute ago vanished. Nobody insulted Mehetabel, not even her own family.

"Mehetabel's safe," she snapped. "But I won't make any promises about me. I bite."

She figured he'd bite right back. Instead, he blinked. Then he threw back his head and laughed.

It was an absolutely beautiful laugh, full and deep and impossible to resist. Merry barely stopped herself from laughing, too.

"Come on, get in," she said. "But don't slam the door too hard or the antenna will fall off."

Mehetabel's rusty hinges screeched as Handsome Hanover wrenched the door open, tossed his briefcase in the back with his shopping bags, and climbed in.

Actually, folded himself in would be more accurate. Volkswagen hadn't designed the Beetle to accommodate topcoated gentlemen over six feet tall, especially not ones with indecently broad shoulders.

He almost fell into her lap trying to pull the door shut. In order to give her enough room to shift, he had to hunch his shoulders and wrap his arms around his knees, which didn't fit under the dash. They didn't fit in front of it, either, even with the seat all the way back.

By the time he got settled, he looked like a half-opened carpenter's rule, all stiff lines and odd angles.

She gave him her sweetest, most innocent smile. "Comfy?"

Those kissable lips twitched invitingly, then curved into a heart-stopping grin. A dimple popped up at the corner of his mouth, neatly matching the slight cleft in his chin.

"Absolutely," he said. "I *like* sitting with my chin on my knees. Really." There was only the tiniest trace of sarcasm in his voice.

Her smile widened. "Good," she said, and put Mehetabel into gear. Neither of them said anything until she was out on the street.

He cleared his throat uncomfortably. "I, uh, I guess I owe you an apology."

She glanced at him, and nodded. "I guess you do."

That made him blink.

She'd been right. His lashes were sinfully thick. She'd have sacrificed her gold necklace and her favorite sweater for lashes like that.

"I hate shopping," he said. "Makes me crazy, all the noise and crowds and—" He waved a hand vaguely. "I *hate* it."

"Well . . ." Merry thought of her brothers. Six of them, all big, strong men, yet they got slightly crazed if someone dragged them to a mall. A sporting goods store, now, or an auto parts place—or, in Ken's case, an art supply shop—they could manage that—but that was as far as it went. Even a grocery store did something to their minds. Send them off for a gallon of milk and a loaf of bread and they inevitably came back with beer, three different kinds of chips, four steaks, two bags of cookies, and no bread or milk.

"All right," she said, giving in. "I guess I can buy that."

"Then my apology's accepted?"

She gave him a speculative look. "On one condition only."

His eyebrows arched. "Which is?"

She grinned. "You spring for coffee at the drive-in stop. I'm *dying* for a good cup of coffee."

He'd happily spring for a dozen cappuccinos, Geoff decided ten minutes later. Especially if it meant he got to enjoy a view like this one.

A pile of old snow banked at the base of the coffee stop had forced Merry to park a little bit farther from the window than normal. Rather than open the door, she'd climbed halfway out the window and was reaching for the steaming cups of coffee the attendant was handing to her. The awkward stretch provided a great view of the back pocket on her jeans . . . and everything else.

She had a great tush. He especially liked the way the jeans had worn to a paler blue right over the best curves. It made him think tight miniskirts were overrated. Although on her—

"Here," she said, dropping back into her seat. "Take these."

Without giving him a chance to object, she handed him the coffees and went back for the rest. The view was as good the second time as it had been the first.

"Here's your change." She held out the handful of bills. Her other hand clutched two stirrers, a fistful of napkins, and what looked like three dozen packets of sugar.

He grimaced and held up the two large cups of coffee. "Just stick it in my pocket." He shifted slightly so she could reach his coat's side pocket. Given how tightly he was wedged into his side of the car, slightly was all he could manage.

"I can't. You're sitting on it."

"Put it in your pocket until we get home, then."

"I can't. I zipped them up and there's no place to put the sugar so I can unzip 'em."

Geoff closed his eyes and prayed for calm. A reasonable car would have a cowl where she could toss it, or a floor that wasn't buried under God knew what. "My inside jacket pocket, then." He held his hands as far from his body as he could—it wasn't very far—in order to give her access to his jacket pocket.

That was a big mistake.

FOUR

She leaned close, so close her wild hair brushed his cheek and his lips, teasing him with its silken touch. It also tickled his nose, which made him want to sneeze. He could smell the lingering traces of an herbal shampoo. He'd never realized the scent of herbs could be so damned unsettling.

It was an awkward angle under crowded conditions. He knew she couldn't help touching him, couldn't help brushing against his chest. So why did his body react as if she were starting to undress him?

Merry held her breath and wondered if a sudden lack of oxygen in the car was making her feel so lightheaded.

This was a mistake. A really big mistake.

She was so close she could see the pulse beating at the side of his throat and a tiny patch of stubble at the corner of his jaw that he'd missed shaving this morning. The scent of his expensive aftershave lingered on his skin, teasing her senses.

The edge of her finger caught the pocket. It was an odd sensation—the silken lining of the jacket rubbing against her hand on one side, the crisp, starched linen of his shirt rubbing against the other, and both sides warm with the heat of him.

Willing herself not to think, she stretched a little

more so she could shove the bills into the pocket, then fell back in her seat, breathing hard. "There."

He let out his breath with a whoosh, like a swimmer who'd been too long underwater. The sound of it seemed unusually loud in the little car.

For a moment, neither of them said a word. Then he cleared his throat and said rather hoarsely, "Want your coffee?"

He didn't even look at her. He was staring at the scuffed and faded Mutant Ninja Turtle sticker on the dash with the intensity of an art collector who's just discovered an unknown da Vinci.

"Miss? Would you mind moving? There are three cars lined up behind you, waiting to order."

The attendant's slightly edgy request wrenched Merry out of her daze. Still clutching the sugar, napkins, and stirrers, she pulled Mehetabel to the side and set the brake.

That's when she realized she couldn't juggle sugar packets and hold her coffee with only one hand.

As if sensing her dilemma, he held her cup out to her. "I'll hold, you stir, then you can do the same for me."

"Deal."

Geoff watched in amazement as she dumped the contents of four sugar packets into her coffee, then another four.

As if sensing his reaction, she looked up and laughed. "I like coffee with my sugar."

He couldn't help smiling back. "Are you sure you got enough? There's only about a dozen packets left."

She made a face at him, for all the world as if she'd known him since forever, and snapped the lid back on the cup. "Willie says I'm getting too fat, but I can't help it. I love coffee, but only if it's really sweet."

"Willie," Geoff said with conviction, "is an idiot."

She laughed. "I'll tell him you said so." She took the cup from his hand and extended the remaining sugar. "Now it's your turn."

It was crazy, but he had a sudden urge to strangle this unknown Willie. If she had an ounce of sense, she'd dump any boyfriend who was that blind and stupid.

Unless he was her husband.

The thought hit so suddenly he almost slopped the coffee. He glanced at her hands. No rings—but these days, that didn't prove a thing.

"Watch it!"

"Sorry." He reclaimed his coffee, then held up the stirrers and the remaining sugar. "What do I do with these?"

"Dump 'em in the back."

"But you might need them sometime and——"

She snatched them out of his hand and casually tossed them over her shoulder, then freed the brake and pulled back into traffic. "I can always dig for them if I do."

He craned for a look at the backseat. "Is this your personal version of a recycling center?"

"That's what I call it, but Neil says I should be honest and call it a compost heap."

Neil. First Willie, now Neil. He hoped she had a hell of a lot of brothers.

Get a grip, Hanover.

Shaking off the thought, he took a cautious sip of the coffee, then a second, more generous gulp. The flavorful brew tasted good on a blustery December evening.

He eyed her, intrigued by the contradictions in her. "For somebody who doesn't approve of shopping bags, you have an awful lot of fast-food wrappers and paper coffee cups back there."

She threw him a startled glance, then fixed her attention back on the traffic. There was just enough light left to see the blush creeping into her cheeks. To his surprise, he found he liked it.

"I—" She gave an embarrassed laugh. "I'm afraid I said that just to annoy you. You were so darned condescending when I introduced myself that I wanted to get in a dig of my own."

He'd been called rude, arrogant, overbearing, and worse, but for some reason, having her accuse him of being condescending bothered him. A lot.

"I'm sorry," he said, and meant it.

She shrugged, clearly embarrassed. "So am I—for being rude right back, I mean. After four hours of shopping, I was getting a little cranky myself."

"Four hours." He shuddered.

Merry laughed. He looked like the kind of man who ate half a dozen hard-nosed businessmen for breakfast, but Christmas shopping clearly unnerved him.

The traffic light changed suddenly. She braked and shifted down. It was awkward, since she needed both hands to drive and another to hold the coffee cup, which was way too hot to hold between her legs. And the passenger's seat, which was her usual cup holder, was occupied by a man who made every nerve ending in her body tingle.

Without warning, he reached over and plucked the cup out of her hand. His fingers barely grazed her skin, but it was enough to make her jump.

"I'll hold, you drive."

"Er . . . thanks." She curled her hand around the gearshift knob to keep from rubbing the spot where he'd touched her.

"Peace?" he said, looking amused.

"Peace.

"So we're friends?"

Friends? A frisson of doubt shot through her. Friends

with a man who could make her think lustful thoughts about Mehetabel's backseat without even trying?

"Good neighbors," she said firmly, and stepped on the gas.

The car was too small and the seat damned uncomfortable, but Geoff couldn't remember when he'd enjoyed a forty-five minute drive more. The warmth—the car's heater was surprisingly good—and the soft glow from the instrument lights made it seem as if they were in their own little haven, cut off from the frosty, busy world on the other side of the windows.

They talked about nothing and everything. They argued over whether latte was really coffee, agreed the instant stuff in a jar wasn't, and that coffee with whipped cream and a dribble of caramel was a wonderfully decadent indulgence. She was a Raiders fan, he rooted for the Broncos. Neither of them cared much for basketball but both loved baseball and hockey. Superman and Batman were the best, but the movies had been a disappointment. Neither of them had ever figured out the appeal of the Hulk.

He hadn't laughed so much in ages.

When she finally pulled into her own driveway, he barely stopped himself from saying he wished it could have been longer.

For a moment, they both sat there, neither one willing to be the first to break the spell. The sudden silence was deafening.

"Well . . ." he said at last, and felt like a fool. He cleared his throat. "Thanks."

"Sure. No problem." She gave him one of those heart-stoppingly radiant smiles of hers. "What are neighbors for?"

"Of course."

Another silence. Neither one of them moved.

He forced himself to grab the door handle. "I'll help you carry your bags in."

"There's no—"

"It's the least I can do. Really."

"Well then, thanks."

He'd had more intelligent conversations in grade school. Deliberately shifting away from her, he yanked on the handle. It was rusty, but it worked. The door swung open, letting the cold air in with a bone-chilling whoosh. He had one foot on the ground and his head half out of the car when she abruptly grabbed his sleeve and pulled him back.

"I don't even know your name. Your first name, I mean. I can't go around calling you Mr. Hanover."

She was so close all he'd have to do was lean down a little bit to kiss her. At the thought, he scooched over on the seat another inch.

"It's Geoff. With a G."

"Geoffrey Hanover." She rolled it on her tongue as if she were tasting it. "I like that."

He grimaced. "My mother thought the medieval spelling was classier. You have no idea how miserable it can be going through life with a name like that." He wasn't even going to mention the III part.

"Oh, don't I?" She laughed, then let go of his sleeve and sat back. That was as far as she went. Their gazes locked, and for a moment something electric and dangerous seemed to crackle in the air between them. Then a gust of wintry air whirled through the open doors, breaking the spell.

"Don't forget your briefcase," she said, and got out.

He took two shoulder bags and his belongings. She took the rest, then led him along a crumbling cement walkway to the front of the house. As Geoff followed her up the broad, well-worn front steps of her house,

the bone-shaking beat of rap music came from somewhere inside.

Wincing—he'd never liked rap—he followed Merry
into the house. His reward was to be greeted with the
tantalizing scent of burning pine logs and fresh bread
baking. He sniffed appreciatively, then set his bags
down and looked around.

To the right of the broad entry hall, through double
French doors marred with smudgy handprints at toddler height, was the living room. Through matching
doors on the left he could see a table already set for a
meal. He only caught a quick glance, but the impression
was of a vast table with what seemed like room to seat
a whole football team plus the cheering section.

Merry darted into the living room and headed for
the booming stereo system. He followed at a more lei-
surely pace.

The room was long and wide and filled with plump
sofas and shabby armchairs clearly chosen for comfort
rather than style. A fire crackled behind the screen of
the massive fireplace that filled the far wall, while lamps
scattered about the room cast a welcoming golden glow
that didn't quite manage to hide the cheerful disorder
of the place. An oversized stuffed gorilla leaned drunk-
enly in the corner, its shiny black eyes seeming alive in
the reflected light from the fire.

Architectural Digest would never clamor for a photo
shoot, yet Geoff couldn't help contrasting the room
with his own professionally decorated house next door,
where everything was new and expensive and in its
proper place and nothing made him want to sit back
and put his feet up.

The music died suddenly, leaving his ears ringing in
the unexpected quiet.

"Who in your house likes rap?" he asked, thinking
of Neil and Willie, whoever they were.

Merry grinned. "My mother, actually."

Geoff's eyebrows shot skyward. "Your mother?"

She nodded. "She says there's a lot of valuable social commentary in rap and that we ought to pay more attention to what the performers are saying and not so much to how they're saying it."

"All of it?" he asked, skeptical.

"Well, no. She picketed one of the groups that staged a concert here a few years back. She opposes anyone who advocates violence, including violence against women."

"Your mother picketed a rap group?"

"Dad, too. He says people need to make their views known instead of just complaining about it. They both marched against the Vietnam War and they've been protesting or promoting something ever since."

Her eyes sparkled wickedly. "Mother framed her first arrest sheet. It's hanging in the hall, if you're curious. She's very proud of it, but don't ask her about it or you'll be stuck here for hours."

Geoff tried to imagine his country club mother picketing anything except her roses, but his imagination wasn't up to it. The most controversial thing she'd ever been involved in was an acrimonious debate with another member of her garden club on the question of hybrid teas. If she were ever arrested, she'd change her name and flee the country.

"Not a word, I swear," he said, and crossed his heart. The gesture caught him by surprise. He hadn't done anything that childish in years. Easy to know who to blame it on.

"Have you followed in your mother's footsteps, then?" he asked, teasing, but curious, too.

"Not a chance. Political protests would have interfered with our schoolwork—or so mother said."

He was strangely relieved. He didn't like the idea of

her in jail, no matter what the reason—not his Merry, with her bright eyes, glowing good looks, and wild hair that made him itch to free it of its restraining combs.

Geoff sucked in his breath. *His* Merry?

"Merry? Is that you? Why'd you turn off the music?" The footsteps in the hall came closer. "What's in the bags? Have you been Christmas shopping? What'd you get?"

Merry's eyes widened in mock horror. "My mother! I have to get those bags locked in my room before she starts digging to see what I got her. I'll be right back."

She was across the room like a shot. "Hi, Mom." She gave an airy wave in Geoff's direction. "Mom, this is Geoff. Geoff, my mom." Then she grabbed her bags and ran.

The slender woman who walked into the room looked like an older version of her daughter—pretty, lively, and totally unfazed at finding a stranger in her living room. "Hi!" she said, extending her hand. "I'm Jane."

"Jane?"

Her eyes narrowed in mock threat. "Don't say it. And if you dare call me Mrs. Doe, you'll regret it for a week."

She ran an appraising eye down the length of him, all the way to his polished Italian shoes and back up again. "Are you a friend of Merry's?"

Without giving him a chance to answer, without even bothering to find out who he was, she stepped into the hall and cupped a hand around her mouth. "Willie," she called. Her voice echoed in the old house. "We have another one for dinner."

FIVE

Geoff's arguments that he had work to do, that he was expecting someone, that he didn't want to impose all fell on deaf ears. A half hour later, he had dumped his bags and briefcase in his own front hall, taped a note as to his whereabouts on his front door, and found himself seated in the middle of Bedlam.

"Pass the potatoes, would you?"

"Who has the butter?"

"So I told him if he wanted to send Peters to Tampa, he could take the expense out of his own budget, not mine, and he said—"

"Hey! Quit hogging the gravy!"

"Of course, Rogers didn't send the part like he promised, which meant I had to tell Mr. Beeson he couldn't have his car—"

Dazed by the half dozen conversations swirling around the table, Geoff filled his plate from whatever bowl or platter came his way and tried not to think of the simple meal his housekeeper would have left for him and the quiet, soothing solitude in which he would have eaten it.

So this was what dinner in a large family was like. He'd run stockholders' meetings that were more organized than this.

He glanced down the long table at the crowd of animated faces. Introductions had been haphazard, but he'd caught most of the names. He'd met Neil and Willie—brothers, not boyfriends—and older brother Dare, who was visiting on vacation with his own family.

"Dare Doe?" Geoff had said before he could stop himself.

Dare had given him a lopsided grin. "Don't ask."

Dare's wife, Steffie, and three-year-old son, Jeffie, were there, as well as a young man and woman who had evidently been fostered in the Doe home some years earlier and were now dreaming of starting their own family.

"But we wouldn't miss Decoration Day for anything," said the woman, whose name Geoff hadn't caught. "We both took some vacation so we could come. Everyone else will be here tomorrow."

She hadn't had a chance to say exactly what Decoration Day was, but the way she'd said the words made it clear the members of the Doe family thought of it in capital letters. He'd have to ask Merry.

He hoped they'd have a moment alone when he could ask her out. He'd take her somewhere elegant, he decided, elegant and expensive. And quiet. She'd be beautiful in a slim black dress with her skin set alight by the candles' glow.

Maybe Sam's Barbecue would be a better bet, though. He couldn't argue about Batman and the Hulk or the chances of the local hockey team over pigeon breast with truffles.

The thought shook him. Since when had comic book heroes and hockey become his conversational topics of choice?

Before he could explore that unsettling thought, someone handed him a basket of rolls and instructed him to take one and pass it on. He dutifully did as he was told, and too late realized he already had half a roll on his plate. He couldn't for the life of him remember eating the other half.

From her seat at the end of the table, Merry watched Geoff and worried. It would have been easier if her mother hadn't separated them. He might be used to high-powered business dinners, but he wasn't accustomed to the free-for-all that passed for dinner in the Doe household.

Not that she could tell it by looking at him. He sat there like a prince in his palace, as poised and well-mannered as if he were dining at the White House. But she'd caught the occasional flash of panic in his eyes, even if no one else had. Her family did that to people—at first, anyway. Afterward, if they had any sense, the guests just relaxed and joined in the fun.

But Geoffrey Hanover was not relaxing, and the last thing she wanted was for her family to drive him off. They might be from very different worlds, but she was sure she wanted to see more of him. A whole lot more.

"Neil!" she said suddenly, cutting into the conversation. "You could fix Geoff's car, couldn't you?" She'd explained Geoff's problems to him earlier but he hadn't shown much interest. His specialty was restoring vintage cars, not repairing new ones.

Her brother looked surprised. "A late-model Mercedes isn't quite in my line, sis. You know that."

"But you can fix anything, and Geoff needs a good mechanic. After all," she added, flashing her guest a deliberately teasing look, "I won't always be there to rescue him when his car breaks down."

"I don't—" said Neil.

"That's really not necessary," said Geoff. "I—"

"Neil can fix anything," she assured Geoff. "He's the one who got Mehetabel running. You should have seen her when I bought her. She was a mess. But now—don't look at me like that! And don't laugh at Mehetabel. Once she gets a new paint job—"

"And a bumper," said Willie.

"And new seats," said Geoff firmly. *"Definitely* new seats."

Everyone laughed.

Merry tried to look insulted. "You guys are just mean. And *you* are jealous," she added, giving Geoff a mock ferocious glare. "All because my car runs and yours doesn't."

"Ouch." He grinned. "That was a low blow."

Neil, forgotten, looked from Geoff to Merry, then back again as a lazy smile of comprehension dawned on his face. He glanced at Willie, who was looking smug, and Dare, who was studying their guest, and at his father, who was looking contentedly benevolent. His mother met his gaze with a twinkling one of her own.

He leaned back in his chair and grinned at Geoff. Poor guy was a goner.

Call it fate, kismet, love at first sight. Whatever it was, Geoff had it bad. Real bad. And Merry had it worse— she had the same sappy look in her eyes Dare had had in his when he'd first met Steffie and Mick had had when he'd met Marcia.

Neil's grin widened. His baby sister didn't even realize it yet, but she'd just found her one and only.

If Geoff was going to be part of the family, then Neil figured he might as well do what he could to help, even if it meant fixing a car that wasn't at least twenty-five years old.

"All right," he said, "I'll check it out. Have your mechanic bring it here. If we have to move it to the shop, I can have my guys do it later."

For a moment, Geoff stared at him with the blank look of someone trying to decipher Martian. "Oh, uh . . ." He shrugged, clearly embarrassed. "That's all right. It'd be too much trouble and—"

"No trouble." Neil gave him a conspiratorial wink. "Merry's the baby of the family, you know. That means she always gets what she wants. So if she wants me to look over your car—"

He ducked as a buttered roll came sailing across the table straight at his head.

Three hours later, Geoff flipped on the lights in his entry hall and closed the front door behind him. For a moment, he just stood there, listening to the silence.

There wasn't so much as a creak from the old house. There was no loud rap music on the stereo, no laughter in the kitchen, no talk of football and politics in the front room, no fussy three year old ready to be put to bed. Nothing.

Quiet at last.

Not only quiet, but clean, well-ordered comfort. Other than his shopping bags and his briefcase, which he'd tossed on the hall table earlier, nothing marred the pristine elegance of the entry. There wasn't a candlestick out of place, no discarded mail, no abandoned toys, no muddy shoes carelessly kicked to one side as there'd been in the Does' front hallway.

He couldn't see much else. The other rooms were dark—there'd been no one to turn on any lights—but he knew they'd be as well-ordered as the hall. Mrs. Sandowsky was a stickler for tidy, and there'd been no one to disarrange so much as a sofa cushion since the housekeeper had left several hours earlier.

For the first time since he'd bought the place, it seemed cold and echoing and empty.

Irritated, Geoff set the dead bolt on the front door and shrugged out of his overcoat. He almost tossed it

from his house it slowed to a crawl. Three blocks away it was down to stop and go, with a whole lot more stop than go.

Geoff frowned and rolled down his window. He couldn't hear any sirens, no one bellowing through loudspeakers, nothing to indicate a fire or a major accident, yet the night sky was alight with a glow that almost banished the dark.

But what, short of a major disaster, could do that?

SIX

It was worse than he'd thought. Worse than he could possibly have imagined.

In spite of the line of cars backed up behind him, Geoff braked to a halt smack in the middle of the street and stared. And as he stared, his grip on the steering wheel tightened until his fingers ached with the strain.

Now he knew what Decoration Day in the Doe household meant.

It meant a three-dimensional Santa and his reindeer and sleigh on the roof. It meant full-size painted cutouts of Victorian carolers under a Victorian lamppost. It meant painted chipmunks and bear cubs and fawns decorating a spruce tree draped in colored lights.

He stared at the tree. Yesterday it had been an average, run-of-the-mill spruce tree about seven feet tall. Nice, but nothing to write home about. Now lights wrapped around all seven feet of it winked on and off while an oversize toy train circled endlessly underneath, chugging merrily and whoo-whooing at every opportunity. Beside the tree, a jack-in-the-box kept popping out to wave at the passersby, a trio of oversize dolls nodded and smiled and blinked, and every once in awhile a shiny red fire engine would raise, then lower its ladder while the big brass bell on its hood clang-clanged.

At the far side of the yard—*his* side of the yard—a

regiment of animated toy soldiers marched across the snow without ever going anywhere. A mouse kept climbing a ladder to string lights from the eaves of his mouse house, but the ladder kept tilting backward, swinging upright, then tilting back again. A polar bear in a red Santas cap and knitted muffler skated around and around a fake frozen pond until Geoff got dizzy watching it.

The center of the yard was covered with a traditional manger scene complete with bales of straw and a flashing star and angels and shepherds and three kings, not to mention a herd of camels and sheep. And a donkey. The beasts were half size, but he'd be willing to bet the Does would have used live animals if they could have gotten around the city's zoning and animal control regulations.

Geoff forced his grip on the steering wheel to ease, but he couldn't take his eyes off the garish display in front of him.

Decoration Day in the Doe household meant three million Christmas lights hung in the trees and dripping from the eaves and strung everywhere—every one blazing so the yard looked like something straight off the Las Vegas strip.

Decoration Day meant a traffic jam big enough to make the downtown planners feel smug. Cars filled the street in both directions as far as the eye could see. People had parked wherever they could find a space and now they lined the sidewalks, gawking and pointing and trampling the once pristine snow into a sodden mess.

Geoff closed his eyes against the sight and swore softly under his breath. He could see it now, *hear* it now. He wouldn't have a single quiet night at home until the madness ended. The racket was deafening. Santa ho-hoed and Merry Christmased, the carolers caroled, the drummer at the front of the marching soldiers thrummed endlessly, and all the while the three kings insisted they from the Orient were, over and over and over again.

And that didn't count the yodeling chipmunk that was putting the star at the top of the seven-foot spruce—at least, Geoff assumed it was yodeling. He couldn't think of any other word to describe the abominable sound that came out of its throat.

Above it all, Rudolph kept flashing that damned red nose of his and looking smugly pleased with his prominent role in the festivities.

So far as Geoff could see, the only thing Merry and her family had forgotten was Gene Autry singing "Rudolph the Red-Nosed Reindeer." Maybe that came later.

A friendly honk from behind him roused him from his stupor. He put the Blazer in gear and moved forward. He'd have to sleep in the guest bedroom at the opposite side of the house for the next few weeks. The lights would drive him crazy if the racket didn't.

A low growl rumbled out of his throat—a growl that had absolutely nothing to do with his empty stomach. His real estate agent should have warned him about this. *I want quiet,* he'd told her. Peace and quiet and a nice, normal, well-regulated neighborhood.

He'd have a few sharp words for her the next time he saw her. She could count on it.

The traffic inched forward and eventually brought him to his own driveway—or, rather, where his driveway used to be.

A minivan and an old Cadillac were parked across it, blocking the two family-size cars parked in the driveway itself. The cars couldn't get out and he couldn't get in, not even if he'd been willing to drive over the rose-bushes that were half buried under the snow.

The roses had already had a tough year. Someone had slid into one of them several weeks ago, smashed some branches and never bothered to stop.

His head throbbed.

If he were smart, he'd find a quiet restaurant where he could have a good meal, a good bottle of wine, and some peace, maybe even a hotel where he could camp until the seasonal madness was over.

Instead, he took the next turn that would lead him back to Merry's house.

It took slightly longer than a half hour to work his way back around. His driveway was still blocked—this time by a pickup and a full-size van—but Merry's driveway was free and clear.

He gunned the Blazer going in, then defiantly parked in the middle of the drive so anyone going in or out would have to swing onto the lawn to get around him.

He climbed out and slammed the door. The sound of it shot through his pounding head, making him wince, but the violence of the action suited his mood. His mouth set in an uncompromising line, Geoff stalked across the lawn.

He frowned when Willie opened the door instead of Merry.

"Hi!" Willie said cheerfully, oblivious to a look that sent secretaries and junior staff scurrying for cover. "Come on in." He swung the door wide, then shouted up the stairs, "Hey, Merry! It's for you!"

A burst of feminine laughter drifted down in response.

Willie grinned. "They're all wrapping presents. Us guys are in the family room watching a tape of the Jets-Dolphins game this afternoon. Pretty good game. Score's tied and they're just starting the third quarter."

"I don't—"

"Merry'll be right down. You can wait in there if you want," he added, giving a vague wave in the direction of the living room, "but if you'd rather watch the game, just come on back. The beer's cold and there's a couple of pieces of pizza left if you want 'em."

With that, Willie sauntered off, leaving Geoff still standing in the hallway, the door gaping open behind him.

He managed not to slam the door, but just barely. What kind of loonies did he have for neighbors, anyway? How did they expect him to complain about that abomination outside if he accepted their invitation to join them for the game?

Besides, he was a Broncos fan.

By the time Merry appeared at the top of the stairs, he had his lines all rehearsed. He knew exactly what he was going to say to her, and he'd pretty much figured out what her response would be, as well. It was plain good business to know what opponents would be thinking long before they got around to thinking it, and Geoff was nothing if not a damned good businessman.

At the sight of her, every single word of it went right out of his head. Geoff might have cursed if he could have gotten any air into his chest to do it.

There was nothing exceptional about her appearance.

Her jeans were as worn and as temptingly form-fitting as the one she'd worn the day before. Her sweatshirt looked as if it had belonged to one of her brothers a hundred years ago. Her hair was mussed, she wore no makeup, and she was in her stocking feet.

Geoff's body jolted alive at the sight of her, in spite of his firm intention to keep things on a nice, neat adversarial level.

"Hi!" She galloped down the steps toward him, graceful and eager as a high-bred colt. "Did you come for the game?"

He opened his mouth and got ready to let her have it. Not a word came out.

"Neil hasn't had a chance to work on your car yet,"

she added, crossing the hall to him, "but he promised he'd get to it as quick as he could."

She stopped not a foot in front of him. That close, she had to tilt her head back to look into his face. Her eyes were even more brilliant than he'd remembered.

"It must really be snowing out there. Look at you!" She flicked her hand across the shoulders of his coat, brushing off the snow that clung to the heavy wool. Then she rose onto her toes and brushed at the snow that had caught in his hair.

He sucked in his breath, fighting for calm. His lungs filled with the scent of her. She smelled like . . . like . . .

"A little more of that white stuff and we could add you to our collection out front," she said, and laughed. "Can I take your coat? Do you want some coffee? Hot chocolate, maybe? Have you had dinner yet?"

He took another, deeper breath, then slowly let it out. She smelled like cinnamon.

"Geoff?" She cocked her head in puzzlement. "Is something wrong?"

The question snapped him out of his daze. He frowned, determined to be dignified, but stern. Calm. Mature. Businesslike. But dignified, above all else.

"There's a damned yodeling chipmunk out there," he growled.

Her jaw dropped. "A what?"

"A yodeling chipmunk." Even to his ears, it sounded querulous, almost childishly aggrieved.

He turned his frown into an outright scowl. It was hard to concentrate on what he wanted to say to her when his mind insisted on reminding him of what he wanted to do to her.

She darted past him and threw open the door, then craned to see. "Where's this chipmunk?"

He came to stand beside her. The doorway was just wide enough for two. "There." He pointed.

Her brow wrinkled in a puzzled frown. "You mean Freddy?"

"That thing on the top of the spruce."

"Freddy.

"Whatever." This close to her, the scent of cinnamon was even stronger. What sane woman wore cinnamon? And why did it smell so damned good on her?

She twisted around in the doorway so she could look up at him. "Freddy is not yodeling. He's chirping. You know, making chipmunk sounds."

He tried to concentrate on the offensive decoration rather than the effect being so close to her was having on him, but it wasn't easy. He felt a little dizzy. Hunger, probably. He really should have eaten that sandwich.

"Chipmunks," he said very firmly, "do not chirp."

Her eyes narrowed. "Whatever."

He braced his hand on the doorjamb opposite, fencing her in, and leaned closer. "Why do you smell like cinnamon?"

"What?"

She was so close. It would be so easy to claim a kiss. One quick, sweet kiss.

"Cinnamon," he said. It wasn't easy getting the words out. "You smell like cinnamon."

"It was the cookies." She licked her lips nervously. His blood pressure shot up ten points.

"Cookies?" He leaned closer. Hunger was making him a little weak in the knees and a whole lot feverish, but this hunger had absolutely nothing to do with the lunch he'd never had a chance to eat.

SEVEN

"Christmas cookies," Merry said. Her breath was stuck in her chest somewhere. It felt as if her ribs had suddenly gotten too tight. "If I smell like cinnamon, it's because of the Christmas cookies. We made the first batches today."

"Yes?" he murmured. He looked dazed.

"Yes." She ducked under his arm and back into the hall. It was a lot easier to breathe once she'd put a little distance between them. "We'd better close the door. We're wasting energy this way."

Geoff shook himself like a bear coming out of hibernation, blinked a couple of times, and growled.

"How can you talk about wasting energy when you have *that* out there?" he demanded, stabbing a finger in the direction of the yard. "Do you realize how much electricity you're throwing away?"

The words came out gruffer than he'd intended, but narrow escapes always made him irritable.

"I do, actually," she said. That hint of a dimple at the side of her mouth was back. "Every year mother frets about how it's not environmentally wise to use all that electricity and stuff, and every year she's the first one to buy another string of lights."

"That's not the point," he snapped, frustrated.

"You don't approve of our decorations?" She wasn't

fooling him. That wounded innocence was a put-on. No innocent woman could elevate his blood pressure like this without even trying.

"No," he said, "I don't. They're garish, unnecessary, noisy, and they're blocking my driveway."

"Your driveway?" She gaped at him. "What do our decorations have to do with your driveway?"

"Your decorations—" He stopped. This conversation wasn't going the way he'd planned. He drew a steadying breath. *Dignity, remember?*

"I can't get into my driveway because your decorations have drawn a lot of ill-mannered people who have nothing better to do than gawk at your tacky display and tie up traffic and park their cars in my driveway. I couldn't get in if I tried, and I went around the block twice."

Somewhere in the middle, his dignified speech had degenerated into a tirade. He wasn't quite sure how or why, but it was when her mouth snapped shut and her eyes took on a martial glitter.

"Our decorations are not tacky." Her hands were fisted on her hips and she was leaning forward on the balls of her stocking feet like a fighter waiting for an opening. "And those people are not ill-mannered."

"You don't call blocking my driveway ill-mannered?"

"Where else are they going to park?"

"How about your driveway? They're your decorations, aren't they?"

"Mine and my family's. And we never heard any objections to them until you came along!"

"Maybe no one had the courage to say anything."

"The bad manners, you mean. *And* the bad taste."

"Bad taste? Hah!"

"Hah, yourself!"

It wasn't the most mature thing she'd ever said, but Merry wasn't in the mood for mature. The man was a nuisance. A menace. He was rude, self-centered, un-imaginative, a stick-in-the-mud of the worst sort—and electricity still skittered along her spine from when he'd been close enough to kiss her . . . if he'd wanted.

Why hadn't he?

The thought brought her back to reality with a snap. The last thing she wanted was to have Handsome Hanover kissing her. The very last thing. "I think you'd better leave."

"I will."

"Good."

Neither of them budged an inch. The energy arcing between them was enough to power every Christmas light in the yard.

That thought galvanized her into action. She grabbed the edge of the still open door. "Well, are you leaving? Or do I have to call my brothers to throw you out?"

"I'm leaving."

"Great. Good riddance."

"Hah!" He turned around and stalked through the door, across the porch, and out of her life.

Merry slammed the door behind him, then collapsed against it, breathing hard.

The air in the hall seemed chillier without him, and it wasn't just the cold from outside that did it.

The gawkers were still out there, tying up traffic, blocking his drive, and crowding the sidewalk until it looked like the Fourth of July parade on Main Street.

Geoff stalked over to his car. He'd drive across the lawn if he had to. Maybe he'd be lucky enough to cut the electric cord that kept that damned chipmunk yo-deling.

His car door was locked. He fumbled in his pockets, then peered in the side. The Christmas lights reflected green, red, white, and blue in the window. They also showed the key in the ignition and his key ring with all his house and office keys dangling from it.

Geoff swore and smacked the glass in frustration. Then he groaned and rested his forehead on the top of the Blazer's door.

He was tired, he was hungry, his head hurt like hell . . . and he wanted nothing so much as to storm back in that house, drag Merry into his arms, and kiss her crazy.

Resigned, he shoved away from the car. Let it sit there. He had other keys in the house and a spare set of house keys stashed in a fake rock under the junipers. He'd reclaim the Blazer tomorrow. If someone in the Doe family wanted to get out in the meantime, they could just go around it. Or they could damned well stay put. *He* didn't care.

Shoving his hands in his pockets, he followed the tracks he'd left in the snow-covered drive out to the sidewalk. That was a mistake. It was worse than the Fourth of July. Worse, even, than fighting the last-minute shopping rush at the mall.

At the mall, people were moving. Here, they just found a spot and took root.

Geoff glared. And then he took a second look.

Old folks, moony teenagers draped around each other like wet socks, parents with small kids in tow—regardless of age, they stared at the lights and the colorful mechanical toys, and for a moment, for the short time they stood in the cold and the falling snow, they had the look of people who believed in magic.

It was enough to make him want to shout *Bah! Humbug!*

He stopped short to let a young family move past. The two older children had claimed their mother's hands and were towing her forward eagerly.

"Look at the bear, Mom! And the fire engine!"

"Look at the mouse on the ladder!"

The father followed them, a child of perhaps two in his arms.

"Daddy, look!" the child cried, pointing and giggling with delight. "Santa Claus!"

The father hoisted the small child higher and grinned. "That's right, son. And Rudolph, too!"

In their eyes, Geoff could see the reflections of the Christmas lights that waved and danced in the wind behind him.

For a long while after the family had disappeared in the crowd, Geoff just stood there, staring where the child had pointed, at Santa and Rudolph and all the other reindeer on the roof. And he knew if anyone had bothered to look, they would see the reflections of the lights in his eyes, too.

Eleven o'clock.

For what seemed like the thousandth time that morning, Merry scowled at her watch. Where was he?

Irritated, she tossed the last section of the Sunday paper, which she'd been perusing with unaccustomed care, atop the untidy heap of papers on the floor.

He should have been here long before now—nine or ten at the latest. She'd planned exactly what she would say, how she would act, right down to the smile she'd give him when he showed up on her doorstep.

So where was he? How was she going to pull this off if he didn't come?

And she was determined to pull it off. Neil had frowned and shaken his head when she'd explained her plan, but there'd been a twinkle in his eye nonetheless, and in the end he'd gone along with it, just as she'd known he would. Willie had laughed and added several adornments to the scheme. Dare had thrown up his hands and refused to be dragged into it, but Steffie had giggled and refused to be left out. King and Ken had promised to help once they were off work. Mick wouldn't be back from his business trip until Monday, but Merry knew she could count on him. Despite taking his responsibilities as oldest son far too seriously, Mick had never let anyone leave him out of a scheme yet, certainly not one as good as this. She'd gotten everyone else on board, which meant they'd have everything ready to go by tomorrow afternoon at the latest.

So where *was* he?

The doorbell chimed. Three times, insistently. Merry was off the sofa before the first chime quit echoing, but she didn't rush. He was up to five before she finally opened the door.

"Oh, hi!" she said brightly, feigning surprise. Maybe she should go into acting. She was *good*.

"Where's my car?" He looked as if he hadn't slept well.

That was good, too. She poked her head out the door and looked around blankly. "Your car?"

"The Blazer," he growled.

He looked great when he growled. Just listening to him sent an exciting little tingle down her spine.

"What did you do with my Blazer?"

"Oh. *That* car." She smiled up at him. "It wouldn't start, so Neil had it towed to his shop. He promised to get to it right after he fixes your Mercedes." Her brow furrowed with mock sympathy. "Do you always have this much trouble with your vehicles?"

He let his breath out with an explosive whoosh. "There was nothing wrong with my car. I locked the keys in it, that's all."

She let her smile widen. "We noticed."

Before he could explode, she added, "We pulled out your briefcase, if that's what you're worried about."

He stared at her. In a night filled with sleep-robbing memories of a woman who smelled of cinnamon and a child whose eyes reflected the lights of Christmas, he'd forgotten the damned briefcase.

"Listen," she said, "I really am sorry about your not being able to get in your own driveway last night. We should have warned you. Most folks have been around here so long—"

I know, he thought, *that's one of the things I liked about this neighborhood.*

"—that they already know what to expect. So I thought I'd treat you to lunch as a way to make up for it."

"Lunch?" He blinked.

"And then I hoped you'd help me pick out one last present. I need a man's perspective and—"

"Shop? You want me to help you *shop?*"

"Great." She gave him her brightest, widest smile. "Thanks. I owe you one."

"I don't—"

"I'll just get my purse." This was going to be a cinch.

Geoff stood in the open doorway and fumed. Every time he turned around, she confused him. He prided himself on being levelheaded, focused, on top of things, yet he hadn't known her for two days and she'd already made him moody and forgetful and robbed him of his sleep twice in as many nights.

It had to stop. Right now. He started to tell her so, but she breezed by him and on down the steps.

"You'll love this place," she shouted as she threw open Mehetabel's passenger-side door. "It's a great place, honest!"

She said something else, but Geoff didn't catch it because she'd bent down and stuck her head in the car. Through the windshield, he could see her furiously pitching things into the backseat, but his attention was fixed on her jeans-clad rump. Even from this distance it looked great, reminding him of how much better it had looked two days ago, when she was hanging out the window for the coffee.

He unzipped his ski jacket at a sudden rush of heat.

Like a jack-in-the-box, she popped back out, still chattering, and went around to her side of the car. ". . . you've gotta try their nachos. The menu's all Tex-Mex and they've got a salsa that's guaranteed to curl your eyebrows."

She threw open her door, then stopped as she suddenly realized he was still standing in the open doorway. "Come on! If we don't get a move on, we'll have to wait for hours to get a seat!"

With a sigh, Geoff closed the door and headed down the steps after her.

EIGHT

The salsa didn't curl his eyebrows, but it came close. He didn't care. Between the laughter and the heated arguments over, among other things, the relative merits of Tarzan versus the Wizard of Oz as childhood icons, he didn't pay much attention to the food or the passage of time. It was only as the waiters began putting the chairs on top of the nearby tables that he looked up.

"Er . . ." He glanced around and realized for the first time that the place was almost empty.

"Oh, my!" said Merry. "Just *look* how late it is!"

Was it his imagination, or was there a tiny little false note in her exclamation of surprise?

"We'd better get going. This may take some time, you know."

He should have known.

Three hours later, they were still shopping. Despite his protests, she'd dragged him back to the mall, but not just to shop. They'd spent an hour playing the electronic games in the arcade, another hour checking out the toys in the toy store (for Jeffie, Merry said, though she seemed to have developed a strong attachment to the bright pink Space Blasters they found in a back aisle), and now he was in the middle of an Eddie Bauer store trying on sweaters while she made him sweat by watching his every move.

It didn't help that the sweater—if she ever found one she liked—was destined for another man. Mick, she'd said.

Mick had damned well better be another brother.

This is a mistake, Merry thought, watching Geoff pull on yet another sweater. He was decently clothed—he had a shirt on under his own sweater, after all—and she'd seen her brothers and their friends pull on sweaters and tug them off again a million times over the years. Not once had the sight set her heart pounding so hard she could feel it thumping all the way down to her toes. Not even a little bit.

"So," she said. "What do you think? Is that a good one?"

"Sure. Just like all the other two hundred I've tried on." He eyed her with unconcealed suspicion. "Are you *sure* this Mick fellow is my size?"

"Sure," she said, flashing him her brightest smile. "Just about. Really."

She stuck her hand behind her back and crossed her fingers. Mick was probably a good three inches shorter than Geoff, and muscular where Geoff was elegantly lean. But she wasn't going to buy a sweater, anyway. She'd gotten Mick a new hat weeks ago to match the hat she'd bought his wife. The shopping had been a ploy. She'd needed to keep Geoff away from the house until it was dark enough that he wouldn't notice what the others had been up to in his absence.

"It's hard to decide," she said. "Mick can be so picky sometimes." That, at least, wasn't a lie.

She ran her hand over the sleeve of the sweater he was wearing and immediately wished she hadn't. Even through the bulky wool she could feel the warmth of him and the curve of hard, lean muscles. She snatched her hand away just as he cleared his throat.

Blushing, and furious at her reaction, she turned away

and pretended to study the pile of sweaters on the table beside her. "Maybe this plaid—"

"*No.*" His hand clamped over hers, then as quickly jerked away.

She turned to look at him, startled, her hand tingling from the contact, but he was already pulling off the latest model. The sweater was up over his head and he was tugging at the sleeves like a kid who'd just spilled a whole bottle of ketchup on himself and was trying to get rid of the evidence fast.

"Here," she said, grabbing one of the knitted cuffs. "Don't fidget like that. If you'd quit—"

"I do *not* need your help," he said the instant his head emerged from the bottom of the sweater.

He was red-faced and a little breathless and his dark-brown hair looked like he'd run through a wind machine, but he irritably waved her away even though his arms were still entangled in the sleeves.

"I can get out of a sweater by myself," he said in a tone that brooked no argument. "And I am *not* trying on any more."

"Right." Merry crammed her hands into her pockets as protection against the almost overwhelming urge to brush his hair back from his face.

He yanked the sweater off, then wadded it up and flung it atop the untidy pile of sweaters he'd tried on earlier.

Merry burrowed into the pile and emerged with his own cashmere pullover. "Here's your sweater." She grimaced. "I'm afraid it's a little rumpled. I didn't—"

"Doesn't matter," he said, and snatched it out of her hands,

"No. Wait! You're going to stretch it out of shape if you pull on it like that. If you'll just—"

The top of his head poked out of the sweater's neck. One eye was still covered. The other gleamed balefully.

"I . . . do . . . *not* . . . need your help." The words were only slightly muffled by being spoken into a sweater.

Merry glared back. She didn't like being flustered, breathless, and crazy, yet he managed to make her all that and worse without even trying.

"Fine," she snapped. "Do it your way."

His visible eye narrowed dangerously as he shoved his fist out the end of one sleeve. "I will."

"Good." Merry swung around to pick up the sweater he'd just pulled off. Before she could do more than untangle the sleeves and shake it out, he grabbed her hand and pulled her away from the table.

"We're leaving. *Now.*" His hair was still standing on end, but he'd managed to tug his sweater into place and grab his jacket.

Long experience and six brothers had taught her all males had their limit when it came to shopping, and Mr. Geoffrey Hanover had clearly passed his. The glitter in his eyes warned it would be risky to cross him, but Merry dug in her heels anyway, caught between wanting to go wherever he took her—which was just plain crazy—and feeling guilty about the mess they were leaving behind, which was normal.

Thank God for normal.

"But I always fold—"

"Not this time, you don't," he grabbed her hand and dragged her out of the store.

He didn't let go even as he trotted her through the mall. She carefully didn't mention that fact. His hand felt wonderful wrapped around hers, big and strong and warm. She tried not to think about what it would feel like to have it on other parts of her anatomy, but she couldn't help it. By the time they reached the parking lot, her thoughts were heading off in very dangerous directions indeed.

Fortunately, it was dark out—dark enough he wouldn't notice her blushing. More than dark enough for her to take him home, though she didn't raise any objections when he suggested they stop for a coffee at a cozy little shop along the way.

"I need a coffee," he said, huddled in his seat and grimly staring out the windshield at the red light dancing in the wind above the intersection. They were the first words he'd spoken since they left Eddie Bauer's.

"You need to comb your hair, too," said Merry, and leaned over to brush it back from his forehead. She couldn't help herself. She'd been thinking about it for so long that she was likely to do much worse if she didn't touch him now, while they were crammed into Mehetabel's front seats, where there wasn't a chance on earth they could get carried away, no matter what her parents had managed in the backseat of another old VW.

He grabbed her hand. Quick, as though he thought she'd hit him.

And then he just held it while their gazes locked and the heat in the car skyrocketed.

Merry stopped breathing—just stopped with the air half in and half out of her lungs. She wasn't even sure which direction it had been going at the time, not that it mattered. There wasn't any oxygen *left* to breathe. It had all been sucked up someplace, leaving a vacuum that was filled by her intense awareness of the man sitting not two feet from her.

She swayed and, without thinking, leaned closer. Maybe it was just her imagination, but she'd swear he was leaning closer, too, that his eyes were sliding shut just like hers, and that, any minute now, they'd meet right over Mehetabel's gearshift. And when they did—

Angry honking from the car behind her jerked her back to awareness. She snapped back into her seat at the same instant Geoff snapped into his. Merry sucked in air—what little there was, which didn't seem nearly enough to get her brain working again. It took a second or two longer for him to let go of her hand—it hadn't even occurred to her she could have pulled it free her-self—and another few seconds to remember where she was and what she was supposed to be doing.

That's when she realized the light had changed to green. By the time she got Mehetabel in gear and mov-ing, it had turned yellow. She was only halfway across the intersection and still accelerating when it turned red, which drew more angry honks, this time from the car behind her and the cars at the cross street, waiting to go if she ever got out of the way.

"Whew!" She hastily rolled down her window, hoping the cold air would help. "That guy was *rude.*"

Geoff grunted. He was slumped back in his seat—as much as he could slump, given the conditions—staring out the windshield like a man whose whole life had just passed in front of him.

"I really, really, *really* need a cup of coffee," he said. "really."

He let out his breath with a low, drawn-out sigh, then slowly squeezed his eyes shut. "And you just drove right past the place."

She had to turn down an alley, then circle around three more blocks to get back to the entrance.

The coffee was great, strong and full-flavored, just the way he liked it. Which was good, because at the moment it was the only thing close to the way he liked it.

Geoff stared at the woman across the table from him and wondered how it was possible for someone he didn't even know existed two days ago to have turned his whole world upside down.

He'd swear she hadn't even been trying.

Bad enough that he'd come close to dragging her into his arms and kissing her cross-eyed right there in the middle of Eddie Bauer's, but to have suffered wildly erotic thoughts about ravishing her at a stoplight in a Beetle with a gearshift between them . . .

Geoff took another gulp of coffee and tried not to think about it.

"I'm sorry about that red light." She looked worried. "Honest. I don't know what came over me. I'm normally a very careful driver. It's just—"

"It wasn't the red light."

She didn't look as if she believed him. Or maybe she didn't want to believe him. "No?"

"No."

"Well, then—"

"I'm tired." He set his coffee cup down with a little more force than was strictly necessary. "I have work waiting for me at home and a long day at the office tomorrow."

"Oh," she said. Her shoulders drooped. "Of course. I hadn't thought . . ."

He never got a chance to find out what she hadn't thought. She resolutely squared her shoulders, then reached under the table to retrieve her purse. "Shall we go, then? Unless you want to finish your coffee first?"

They drove back in silence. The old car's heater was working perfectly, but Geoff had the uncomfortable feeling there was more frost inside the car than out—which was too bad, because he had lots of great ideas for steaming up the interior. None of them were appropriate for when they were still driving, of course, and she probably would slap him silly if she had the slightest idea what he was thinking, but still . . .

The traffic jam was just as bad as it had been the night before, but this time, miracle of miracles, his driveway was clear. Or maybe not such a miracle.

As she cautiously nosed old Mehetabel over the sidewalk and onto his drive, he spotted a large, neatly lettered sign nailed to a stake by the drive. It read: *Please do not block the driveway! Thank you, and Merry Christmas!*

"Oh," he said, remembering his angry diatribe of the night before. "Er . . . thank you. I appreciate it."

She didn't glance at him, just roared up the drive as if a pack of wolves were after her. For a minute, he was afraid she'd plow into the back of his Blazer, which was pulled up in front of his garage, but she put on the brakes just in time. He closed his eyes for a moment of silent prayer, then cautiously let go of the hand grip Volkswagen had thoughtfully provided for nervous passengers.

"Well." He couldn't think of a single thing more to say.

"Yes." She glanced at him out of the corner of her eye, then abruptly looked away. "Looks like Neil got your car fixed," she said. "I think I know where he would have put your keys."

"I've got another set—" he said, but she was already out of the car and headed up his front walk, leaving Mehetabel still chugging contentedly behind her.

He had to slam her car door twice before it would shut properly. By the time he reached her, she'd fished a small, lumpy package wrapped in waterproof black cloth out of the middle of the juniper bush at one side of his steps. "Here it is."

"Merry—"

"I—"

They froze, gazes locked together, tongues securely tied.

She glanced down at her sleeve, then carefully flicked off the bits of dead juniper that clung to it. Her breath plumed in the frosty air. "About that red light—"

He gritted his teeth. "It wasn't the red light."

"No, but—" She licked her lips nervously, then looked up at him with eyes that seemed big enough to swallow him whole. "You see, I was really hoping you were going to kiss me, back there at that traffic light. But I guess I was wrong and—"

He grabbed her arms and pulled her against him before she had a chance to finish. He gave her a little shake because he couldn't think what else to do and because his frustration level was at explosive.

"You *what*?"

"I wanted you to kiss m—"

Merry got what she wanted—in spades, with bells and whistles and a trumpet voluntary that tingled all the way down to her toes.

Vaguely, from a distance, she heard "Angels We Have Heard on High" in a full-chorus version, and for a minute thought it was being sung for her. Good thing she'd wrapped her arms around his neck, or she'd have collapsed right there on the step in a puddle of happy mush.

The man could *kiss*.

Not that she'd had any doubts.

She'd wanted to kiss him back there at that traffic light, in the coffee shop, and all the way back home. She'd told herself fishing his keys out of the bushes was an extraordinarily clever ploy to get him up to the door without his having a chance to notice the additions made to his house during his absence, but she'd *really* wanted him to kiss her silly and have the chance to kiss him right back.

If she was a good little girl, she remembered her mother saying, Santa would come early and bring her exactly what she wanted.

He drew back at last, gasping for air. "Wow!"

She laughed and leaned into him. "You should have tried it at the stoplight."

He eyed her warily. "Why? Do you make a habit of kissing guys at intersections?"

"Haven't yet, but I was feeling inspired. It might have been, well—"

"Wonderful? Incredible?" He grinned. "Absolutely stupendous?"

"For a start." She loved the way he laughed. He ought to it more often.

"A start?"

He opened his mouth to say something, but not a word came out. A funny look came over his face, then his mouth snapped shut and he gently but firmly removed her arms from around his neck.

She started to protest, then suddenly blushed as she realized what followed a round of really passionate kissing, especially in a Bug.

It would be great, actually, but not at a stoplight. And *not* in the front seat.

As one, they glanced at his front door, then as quickly looked away again. His hands dropped to his sides. She stuck hers in her pockets.

"Yes," she said. "Well."

He cleared his throat and stuck out his chin the way a man does when his collar's suddenly gotten too tight. "You probably have to get home. I didn't realize it was so late."

"No."

"And your car's still running."

"Yes."

"Wouldn't want to pollute the air."

"No."

He looked at her. She looked at him. They both burst out laughing.

And then he did what he'd been wanting to do for a long, long time. Ever since he'd met her, in fact. *Was it really only two days ago?* He slid his hands up each side of her throat and ran his fingers into her hair until the silken curls tangled around him like ribbons, binding him to her. He kissed her again, an exquisitely hot and dangerous kiss that seemed to go on forever.

She was the first one to let go. He stepped back and, without taking his eyes off her, reached for the doorknob. It took a minute of fumbling for him to realize that he'd never gotten around to unlocking it.

He dug the keys out of his pocket. She picked up the set he'd locked in the Blazer the night before, then dropped on the steps when they'd kissed. For a moment, for one wildly insane moment, he thought about telling her to keep the extra set.

Fortunately, his brain kicked into gear before his libido could get him into trouble. He hoped it was his libido. If it was something else, something insane like his beginning to fall in love with her, he was in a lot more trouble than he'd thought.

Merry started down the steps, but stopped halfway and turned to look up at him. "Thanks for helping me with the shopping."

"It was . . . fun." He realized, to his surprise, it really had been fun. He'd never had a chance to spend time in toy stores checking out bright pink Space Blasters, even as a kid.

He had to repress a wild urge to forget work tomorrow and spend the entire day with her, exploring arcades and toy stores and traffic lights.

"Maybe this isn't the time to ask, but my family wondered if you had plans for Christmas."

"Christmas?" He frowned, trying to remember. "I usually go skiing in Switzerland for Christmas."

Her face fell. "Of course."

"But I'm not going this year."

Her smile returned. "No? Well, if you're not, you're welcome to join us, if you want. I have to admit it's a little crazy—you know, big dinner, kids running around, lots of noise, everyone talking at the same time." Her smile got a little uncertain around the edges. "Probably not your style."

Actually, he *didn't* know. Christmas with a traditional dinner and a huge family complete with screaming kids was about as far as you could get from the civilized gatherings he was used to. It sounded absolutely wonderful.

This time his face fell. "I did say I'd join some friends."

"Oh," she said. "Of course." She shrugged. "It was just a thought."

Was it his imagination, or did she seem a little disappointed? Maybe even a whole lot disappointed?

She got all the way to the bottom of the steps this time before she stopped. "But if something happens or you change your mind . . ."

"Thanks. I'll remember you asked."

He knew he wouldn't be there. He'd already promised Grace and Jeremy he'd join them for dinner at The Chateau, the city's most expensive restaurant. Besides, he couldn't barge in on a neighbor's family gathering after a few days' acquaintance, not even if you'd kissed their daughter—*especially* not if he'd kissed her the way he'd just kissed Merry.

Merry climbed into Mehetabel. She slammed her door three times before it finally stayed shut, a quick reverse U that barely missed clipping the hedge on the far side, and shot off down the drive. With the traffic, it would probably take her ten minutes to get from his driveway to hers, maybe longer. They could have walked over in half that time.

Determinedly shoving aside the thought of a walk through the snow with Merry, he unlocked his door and flicked on the hall lights. The overhead fixtures cast a soft, golden glow that barely touched the shadows of the rooms at either side of the dark stairwell.

It was, of course, his imagination that the house seemed as cold as the winter night outside.

NINE

"Hey, Geoff!"

Geoff scowled at the phone, then at the stack of files Ms. Gompers' temporary replacement had just dropped on his desk, half of them with sticky notes full of questions. Barely nine o'clock and already the day was shaping up to be a bad one. Next year, it was St. Moritz for sure—and no vacation for Ms. Gompers.

"I'm a little busy this morning, Jeremy. What's up?"

"Christmas. Grace's brother and his wife are coming up after all and Ted Deaver and his significant other thought they might join us, too. You don't mind, do you?"

"No. No, of course not." Did he know Ted Deaver? Geoff couldn't remember. He was sure he'd never met Grace's relatives.

"Grace says The Chateau can still take us, seven o'clock sharp. And, Geoff?"

"Yeah?" He barely stopped himself from swearing as he read the scribbles on the first sticky note.

"It's formal. Tux. I told you that, didn't I?"

Hell. "Tux. Right."

"Great! Catch ya later!"

And then the day got *really* bad.

* * *

Bad day, bad traffic, and a really bad mood. He'd quit early, but even leaving the office while it was still light out hadn't helped.

Geoff glared at the traffic and the snow and wondered if he was going to spend the rest of the year like this.

Why hadn't he gone to St. Moritz? At least there he never felt the pressure to get in the holiday mood. It was just another vacation. A tradition, really. This time of year was supposed to be for traditions, so why hadn't he kept his?

He knew the answer, of course. The thought of one more un-holiday holiday spent with friends he seldom saw, doing the same thing he'd done every year since he was nine, had been too depressing to contemplate.

Though he hadn't been able to put it into words, he knew now he'd wanted, for the first time in his life, to have a traditional Christmas like the ones he'd read about in books and seen in magazines, the kind that came complete with a big tree and the laughter of children and the company of people who didn't spend all their time talking about the latest mergers and acquisitions.

It was crazy. His family had never celebrated Christmas like that. His parents had been too busy; his brother had been much older and always had plans for the holidays. He didn't even own any Christmas ornaments! After all, you didn't need ornaments when you spent Christmas in St. Moritz.

As for his friends, well, traditional Christmases weren't their style, either. The ones who had kids also had nannies who took care of them, and those who didn't have kids didn't want to be bothered by anyone else's. If they weren't talking business, they were talking about the latest museum opening or their last trip to Paris or the wine they'd just bought direct from the vintner. No one he knew had ever read the Tarzan books, let alone argued about them over nachos and hot sauce.

Except Merry.

Just the thought of her was enough to warm him on a wintry day like this. A Christmasy kind of day, he thought, peering out the car window at the softly falling snow, even if there was still a week and a half to go.

The thought made him scowl again. A whole week and a half, and he was going to spend every day of it working. His shopping was done; the gifts he'd bought at Dailey & Sage the Friday before had been distributed around the office or carefully boxed by his mailroom staff and shipped off to the appropriate destination. Jeremy had confirmed the plans for Christmas Day dinner. His corporate attorney had invited him to a Christmas Eve cocktail party, so that was taken care of, too. There was nothing left but work.

That thought didn't help his mood.

He took the shortest route home this time. At least it was still light enough out that the Does' Christmas display wouldn't be turned on yet, and he wouldn't have to deal with a traffic jam in front of his house.

But there was still enough light left for him to see what the neighborhood elves had wrought in his absence.

His mouth gaping, Geoff pulled into his drive.

Yesterday morning, his lawn had been an unbroken sweep of white. It had been dark when he got home with Merry last night, and dark when he'd walked out his front door this morning, so he hadn't noticed anything different.

But between yesterday morning and now, his lawn had sprouted a snowman made of wire and wrapped with lights, an oversize teddy bear, a six-foot tall candle, and a fat little elf with an enormous top hat. Whoever had put up the figures had taken care to brush away their tracks, making it look as if the figures had magically dropped into place, but it wasn't hard to tell someone—several someones, in fact—and been mucking around on his lawn.

They hadn't stopped at lawn ornaments, either. They weren't so easy to spot against the dark brick of his house, but he could see strings and strings and *strings* of lights hung from his house and his trees and wrapped around his bushes. When everything was turned on, his place would be almost as garish as the Does'.

Muttering, Geoff switched off his engine and got out of the car. He'd deal with this later, he decided. Much later. Right now—

A snowball smacked his ear.

He whirled around. There was nobody in sight except the snowman and his colleagues, and they were all facing the street, not him. He swiped at his ear. The snowball hadn't been hardpacked, but it had been icy cold and just wet enough for some of it to cling to his hair and slide down his neck and under his collar.

His attacker couldn't have hidden behind the bushes. Even under their burden of snow, they couldn't hide a finch, let alone a snowball-flinging fiend—but the big spruce that sat on the property line between the two houses could hide a dozen of them.

If he had stopped to think, he wouldn't have plunged off the walk and into a foot and a half of snow, because good Italian leather shoes weren't designed for cross-country winter travel. He didn't stop. Geoff charged the spruce. He was three-quarters of the way there when Merry squealed and sprang out of hiding.

"Gotcha!" she crowed, then turned and fled, laughing.

She had the advantage, but he hadn't played varsity football for nothing. She was still a good five feet from her own front walk when he brought her down with a flying tackle.

"Gotcha!" he crowed.

In the blink of an eye, she rolled out from under him. "Hah!" she said, and hit him square in the face with a handful of snow.

He grabbed her sleeve and pulled her back. "Oh, no, you don't!"

He might have had her if he hadn't made the mistake of trying to stand. Off-balance and fighting to maintain his grip on his laughing, squirming assailant, he couldn't dodge when she wrapped her legs around his ankles and twisted. His expensive leather shoes slid out from under him as he toppled smack dab on top of Merry.

"Oof!"

"Unh!"

The fall knocked the breath out of both of them and for a minute all he could do was lie there, fighting for air and blinking against the snow crusting his lashes.

Merry giggled, then shoved at his shoulders. "You almost flattened me, you big oaf! Get off of me!"

"I wouldn't have if you hadn't pulled me over on top of you."

"You tackled me first!"

"And you threw the snowball!"

She laughed and stopped squirming. "Gotcha good, too!"

He shoved onto his elbows but made no effort to roll off her, even though he lay between her sprawled legs with his hips pinning hers to ground. It was a dangerous—and dangerously tempting—position to be in, but he had no intention of letting her up before he had to.

"Surprise attacks don't count," he said firmly.

"Says who?"

"Says I!"

She lay there, half buried in the snow, and grinned up at him. Her knit cap had come off in the struggle and her hair spilled across the snow like a tangle of red Christmas ribbon the cat had gotten into. Snow dotted her lashes and drops of melted snow glistened on her cheeks, which were flushed from the cold and the struggle. More snow glittered on her mouth.

Before he could stop to think, before he had any idea of what he was doing, Geoff bent his head and gently licked the icy droplets from her lips. She sucked in her breath, startled, then slowly let it out. It brushed against his mouth, warm and sweet. He bent for another kiss.

She didn't seem to mind. With a sigh of pleasure, she wrapped her arms around his neck and drew him down on top of her.

It was mad. Snow had snaked its way up his pant legs. He wore no gloves, no hat, and his coat, unbuttoned because of the warmth of the car, was open. It covered them like a blanket but gave him no protection against the snow that coated her jacket and jeans. Dimly he was aware that melting snow was working its way under his jacket and through the fine wool of his trousers—not that he cared right now.

With great deliberation and attention to detail, he licked off another bit of snow that lingered at the corner of her mouth. It melted on his tongue, tingling and sweet. "Mmmm."

Her tongue flicked out to claim the last drops, licking where his had licked. "Mmmhmm." Her lips curved in a wicked smile. "Did you know you have snow on your eyelashes and eyebrows?"

"If I do, it's all your fault."

"Here," she said, lightly brushing his brow with her mittened finger. "And here, and here, and he-"

He didn't let her finish. Ruthless, he claimed another

kiss, then another and another. With each kiss, she kissed him back, deeper, more demanding, opening to his touch, moaning softly in the back of her throat.

"Myself, I've never tried making love in the middle of a snow drift, but to each his own, I guess."

The rumbling masculine voice, rich with scarcely suppressed amusement, shattered the spell. Geoff raised his head and found a tall, handsome man he'd never seen before staring down at him with undisguised interest.

"Hi, Mick," said Merry. "Geoff, this is my big brother, Mick. Mick, meet Geoff."

Geoff cleared his throat. His face and the back of his neck were growing hotter by the second despite the snow that had worked its way under his collar. "Er . . . how do you do?"

Mick grinned. "Not as well as you, it seems."

"Go away, Mick," said Merry agreeably.

"Right." Mick nodded at Geoff. "Nice to meet you." He ambled on up the walk, clearly unperturbed at finding his baby sister being ravished in a snowbank. The sound of the front door closing behind him seemed extraordinarily loud in the frosty air.

Cursing, Geoff rolled off Merry and struggled to his feet.

Merry just lay there in the snow, grinning up at him. "Coward."

"Cold feet," he said, shaking snow out of his pants legs. "Literally."

"Help me up." She extended a hand. Her smile was innocently enchanting.

Geoff shook his head and backed away, safely out of reach. "Not on your life. You'll have to get up on your own."

"Huh!" said Merry. "You, sir, are no gentleman."

"Maybe not, but I'm no fool, either." He picked his

way through the tumbled snow to the walk, but carefully avoided glancing toward the house. The back of his neck prickled, a sure sign he was being watched.

"Oh, well." Merry climbed to her feet. He was already headed down the walk when she grabbed his sleeve and pulled him back. "Oh, no, you don't! Not until you've had a chance to dry off and warm up first."

She didn't let go even when she tried to brush off the snow that coated her from head to foot.

"Here, let me help," said Geoff. He swiped at her sleeve, her shoulder, then the front of her jacket.

"Opportunist."

He looked up to find her grinning wickedly. "What do you mean?" His hand froze in mid air, right over her left breast.

"Oh." He jerked his hand away.

"A coward *and* an opportunist," she said, triumphant, as she led him into the house. "You can hang your coat up there," she added, pointing to one of the already overburdened coat hooks, then casually tossed her own wet coat over another. "Come on back to the kitchen and I'll find something to dry your shoes."

"I don't—" He was already talking to her back.

The kitchen was as warm as promised and redolent with the savory smells of stew and fresh bread. Geoff's stomach growled approval.

"Here's a chair and a towel. Just take off your shoes. I'll be right back." Before he could catch his breath, Merry sailed out of the kitchen.

Because he couldn't think of anything else to do, Geoff took the chair she'd indicated and mopped at his wet face and soggy collar. He was damned if he was taking his shoes off, however, no matter how much Merry nagged him.

Mick strolled in a couple minutes later. At the sight

of Geoff, he grinned. "Let you up, did she? Like the decorations?"

Geoff blinked. "You put them up?"

Mick's grin widened. "We all did. Merry made us. And when Merry decides you're supposed to do something, you might as well give in and do it. She won't give up until you do."

"I'm beginning to find that out," said Geoff with a wry grimace.

Mick opened the refrigerator door and peered inside. "Hungry?"

"No, thanks."

"Hah! Some of Willie's fried chicken!" He emerged with a drumstick in one hand and a jug of milk in the other. "Sure you don't want something? It's an hour at least till dinner and Willie makes the best fried chicken in three counties."

Geoff shook his head, then cleared his throat. "Look, about what you saw out there. It wasn't—I mean, I didn't—"

Mick grinned. "I didn't think you did."

Geoff's head came up. "You didn't?"

"Fellow dressed like you"—Mick waved the drumstick to indicate Geoff's tailored suit and sodden shoes—"doesn't usually jump into a snowbank for the hell of it. Not without provocation. And Merry can be pretty provoking when she wants to be." He set the milk on the counter and took a glass out of the cupboard. "What'd she do? Clobber you with a snowball?"

Geoff grimaced. "Got my ear. Half of it went down my collar."

"Merry's good." Mick's grin widened. "Taught her myself." He took a sizable bite out of the drumstick, then carried the chicken and the glass of milk over to the kitchen table and sat down. "Sure I can't offer you something to eat?"

Geoff shook his head.

"Merry's stew is pretty good, too. You'll like it."

"I'm not staying for dinner."

"Sure you are!" Merry sailed back into the kitchen with all the energy of a small tornado. "There's lots of stew. Mom would be upset if you didn't stay. *I'd* be upset if you didn't stay. Hey! Didn't I tell you to take off your shoes so I could dry them for you?"

"I—"

"Never mind. You can do it in the living room. Dad's got a fire going and you can warm your feet while your shoes get dry."

"I don't—"

She grabbed his hand and pulled him toward the door. "Come on. What else would you do? Go back to that big empty house and spend the rest of the evening reading a bunch of papers?"

That was exactly what he'd planned to do, but suddenly the prospect of an evening spent alone with the house's silence echoing around him didn't hold much appeal.

Sighing, Geoff followed her out of the kitchen.

Mick watched them go. Neil had been right, Merry had bagged her gentleman. All that remained was for the poor guy to figure it out for himself.

He grinned, then took another bite of chicken.

The fire felt good on Geoff's stocking feet, and the conversation—a spirited discussion on city planning that somehow segued into third world development concerns—kept him on his toes. Dinner was wonderful, as promised. When it came time to reclaim his dry shoes and say good night, Geoff had to admit he didn't want to leave. But work was waiting, and he didn't want to wear out his welcome.

"I'll walk you back." Merry followed him into the hall.

"That's all right."

"Here's your coat." She handed him his topcoat, then pulled hers off the hook.

He didn't argue. The minute she'd pulled the front door closed behind her, he tucked her hand into the crook of his elbow and led her down the walk.

They didn't rush. The sidewalk was too crowded for that, even if they'd wanted to. He definitely did not want to. Their breath plumed in the cold, while overhead the sky was clear black velvet.

At the edge of his property, Geoff stopped short, stunned by the transformation of his staid house and yard.

He'd forgotten the lights.

Merry's family had hung them everywhere. They ran along the eaves and dripped down the sides of his house. They outlined his windows and wrapped around his bushes and arced from tree to tree in a dazzling web of color.

Better than the lights, however, were the figures on his lawn. The red lights on the snowman's muffler glowed against the tracery of white lights that outlined its wire-frame. The teddy bear waved and nodded, the electric flame on the six-foot candle flickered, and the elf tipped his hat to the delighted gawkers who lined the sidewalk.

"Like it?"

Geoff looked down at Merry. She had a grin on her face as broad as the grin on that teddy bear on his lawn.

He sucked in his breath. In her eyes he could see the reflections of the lights. *His* lights. His special Christmas gift from Merry.

When he didn't answer, her smile faded. "Don't you like it? I thought—"

He laughed. *Really* laughed. Her gift, too, even though it hadn't come wrapped in shiny ribbon.

"I *love* it!" He turned back to stare at this miracle she'd given him, she and her family.

"I really love it," he said, wrapping his arm around her shoulders and drawing her to him. She came willingly, fitting against him as easily as if she'd always been there.

And that, Geoff realized, was a bit of a miracle, too.

Christmas Eve. Already.

Geoff stood on his sidewalk staring at the lights that wreathed his house. He'd been out here every night for the past week to look at them, but this was the first time Merry hadn't been there to share them with him. It felt a little colder without her beside him.

They'd spent most of the past week together. He'd finally realized his office could survive without him over the holidays, just as it had all those years he'd gone to St. Moritz. He'd declined his Christmas Eve cocktail party invite, pulled out of Christmas dinner with Jeremy and his wife and whoever, then left a message for his temporary secretary telling her to cancel all of his appointments and have a great Christmas, that he'd be back in the office after New Year's.

Then he'd spent every minute he could with Merry.

They'd kidnapped Jeffie and taken him to see the zoo lit up for Christmas. She'd spent an afternoon teaching Geoff the secrets of baking Christmas cookies and laughing at his lopsided reindeer and cross-eyed gingerbread men. He'd dragged her off for a neighborhood game of hockey. Together they'd stormed the toy stores, hit the game arcades, gone sledding, watched every Tarzan movie they could find in the video stores, downed gallons of coffee and talked and laughed and talked some more, yet somehow never run out of things to say. Whenever he got a chance, he'd kissed her.

She'd made sure he had a lot of chances.

Yesterday he'd casually mentioned he'd never had a Christmas tree. Once she recovered from the shock, Merry had dragged him off in search of a tree—no easy thing, this close to Christmas—immediately followed by a sweep through the stores for lights and ornaments and all the assorted paraphernalia that went with it.

"Not that it's perfect," she'd said last night, critically eyeing their creation. "To be perfect, it needs a few really tatty things made with popsicle sticks or paper plates that some kid brought home from school. But it'll do for now."

Geoff, who'd been thinking his first tree was an outrageously splendid achievement, had looked at the shiny glass balls and the twinkling lights and for the first time he'd seen, clearly and without confusion, exactly what it was he wanted in his life.

He wanted kids. Lots of kids. He wanted the smell of bread baking in the kitchen and laughter on the stairs and furniture that looked like it had been used as a trampoline instead of set in a salesroom window. He wanted a house that was a home, and a dog that tracked in mud, and a Christmas tree dripping in funky ornaments made with glue and bits of yarn and lots and lots of love.

More than anything he could imagine, he wanted Merry, because none of it would matter if she wasn't there to share it with him.

He hadn't said so, of course. How could he ask a woman to marry him when he hadn't even known her two weeks? But last night, long after she'd gone, he'd sat by the fire and watched the lights on the tree blink on and off and on again, and he'd dreamed of the years ahead.

He was drifting back into dreams when a small flock of children raced past him on the sidewalk, startling him from his thoughts.

"Look at the elf! And the snowman!" they cried.

The biggest one took one look at the snow heaped at the side of the walk and toppled over backwards into it. "Look! I'm making a snow angel!" An instant later, three other small bodies were flailing away in the snow beside him.

Geoff was watching them, laughing at their enthusiasm, when their father stopped beside him. "Great display, isn't it?" he said.

Geoff nodded. "Yes, it is."

"We drive by every year on our way home from church. It's become part of our family's Christmas tradition. I'm glad to see the folks in this house have finally joined in."

"Oh?" said Geoff, startled.

"Always looked sort of empty before. You know, no lights, no decorations. Some years they didn't even have a Christmas tree. Traveling, somebody told me."

Geoff thought of St. Moritz. "Doesn't sound very appealing."

"Nope. But the house sold this year, I heard." He grinned as his youngest child squealed with excitement when the teddy bear waved at her. "This is definitely an improvement."

"Yes." Geoff meant it. "It's definitely an improvement."

"Well, we'd best get going," the man said, smiling. "We have to check out *all* the lights, you know, and try to get everyone in bed so Santa Claus can come."

He hoisted his youngest on his shoulders and strolled off toward Merry's house. Geoff watched them for a while. Then, with one last look at the pint-size snow angels that now decorated his lawn, he retreated to the fire in his fireplace and his not-quite-perfect Christmas tree.

An hour later he was dozing over a brandy and a copy of Dickens' "A Christmas Carol" when his doorbell started pealing. Hope blossomed. All he wanted from Santa this year was to find a certain redhead on his doorstep.

Still in his stocking feet, he padded to the door.

Merry was there, just as he'd hoped—along with everyone else in the Doe clan. "Surprise! Merry Christmas!" They poured into his hall.

"Merry made us come," said Willie good-naturedly, casually tossing his coat over a chair. "But I managed to bring the wine and Mick's got the spices for it and Steffie grabbed all the makings for hot chocolate, so I guess we'll manage."

"An' I got the cookies," said little Jeffie, handing Geoff a basket filled with them.

"And I've got the most important stuff of all." Merry stood on tiptoe to give him a kiss. "See?" She held up a cluster of paper plates strung on loops of red yarn and covered with childish crayon drawings of Santa Claus and Christmas trees and a few things only the artist would ever be able to identify. "I raided one of the church Christmas trees—with the pastor's permission! Can't have a tree without 'em."

She was only partly right, Geoff decided a little later, contentedly sipping the spiced wine Mick had brewed. A perfect tree also needed people around it and laughter and a few off-key choruses of "Jingle Bells" and "Silent Night," topped off with the hot chocolate that Jeffie spilled on the carpet.

When they eventually collected coats and gloves and hats for the walk back home, Geoff lost Merry in all the confusion. As he stood on his front steps watching his neighbors make their way down the sidewalk, he couldn't help feeling a little hurt that she'd left without so much as a good-night kiss. Only when he'd shut the front door did he realize there was one coat left of the pile that had buried his hallway table.

She was sitting on the floor in front of the fire, dreamily watching the winking lights on the tree while the firelight cast a golden glow across her face and set her wild red curls aflame.

"I thought you'd left."

She looked up at that and smiled. "I told Mom I'd be over a little later. I love my family, but sometimes it's nice to have a little quiet, and tonight . . ."

Her words trailed off as her gaze shifted back to the Christmas tree they had decorated together. His imagination or a trick of the firelight that made him think she was blushing.

"Tonight?" he prompted gently, settling on the floor beside her.

"Tonight I wanted to be alone with you," she said simply. "Just for a little while. Sort of a special birthday present, all for me."

"*Birthday* present?" He frowned as an odd little suspicion suddenly struck him. "How do you spell your name?"

She smiled.

He tried to look stern "It's not with an 'a,' is it?"

She shook her head, eyes alight with sudden mischief. "No, it's not."

"And I suppose your middle name is—"

She nodded. He laughed.

She playfully punched his arm. "Don't laugh. You don't know how awful it can be to have a name like mine. As if having your birthday on Christmas wasn't bad enough already!"

His laughter died. "If it were your birthday and I could be sure of sharing it with you . . ." He hesitated, but the words came tumbling out in spite of him. "Merry, will you marry me? I know it's too soon to ask you, that we've only known—"

"Yes."

"—each other a few days and—" He stopped. "What?"

She smiled. "I said yes. Yes, I'll marry you. Of course I will! I was beginning to think you'd *never* ask!"

His head was still spinning when she pulled him down on the rug and started kissing him so he couldn't think, couldn't breathe, couldn't do anything except kiss her back.

One kiss naturally led to another, and then another and another. There was hunger in those kisses, and excitement, and something sacred and infinitely sweet.

She was his! *His!* If he weren't a grownup, he'd race outside and make a dozen snow angels all his own, just for the joy and wonder of it.

"Promise me one thing," she said.

"Anything."

She cupped his face in her hands and looked deep into his soul. "Promise me that when we have kids they'll have names like Sam and Frank and Judy."

He grinned. "I promise."

"Then kiss me again," she said. "Just to make it legal."

And of course, he did.

SILVER
CHRISTMAS

by

Vella Munn

ONE

Shannon Hastings speared lettuce from her salad bowl and concentrated on what was being said. Still, she couldn't quite believe her business, Country Quilts, had become reality and she had every right to be here.

"No, of course it's not too late to pull it off," Myra Cummings insisted, the handsome, older woman's take-no-prisoners voice echoing off the restaurant's high ceiling. "We want this to be Oro's best Christmas, don't we? The one that'll put us on the map once and for all."

"But a sleigh and horses?" William Thrasher, owner of a secondhand store, had been quietly drinking coffee while Myra expounded on her plans, but now he creaked to his feet and stared at Myra from his position at the opposite end of the long, crowded table. "I don't know squat about horses and even less about how we're going to get an historically accurate sleigh up and running in the next week."

"I've been talking to Brad," Myra insisted. "He says they aren't that complicated to make. Children will love being pulled around in it; you know they will, and they'll insist their parents bring them into town, which means even more customers."

William sighed. "I don't suppose you got Brad to agree to build the thing?"

"Of course not!" Myra snorted and pushed down her glasses, staring at William over the top of them. "He's much too busy. We're just fortunate he's been willing to share his expertise with us."

By 'us,' Myra was referring to the members of Oro's Merchants' Association, but that didn't particularly concern Shannon. This was the second meeting she'd attended, but fortunately as the small, southern Oregon town's newest merchant, she wasn't expected to contribute much—just somehow keep from drowning under the tidal wave of her friends' enthusiasm.

"I'm as appreciative of our esteemed museum director's expertise as the next person," William continued, "but I daresay he'll think we're going off the deep end trying to recreate what happened here over a hundred years ago. Customers aren't going to care whether we use plastic or wood on the sleigh or even if we have one. They just want to get their Christmas shopping over with. Shoot, a lot of 'em are going to order everything over the Internet, just so they don't have to set foot outside."

That elicited a few nods of agreement, but, as Shannon had already figured out, most of the nearly twenty shop owners sided with Myra and her gang. They were determined to pull in customers from the larger surrounding cities and were willing to go all out in order to make that happen. The 'all out' revolved around exploiting Oro's early years as a gold mining camp—something much more interesting than the Internet, a catalogue, or the mall.

"If we're done with that," Myra said, dismissing William, "I want to get onto the next order of business— the tree lighting ceremony. Brad pointed out that historically, trees were decorated with burning candles secured to the branches, not multicolored lights. However, the fire chief—"

Burning candles, Shannon thought, spacing on the rest of what Myra had to say. One semistiff breeze and the tree would catch fire and put an end to the ambitious undertaking she'd unwittingly become part of. Brad, whoever he might be, was a fool if he didn't realize Myra and the others would take everything he said as gospel. Why couldn't he just keep his mouth shut?

"Anyway," Myra was saying, "Brad agreed with the fire chief on that. We still need to decide whether we're going to have lights on the tree or just what the children have been making in school, but I thought it would be a terrific idea to share what Brad knows about the origins of holiday tree decorating. Shannon, you're so artistic. I was thinking you could design a flier detailing early customs that we could pass out in our shops as a goodwill gift. Nothing too fancy. Maybe drawings of pioneer Christmas preparations, tree cutting ceremonies, snow falling, smiling children, and beaming parents."

She was a seamstress and quilter, not an artist, and the thought of putting all that on a single-page flier exhausted her.

"We're really excited about this, Shannon." Myra indicated her fellow committee members. "It's a perfect way to bring you on board, and Brad says—"

At the mention of the museum director's name, an image formed in Shannon's mind, once again shutting out Myra's voice. She had yet to meet the man—not that she was looking forward to it—but there was nothing she'd like better than to see him slowly sinking to the bottom of a vat of hot candy syrup, homemade candy-making being something else Brad had educated Myra and her crew about.

Was the man off his rocker? Okay, so he was responsible for maximizing Oro's ties with the past; it probably wouldn't hurt his career to have the local merchants go all out to recreate the town's early years, but enough was enough.

It had gotten quiet all of a sudden. Everyone was looking at her. Wincing, she guessed they were waiting for her to respond to Myra's suggestion.

"I don't know," she said. "I-I guess I'll have to discuss it with Brad." She almost bit her tongue saying the last.

"Of course, of course. In fact"—Myra glanced at her watch—"he's going to be joining us any minute. I know it goes without saying, but I hope you'll all show proper appreciation. We've already taken and will continue to take a great deal of his time and expertise. In order for—"

Yes, teacher. We know how to say please and thank you.

Myra was off and running again, but dinner was being served and Shannon allowed herself to be distracted by thoughts of how wonderfully hot the stew she'd ordered would taste. If only she could get warm.

"Ah, there he is!" Myra gushed as Shannon dipped her spoon in the concoction.

She filled the spoon and lifted it, idly wondering if she could flip it with enough force to hit the esteemed and pain-in-the-neck Brad full in the face. That was before she focused on the man. .

Plain and simple, this wasn't a museum director. Where were the horned-rimmed glasses, tweed jacket, gray and receding hair, pipe clamped in false teeth? Instead, this man was—was—like wow!

Her meal and chilled fingers and toes forgotten, she took inventory. He had to have been an athlete in school and probably still was, judging by the easy way he walked to the head of the table next to Myra. With three brothers, she'd had a thorough indoctrination in all things athletic and came to the quick if less than scientific conclusion he'd played baseball, not football, although he could have been a quarterback or receiver. He was tall, a few inches over six feet, and built along the lines of an inverted triangle—something his open-necked dress shirt and slacks didn't begin to conceal.

His hands were large and broad and capable, she noted with no little surprise as he shook hands with those closest to him. Instead of being a short breath from retirement, as she'd thought he'd be, he had to be in his mid thirties. Not that it mattered, but she checked his left hand again. No wedding ring.

She turned her attention to his eyes. Lordy, lordy, a deep-throated inner voice kept saying. They were brown, chocolate brown—large, deep, gorgeous. They captured and reflected half of the light in the room. Long lashes. Quick blinks. And now—lordy, lordy—focused on her.

Myra was making an introduction and nodding like one of those spring-necked dogs in a car's rear window. Brad was smiling a white-toothed smile.

"I'm glad to meet you, Mr. Reading." She felt brilliant for having remembered that Myra had supplied a last name.

"Please, call me Brad," he said, smile still in place, his gaze maybe lingering on her longer than necessary. "I always think people are talking to my father when I hear 'Mr. Reading.' So you've moved into where the real estate office was, have you? Fortunately they did some major repairs while they had it. Not long ago the building was falling apart. If you're interested in its history, I'd be happy to supply that."

That's not what I want you to supply. Deeply, deeply glad he couldn't read her mind, she nodded, although at the moment she couldn't care less when or how or why the long, narrow brick building she'd leased had come into being. However, if it gave her an excuse to see him again . . .

Apparently Brad often ate at the Italian restaurant the merchants' association used for their meetings, be-

cause the waitress asked if he wanted lasagna or spaghetti and he opted for the lasagne without consulting
a menu. Once that detail had been tended to, Myra
explained Brad had brought a number of pictures of
early Oro Christmases. Shannon remembered to eat
her stew, but if anyone were to ask what it tasted like,
she'd be in trouble.

It wasn't just that his shoulders took up an inordinate
amount of space or that his thick, black hair begged to
have her fingers run through it or that his voice reminded her of low drumbeats. What made her oblivious
to everything else was that he still hadn't taken his eyes
off her.

TWO

It was drizzling when Shannon stepped outside, water dripping off the overhang and sliding down the single step to the sidewalk. She considered asking if she could spend the night in the garlic- and cheese-scented restaurant, but they'd probably put her to work washing dishes until midnight.

"Be brave," a male voice she instantly recognized said behind her. "This isn't a real rain."

She'd been certain Brad wouldn't be able to extricate himself from Myra and her cronies for a while, which was why she'd given up on any thought she might—accidentally, of course—find herself alone with him.

"It looks real to me." She pulled her collar up around her neck and glared at the drips to emphasize her point. "I *have* to buy an umbrella."

"You don't have one?" Despite the dim lighting, she could tell he'd pasted on a somber tone. He pointed a rolled up umbrella at her. "You're not an Oregon native, are you?"

"How could you tell?"

"Oregonians are born knowing how to deal with rain. Please don't tell me you're from California. Sometimes I think we ought to close the border."

"Hardly." The wind was blowing from him to her.

With his greater height, if she slid closer to him, she'd be well protected. "I'm from Arizona."

"No kidding." The somber look was replaced by surprise. "Are you suffering from dry air withdrawal?"

She chuckled. "A little."

"I bet you are. If you can hang in until spring, I promise you'll love that and summer. Actually, winters aren't bad either. There are a number of ski resorts around and—"

"I've never worn skis in my life."

"No kidding? Well, we're going to have to change that, aren't we?"

Before she could think of anything to say, the front door opened and several people, William among them, stepped outside. In order to make room, she stepped onto the sidewalk. Although the older woman with William started talking to Brad, he kept looking at her.

Despite the cold and drizzle, she didn't leave. Instead, she took in as much of the main street as she could see at night. There was a light at either end of the four-block-long business district. Most of the shops had lights in their display windows, but the brick fronts absorbed rather than reflected the illumination. In the process of getting her shop ready to open, she hadn't had time to take more than a cursory look at what her fellow merchants had to offer. Because the buildings shared common walls and the street was only two lanes wide, with limited parking in front of each building, it was a far cry from a mall shopping experience, thank heavens.

The surrounding hills were covered with evergreens that nestled around and protected the town. The county seat of Brabury was less than ten miles away, but the city's impact was barely felt here, something else she was thankful for.

"Sorry about that," Brad said when he finally joined

her on the sidewalk. "That's something about living in a one-horse town. Everyone knows you."

That was the primary reason she'd been willing to leave Phoenix. Although she'd made it her home since graduating from college four years ago, many of her closest neighbors had remained strangers.

"So," he continued, his attention torn between her and the drizzle, "do you live in Oro, or is this just where you do business?"

"I'm over on Stagecoach Street," she explained. In the city she would never have given her address to a man she'd just met, but Brad Reading was a far cry from being a closet ax murderer. Besides, he had an umbrella, even if he hadn't yet unfolded it. "Just a cottage I'm renting behind—"

"I know the place. Bob and Shirley, the owners, built the cottage for Shirley's mother, but Carol only lived in it for about three years before she broke her hip."

He probably knew something about everyone who'd made Oro home for more than a few weeks. She found that concept foreign, but also intriguing.

"The bungalow suits me," she admitted. Was it her imagination, or was the rain picking up?

"Hmm," he said. "It's kind of small, isn't it?"

"Not for one person." She wasn't sure saying that was wise. Maybe he'd think she was advertising her marital state.

"Then you came here by yourself?"

She started to tell him her aunt and uncle lived in Brabury, but in truth, being this close to him was exhausting her. Her nerve endings, all five billion or more of them, had gone on alert, and although he'd put on a windbreaker, she remembered the strong line of his collarbone, the way his thighs strained his slacks, the flat plane where a lot of men his age had bellies.

"I have relatives around," she managed in an offhand

way. "I, ah, appreciate the time you've given our organization. I hope you haven't shorted yourself because of it."

Brad laughed and waved as another group exited the restaurant. "Given? I'm not sure how much say I had in the matter. When Myra gets the bit between her teeth, she can be a steamroller."

She'd never heard that particular analogy before; it made her smile.

"What do you think of everything they've planned for the holiday?" he asked.

"I'm not sure. I don't have anything to compare it with."

"It's going to bring in more business. The advance publicity is already having an impact on the number of people calling about or coming to the museum."

"That's good."

"I guess."

"You guess?" she asked. As she did, she looked up and into his eyes. At least she tried to, but he was turned so the restaurant lights didn't touch his face. She was still fascinated by his voice, by the impact his physical presence made on her nerve endings, but even more of the association members were leaving, their good-byes distracting her.

"I'm sorry," he said. "Forget I brought it up. So, are you going to design that flier? I have the information in my office, probably more than you could ever use. You can come by anytime and pick it up."

She hadn't agreed to do it. In fact, she had been trying to find a way to gracefully beg out of it, but now he'd invited, asked, whatever, she'd be a fool to turn him down. After telling him she'd try to find time tomorrow, she slowly drew her keys out of her purse.

"I'll walk you to your car," he said. With that, he

snapped open his umbrella and started to hold it over her head.

"I don't think so."

"What?"

"Look at it."

He did. The umbrella appeared to have been hit with shotgun pellets and more resembled a sieve than something designed to keep off the rain.

Laughter bubbled inside her. "If that's a new marketing concept, I don't think it's going to catch on," she told him.

"Darn that Yapper."

"What?"

"Never mind." He sighed. "It's a long, weird story. Here I was thinking I could play the gentleman, and I wind up making a fool of myself."

"No, you're not." Curiosity about the reason for the umbrella's condition was driving her crazy, but someone had opened the faucet on the clouds. If they didn't head for shelter now, they were in trouble.

"I say I am." Laughing, he collapsed what there was of the umbrella. "Look, they're going to lock us up if we stay out here much longer. Anyway, welcome to town."

"Thank you." Thanks to the sudden downpour, her hair was already plastered to her head. So much for impressing him with her physical charms. "I really appreciate all the help you've been giving us," she said, nearly yelling in order to be heard. "As someone with a brand new store, I sure hope all this effort results in a successful holiday season."

He grunted. "As in financially successful?"

"Is there anything wrong with that?"

"Wrong? Not really. Let's just say I have problems with the commercialism. Remember, I deal with the past, when Christmas was celebrated simply, not the frenzy we have now."

Frenzy? She'd never thought of it quite like that. "I can't look at it that way," she told him. "Brad, I've wanted my own business as long as I can remember. I'm about to find out whether I have what it takes to make that dream come true."

She hunched deeper into her coat and started down the sidewalk, now speaking over her shoulder. "So, yes, I want to see a lot of shoppers come through my door. And I'm not going to apologize for feeling that way."

He'd gotten the young lady's hackles up, Brad realized as he let himself into his house some ten minutes later. It was a shame things had ended on that note, since he'd completely and thoroughly enjoyed speaking with her—enjoyed standing near her in the rain with her head upturned and the restaurant lights highlighting her dark eyes, her soft, slightly parted mouth. It obviously hadn't mattered to her that her long, rich brown hair was getting wet. He hadn't minded her jacket had hidden what he'd already determined back in the restaurant was a healthy and nicely contoured body—not that he wasn't intrigued by the possibility of seeing her with less on. A lot less.

Whoa up there, old man, he admonished as Yapper, his six-month-old mostly Irish setter bounded toward him. He was getting too old for that kind of thinking.

"You aren't going to be any help, are you?" he asked Yapper. "And thanks for the job you did on my umbrella. It caught a certain lady's attention. Made me look like an idiot, not that you care. You're still too young to care whether the neighbor dog is male or female and what the difference can lead to, aren't you?" He frowned. "At least I hope you're too young."

In the time since Yapper had shown up on the museum grounds, he'd learned the dog needed a rough-housing session before he could settle down. Brad got down on his hands and knees and growled at him. The nearly seventy-pound mutt growled back, then tried to bowl him over.

"I saw that move coming," he informed Yapper as he knocked the dog's legs out from under him and started pushing him first one way and then the other on the carpet. "If you're ever going to go anywhere with your wrestling career, you have to quit telegraphing what you're doing."

Having a pet—or was it the other way around?—took years off Brad's life and put that life's complications into perspective. The basics of existence, plain and simple, were rest, play, food, and water.

When the dog finally ran out of steam, Brad let him out back, then went into the bedroom of the 1892 house he'd bought last year. There were still moments—as when he'd determined all the plumbing needed to be replaced—when he wondered if he'd gotten in over his head, but he'd become a museum director because history fascinated him. What didn't turn his crank was being arm-twisted into exploiting Oro's past.

"That's what I didn't tell you," he said aloud, as if Shannon were in the room with him. "You might be the first breath of fresh air to come to town in a long time, but that doesn't change the fact you and the rest of your organization have gone off the deep end."

Sitting down on the side of the bed, he untied his damp shoes and kicked out of them. Because he didn't own any pajamas, he traded his shirt and slacks for a pair of sweats. By then, Yapper was ready to come inside and sit quietly beside him as he went through the day's mail. Thanksgiving wasn't until next week, but the avalanche of holiday advertisements had already picked up. He thumbed through a glossy catalogue offering exotic cheeses, smoked meats, and wines, then let it drop to the floor. Yapper started to gnaw on it.

"At least you've found a use for it," he told the dog. "All I want is for this nonsense to be over with." He sighed. "If I had been alive around the time this house was built, I wouldn't have had to contend with the insanity. Why can't things still be simple like that? Stockings filled with nuts and fruit, maybe some new winter clothing under the tree, period. End of story."

Of course if he'd been alive in 1892, Shannon Hastings wouldn't have been there, either.

THREE

"He put the tree in the nursery?" Shannon asked. "Not the living room?"

Brad nodded. "Seems a little risky, doesn't it? Especially since he used candles to decorate it. However, his heart was in the right place."

"Yes, it was. It never occurred to me the tradition of having a Christmas tree originated in Germany—with Martin Luther, of all people—but I love the idea that he had a nativity scene in addition to the tree. A connection with what was the true spirit of Christmas. It didn't take long for the custom to spread, did it?"

"No, it didn't."

She and Brad were sitting in his cramped office at the rear of the large brick museum, he in his a-little-the-worse-for-wear office chair, she settled on the part of the couch that wasn't taken up with books, magazines, newspapers, photographs, and files.

He'd looked pleased, if slightly reserved, when she showed up a little after five in the afternoon. Although the staff and volunteers were getting ready to leave, he invited her into what he called his cave. She tried to hide her reaction to the clutter as he explained that the museum had recently been bequeathed a small historic house and its contents, and before the material could be shown to the public, it first had to be catalogued, and certain items placed in protective wrapping. A great deal of that process was taking place under Brad's watchful eye.

She'd been prepared to take notes for the flier she'd allowed herself to be roped into doing, but Brad had presented her with a folder full of more than she'd ever care to know about Christmas tree traditions. Although she kept getting distracted by his nearness and the way his voice echoed off the high ceiling, she managed to thumb through most of it, not that she'd get an A for concentration.

"Do you think that's going to do you?" He indicated the folder.

"I'm overwhelmed," she admitted. "I just hope the association doesn't expect me to come up with a book."

"You wouldn't have time even if they twisted your arm. After all, you're stocking shelves and doing whatever it is merchants do this time of year, aren't you?"

Something about his question wasn't actually hostile, but wasn't quite approving. Either that or her senses had been knocked out of whack because she'd discovered that his eyes were even darker than she'd previously thought.

"I'm busy, all right, but I have to do my part," she explained. "We're inviting everyone to the tree lighting. You'll be there, won't you?"

"I'd be in trouble if I weren't."

Although that was about the way she felt, she didn't tell him. "You sound as if that isn't your favorite thing to do. If they manage to get a sleigh operating in time, they'll be offering rides for children before and after the ceremony. You'd enjoy seeing that, wouldn't you?"

He didn't immediately answer, which allowed her to again take her measure of him. Apparently his job didn't require him to wear a suit, since he was as casually dressed as he'd been yesterday. Today he'd chosen a deep green knit pullover with white piping on the collar. His tan slacks were pressed, forcing her to wonder whether a woman was responsible. Last night she'd noticed a shadow of stubble on his face, but he looked clean-shaven now. Unfortunately, he was sitting too far away for her to determine whether he wore aftershave. She liked being aware of him, liked feeling alive. Slightly charged.

"Shannon." He spoke slowly. "My career calls for me to spend much of my time in the past. Although there are certain things about this town's early years I wouldn't care to repeat, such as untreatable diseases and infections, not enough of the right kinds of food for healthy bodies, dreams of gold that turned to nothing, there's a lot to be said for getting back to basics—to keep things simple, family centered, not commercial."

"I agree," she admitted, then held up a drawing of a pioneer family gathered around a barely decorated tree, their rustic cabin in the background. "This is about as basic as things can get, but that's not the world we live in. We're an industrial nation, no longer pioneers."

"We can still take lessons from the past." Groaning, he pressed his hand against his forehead. "I'm sorry. I told myself I wasn't going to pontificate when you have every right to succeed at your business. So, tell me, what brings a desert woman to Oregon?"

Did she want to get into that? Not really, but if she gave him some of the details, maybe he'd tell her things about himself and she'd learn whether he was married, engaged, living with someone, in love, or, maybe, free to explore.

"A man," she blurted.

"What?"

"A man," she repeated. Now the cat was out of the bag, there was no putting it back in. "What I mean is,

I'd been going with the same guy since my last year of college and when that ended, I . . ."

"You needed a change of scene?"

"Something like that," she said, although it was much more complicated. "We were going to get married. For five years we were going to get married, only the timing was never right or he didn't feel he was in a position to support me or—"

"You wanted to be supported?"

"Perish the thought. Only I could never convince Mike of that. Finally the lightbulb went on and I realized he was scared of the whole institution of marriage."

"How long ago was this?"

"A few months before I left Phoenix. I thought about staying, but Mike and I, well, he didn't have a lot of friends and wasn't particularly interested in mine, so over the years, we'd pretty much isolated ourselves."

She shifted her position on the couch, aware for the first time of the slightly stuffy smell to the room. "Anyway, I wanted to open my own business, so when my aunt and uncle told me about Oro . . ."

Instead of finishing, she glanced at him. There was no doubt his attention was fixed on her every word, and that she was presenting him with a major chapter in her life story.

". . . I decided there was no better time than the present to take the plunge."

"Your timing's good. You should get a lot of customers over the next month."

"I'm pleased with how things are going so far. Still . . ."

"Still what?"

"You want the truth?"

"Of course I do." He nodded, emphasizing the point.

"Okay." She took a steadying breath, looked into his

eyes, believed in the intensity she found there. "I'm scared."

"Scared?"

"Of falling on my face," she admitted. "I've worked for several small businesses and taken some classes on being self-employed, so I'm not completely naive, but I've got my fingers crossed I'm not in over my head. I envy you. You have an employer who tells you—ah, what I mean is, there must be some formal guidelines, some . . ." *Shut up. You don't have a clue what you're talking about.*

To her relief, Brad chuckled. "If you want to see my job description, I'll be happy to show it to you—not that it'd tell you what I do with my days."

"At least I know what you do with some of your evenings. You have dinner with the merchants' association."

"True."

She'd hoped he'd say something about what he did with the rest of his nights, but he didn't. Instead, he picked up an orange scrap of paper she took to be a message. He started to pick up his phone, then stopped.

"Do you have to get back to your shop right away?" he asked.

She shook her head, then explained she'd hired a local high-school girl to come in for a few hours in the afternoon. The arrangement allowed her to work on replenishing the stock that had sold—or, like today, touch base with the world beyond her walls.

"You sell quilts, right? Don't they take forever to make? Historically, sewing bees were held so all the local women could work on a project."

"And gossip, I daresay." He'd barely moved since she walked in. Did that mean he was in no hurry to have her leave? "I sell a number of handmade quilts on consignment, but I use machines for what I create."

He frowned, the gesture creasing his brow and robbing her of a little of the impact of his dark, striking eyes. Although her most recent employer, a divorcée in her late thirties, was fascinated by men's rear ends, she herself had been drawn to men's eyes since she'd discovered boys might have a purpose in life after all. On a scale of one to ten, Brad's were off the chart.

With a start, she realized he'd just told her he hadn't been inside her shop but had taken note of her front window display.

"My mother would love hanging around your place," he told her. "You get a lot of older women customers, do you?"

"Yes, but I'm surprised by how many young people come in, too, a lot of couples. They tell me they've been looking for something for their beds but are put off by commercially made coverings. I keep hearing the words timeless and romantic."

"That's good."

That couples considered her quilts romantic? Although she wanted to explore that particular topic with Brad, she wasn't sure it was wise, given there was some kind of physical attraction going on here—at least on her part.

How long had she been in his office, taking up his time, talking instead of tending to some overdue record keeping? Sighing, she got to her feet and bent to pick up the material she'd be taking with her. She was still shuffling it into a manageable pile when Brad stood.

"What are you doing for dinner?"

"What?" Stupid, stupid.

"I said, what—"

"I know what you said. I'm sorry. I didn't mean to sound like an idiot."

"You didn't. Besides, if we're going to get into an argument over who could improve on the impression

they're making, I'm the one with the dog-bitten umbrella, remember?"

"Dog bitten?"

He sighed. "You'd have to see Yapper to understand.
Nothing he can get in his mouth is safe. It's a good
thing he has such a tight hold on my heart, or I might
make him get a job to pay for the damage."

Fifteen minutes later, they were sitting at a window
booth in a small cafe near the town's one bank. The
cafe specialized in vegetarian dishes and Brad, who obviously was friends with the owner, suggested a pita sandwich stuffed with everything from mushrooms and Swiss
cheese to artichoke hearts.

It was early on a week night, but the place was packed.
Piped in Christmas music played, and the chubby waitress wore a red and white Santa Claus hat and a necklace made of silver bells. From the way she hovered
around their table, Shannon sensed her interest in Brad
went beyond the casual. She couldn't blame her.

"You do stand out," she pointed out as someone at
an adjoining table waved at him. "Maybe you ought to
run for mayor."

"Not in this lifetime, although it has been suggested
several times. I don't have a political bone in my body.
However . . ."

"However what?" They'd been served homemade
sourdough bread and creamery butter. Calories be
hanged. The smell alone was her undoing—that and
the simple yet telling act of sharing a meal with Brad
Reading of the compelling eyes, sitting at an intimate
table that would have their knees touching if she
weren't careful. If he had a wife, wouldn't he have invited her to join them? Besides, there'd been no pic-

tures of children or women on his desk—not that she'd
gone looking, of course. And so what if she had?

"There's something I *am* getting involved with," he
said, jerking her back to the present.

"Oh?"

His voice low, yet filled with a barely restrained passion, he told her about having found a stray puppy—the
infamous umbrella eating Yapper—and taking it into
his home. He'd contacted the local dog pound and humane center in addition to taking out a newspaper ad
and posting notices around town. Nothing had come
of those efforts. He'd welcomed Yapper into his life—
and come face to face with the reality of how many
unwanted dogs there were.

"There's a local private organization that deals with
stray cats. They offer low-cost neutering and adoption
services and provide educational programs anyplace
they can get people to listen, but there's nothing com-
parable for dogs. I'm not sure why, except that the cat
people are passionate. The pound and humane society
do the best they can, but they have their hands full
rounding up, sheltering, and trying to reunite or adopt
out what comes through their doors."

"And sometimes putting them down."

"Unfortunately," he said. "Anyway, to make a long
story short, I've become part of a new group made up
of dog lovers—or should I say people who have been
suckered by floppy ears and wagging tails? Because I've
done a lot of public speaking, they're asking me to handle that."

"That's wonderful. Brad, I can't imagine anything
more worthwhile." Reaching out, she squeezed his
hand.

Whether that was a mistake or not she couldn't say;
his flesh felt warm and alive, a little roughened, part

and parcel of him. She let her fingers linger a moment longer than necessary.

"I'm glad you feel that way." His voice continued its low, rumbling tone. He was looking at her hand, caressing it almost. "Shannon, no matter how much the merchants of Oro want me on their holiday bandwagon, there's a limit to what I can and frankly want to do. Winter's hard for stray dogs. That's what I refuse to lose sight of."

"Of course." Suddenly, in this warm and aromatic place, with Christmas music playing and red and green lights holding the night at bay, her concerns for her business's success seemed petty. "I—have you told the merchants that?"

He shook his head. "MUTTS—that's what we're calling ourselves—is taking off much faster than any of us could have imagined. Commitment runs amok, I guess. I have all I can do to decide what direction my presentations are going to take, how to get through to people."

It was on the tip of her tongue to ask what she could do to help, but would he think she'd jumped on board because he was part of it—because she was pursuing him? How little she knew about how the dating game was played these days!

Dating game? Was that what tonight was, a date?

Dinner had gone well, Brad admitted to himself as he paid the bill. Shannon had wanted to go Dutch, but he'd explained that he'd invited her which, according to some regulation he didn't specify and she fortunately didn't question, made the tab his responsibility. He was waylaid twice by people wanting to talk, but finally he steered her toward the door.

Last night, she'd had her car and he'd had to content himself with waving her off. Tonight, however, he was going to walk with her back to her shop, into the night, no one interrupting or distracting them, so she could pick up her vehicle.

They'd just stepped outside when she shivered. It didn't take much for him to realize her jacket had been made with an eye to style, not warmth.

"You still need some lessons in becoming an Oregonian," he said. "To provide decent protection, a coat needs to cover the—the hips."

She tugged on her coat's bottom hem, but it remained at her waist. "So I see. It gets darned cold when the sun sets this time of year, doesn't it? It's like that on the desert—the temperature difference, I mean— but my nose never frosted." To demonstrate, she covered her nose with her hand—her small, pale, yet strong and competent hand.

Although he'd like nothing more than to cover her fingers with his, he didn't. His nerves still hummed from when she'd touched him. Still, when they stepped away from the cafe, he guided her around him so his body provided at least some protection from the breeze. Fortunately it wasn't raining.

The storefront decoration project handled by the volunteer fire department wasn't until this weekend, but the town already felt like Christmas. Some of that was due to the time of year, but the majority of window displays already proclaimed the season—some with more dignity than others. Because most of the glass was single pane, the windows tended to collect moisture, giving them a frosted appearance.

From the corner tavern came a scratchy rendition of "Rudolph the Red-Nosed Reindeer." A weathered wooden storefront Indian stood holding a handful of cigars in front of what was now a barbershop. Someone had put a Santa hat on him and a red wool muffler around his neck.

"Now that's what I call class." Shannon laughed as they paused to look at it. "All it lacks are some plastic reindeer."

"Plastic with blinking red noses."

"Do you think he'd like that?"

"I think he'd try to scalp whoever was responsible."

He looked down at her, decided she must still be cold, and placed his arm around her shoulder. She stiffened, but just for a moment. Then, bit by bit, she leaned into him. He wished he could see her expression, but having her against his side was even better.

Thanks to the streetlight they were approaching, he caught a glimpse of the auburn highlights in her hair and was slightly surprised she wasn't wearing a bonnet, her legs covered by a long skirt. When she'd come into his office earlier, his mind and appointment book had been full of everything he needed to accomplish before Christmas Eve, when he'd drive some twenty miles north and have Christmas with his sister and her brood.

Now nothing mattered except that he was walking Shannon to her car.

"I take it Myra and her cronies have filled you in on the decorating extravaganza," he said, gathering his thoughts. "The firemen really get into it. No matter what the weather, they're out there, heckling each other and yet somehow accomplishing what they need to."

"I know it's a big deal."

He'd gone to considerable effort to keep the conversation going so he wouldn't make the mistake of imagining himself as the town sheriff and her the maiden schoolmarm, and yet maybe it meant little to her. Now he slowed his pace to match hers, to make the most of the ambling pace she seemed content to set. She paused to look in each window, yet didn't comment on them. And she remained against him, warmth and long legs, slender shoulders beneath the layers of clothing, smelling oh so faintly of roses.

"I like your perfume," he heard himself say.

"My aunt makes it. I'm not sure now except that she uses the roses from her garden." Her voice became almost dreamy. "She also uses lavender and carnations. The aroma reminds me of my grandmother's house."

Hm. What it reminded him of was that she was a beautiful, intelligent, desirable woman and he a man who'd been without that in his life for too long.

They reached her car before he was ready to let her go, but he had to release her while she pulled her keys from her purse and unlocked her door. He nearly told her to let the engine run a while before getting in so the interior would start to warm, but he'd sound like an overbearing male. He wished he could take her home in a buggy pulled by a matching pair of horses.

"Thank you." She was almost whispering, standing close and yet not close enough. "For your help this afternoon, for dinner, for everything."

He should be thanking her for reminding him how exciting it could be for a man and a woman to walk together while their bodies—at least his—discovered things about each other.

"You're welcome," he said.

Then, because she was looking up at him and her lips were slightly parted and he could still smell roses, he bent down and kissed her.

Lightly.

Not long enough.

FOUR

"I saw you with him; everyone did."

Shannon winced. "I doubt *everyone* did," she told Myra, then switched the phone from her right hand to her left so she could sort through a stack of cloth triangles. She'd been so busy with customers all morning that this was her first opportunity to sit at her sewing machine. Now she would have to handle what she hoped was no more than Myra's curiosity.

"Close enough." Myra laughed. "The way you had your arms around each other, it appears cupid has struck."

They hadn't had their arms around each other; he'd simply been making sure she didn't freeze. However, she didn't try to tell Myra that. The older woman would punch holes in her explanation, especially if someone had seen what had happened at the end.

Feeling warm all over, she struggled to find a way to change the subject. Fortunately, Myra spoke before Shannon was reduced to stuttering.

"I'm delighted my dear, delighted. There's nothing like a little added ammunition."

"Ammunition?"

"In getting Brad's cooperation, of course."

Myra's words set Shannon's teeth on edge, but she forced herself to remain silent as the other woman

launched into a lengthy explanation of what she had
in mind. During a brainstorming session the previous
night, Myra and the rest of the steering committee had
decided to modify their plans for a sleigh, since they
didn't have time to make one. They'd decided more
bang for the buck, so to speak, would come from placing authentic pioneer buckboards, stagecoaches, and
covered wagons along the main entrance to town.

"It's such a magnificent idea I'm surprised we didn't
think of it before!" Myra gushed. "Let's just see cyber-
shopping try to compete with that. Carol and Cliff Jensen must have tens of thousands of Christmas lights they
use to decorate their place—they have the historic
Nichols House—you know. They've agreed to donate a
portion of those lights as long as one of the stagecoaches is placed on their property. They're going to
have a tour there with the profits from what they charge
going to the city park improvement fund. They're very
civic minded. Even with all their money, they're willing
to—I'm sorry, I'm getting sidetracked, aren't I?"

Since she didn't know where this conversation was
going, Shannon couldn't say.

"Has Brad shown you the museum's collection?"

Of what? she nearly asked before it occurred to her
Myra must be referring to what the museum had in the
way of horse drawn conveyances.

"He's always been so protective about them," Myra
was saying, "keeping them in storage like that, not letting anyone sit on them or go into the room where they
are unless staff members are there. I realize they're fragile and there are probably some regulations or something, but we have that all figured out."

She explained the committee would build lean-tos to
shelter what they hoped Brad would lend them. They'd
already coaxed the city administrator to look into in-
surance coverage, and they planned to ask the police

department—all three officers—to provide around-the-clock protection.

"The hard part was going to be convincing Brad," Myra added. "but now we've found his soft spot—"

"You want me to do the convincing?"

"Put like that it sounds rather harsh, doesn't it? We know he thinks we're going overboard in making Oro *the* place in the county to shop this season, but if he understands how this will benefit the town and how many people are committed to seeing it work, and if that explanation comes from you, well, you understand—"

Myra had a lot to say after that. She pointed out the town was on the national register of historic places and had favored status with a number of federal agencies. Unfortunately, the town was vying with every other place on the register for federal grants. However, if more and more people came to Oro and their experience was so favorable that they told their congressmen and senators, it could add up to considerable money coming the town's way.

By the time Myra was done, Shannon felt exhausted. All she wanted to do was provide her customers with a large selection of quality quilts and herself with a means of support. She'd had no idea how complicated it would be to get those customers to come through her door.

"You want to succeed here," Myra was saying. "That's what all of us want. If we can get people to realize shopping here is more satisfying and fulfilling and—and historically educating or whatever you want to call it than any of the other options . . . you'll do it, won't you?"

"Do what?" Shannon asked, the image of a trapdoor opening in front of her coming to mind.

"Convince Brad, of course."

* * *

If anyone had asked Shannon what she had in mind when she invited Brad to her shop after work, she wouldn't have had a clue. True, Myra had presented a powerful argument. The image of the historical artifacts set up around town had an undeniable appeal, but she couldn't shake the feeling she was being used—and would be using Brad. Still, she wanted to see him again.

So he likes rose-scented perfume, does he, she thought as she dabbed a little behind her ears. She'd never been one for much makeup, but she took a moment to reapply lipstick and run mascara over her lashes, pleased that some of her Arizona tan remained. Then she inhaled the mix of simmering spices near the cash register that reminded her of pumpkin pie. The whole shop smelled of cinnamon, nutmeg, and cloves, which meant he'd have to stick his nose behind her ear to catch a whiff of roses—a thought that sent a small shiver through her.

Restless and excited and wishing she knew what she'd say when he stepped inside, she walked over to the window and looked out. The day was gray, the sky heavy and close. There'd been snow in the mountains, and the area's ski resorts were hopeful they could open once a few more inches fell, but all she could think about was how drab everything looked. She could hardly wait for the public decorations to go up, and the thought of seeing old carriages, stagecoaches, and even hay wagons festooned with multicolored lights brightened her spirits.

Movement at the corner of her eye caught her attention. Brad, oblivious to the weather, was walking her way, collar pulled up around his neck, hands jammed in his pockets, athletic body meshing with each step. He nodded at an elderly couple coming out of another shop but didn't stop to speak to them.

Maybe he's eager to see me.

"Good afternoon, Mr. Reading," she said cheerfully when he opened the door. "Brisk enough for you, is it?"

He came closer, drawing her attention once again to his remarkable eyes and the fact that moisture glistened in his dark hair. She started to comment on it when he suddenly shook his head like a dog. A few drops hit her face, cooling a little of the unexpected but tantalizing heat she'd begun to feel the moment she spotted him.

"In case you're curious, yes, it is raining," he said. Then he surprised her by capturing her wrists and bringing her hands to his hair. It was wet to the touch, thick and rich and altogether wonderful.

Feeling every bit as off balance and alive as she had back in high school when Bobby Thaks, quarterback and all-around heartthrob, had asked to look at her homework, she drew back. Then, although no sane and sensible woman would do such a thing, she licked her palm. It tasted of cool, clean water.

His smile all but melted her down. "So you're not entirely opposed to rain?" he asked, his voice a deep rumble.

"I—I—of course I'm not. Without rain, we wouldn't have all those evergreens in the mountains, no water flowing into the dam, no . . ." She had to shut up before he took her for a fool.

"You'll be tired of it by spring," he said. "Everyone is. But it isn't so bad if you can think of it the way my grandfather did."

"Your grandfather?"

"Homer Eon. I love that name. He had a farm in the Willamette Valley back when success or failure depended almost entirely on the weather."

Love and respect for the man flavored Brad's words, and she fell just a little bit in love with him as a result. "What did he say?" she managed, very, very glad they had the shop to themselves.

"That gold brought people to this part of the country,

but it was the rain that kept them. That and good earth. He called the rain Oregon's silver."

Her throat tightened and her eyes felt hot. "That's beautiful."

"I think so." His features sobered. "I wish he'd lived until I became an adult so I could have truly appreciated his wisdom. He was a basic man, tied to the earth. He paused and looked around. "So, this is where you hang out. It smells great."

As she gave him a tour—it didn't take long, since the entire building was less than a thousand square feet—she kept thinking of what he'd said about needing an adult's wisdom in order to really understand one's grandparents. Maybe it was his respect for the past's lessons that made his career right for him.

And maybe, if he continued to pass his wisdom on to her, she'd continue to fall in love with him.

"The price on the handmade quilts is so much more than those you make on the machine," he observed. "I understand the difference in labor is the reason, but can you sell many of the handmade ones?"

"Oh, yes." She fingered a queen-size spread with a double wedding ring pattern, the muted blue and green colors highlighted with white edging. "People are looking for something that'll increase in value—at least a certain percentage of them are. Handmade quilts will, while mine—some of my customers tell me they want to be reminded of their grandparents or great grandparents, which is why they invest in something that never came near a machine."

"Good."

"Good that all I get is a commission on them?" She'd put up as many display racks as she could fit into the space. As a result, only narrow aisles existed between the piles of quilts. It made her feel as if she were standing both in the past and present. When she had customers, she tried to stay out of the way, but Brad had remained close to her. She felt surrounded by him. It was a little frightening but also exciting, tantalizing. Vital.

"What I mean is—" He ran his hands over the quilt. She could never picture his large fingers doing the kind of precise stitching needed to complete one. Still, she believed in his admiration for what an elderly widow had created.

"What I mean is," he continued, "I'm glad your business carries over into our heritage."

"So am I," she agreed.

And then his arms were gently around her and she was searching his eyes and her mouth had gone slack and then his covered it and she couldn't think anymore.

She felt him, smelled him, heard his breathing and his heartbeat, remembered what his voice sounded like and the feel of his wet hair, his passion for so many things. She'd thought herself substantial enough to face the modern world, but with his hands running down her arms and their bodies kissing, she wondered if she might float away—either that or be consumed by heat.

It was happening too fast. Wasn't it?

No. She parted her lips just enough to taste him, to delight in sensitive flesh against sensitive flesh. This wasn't youth's passionate and untutored kiss. They were in the middle of an exciting, wonderful exploration, taking it one sliding step at a time. She couldn't help trembling and was all too aware of her growing weakness. Still she continued the journey.

He had muscles, the kind honed by honest labor and not slavish devotion to machines. He was strength and health, radiated youth, and yet was filled with a seasoned quality she admired and hoped she was capable of matching.

"You don't mind?" he whispered when they were

done—when it wasn't safe to go any farther than they had.

"N-no."

"I can't help it. I see you and I want—you talk about things that matter to me and I . . ."

She wanted to tell him his stumbling words were precious to her, but his hands cupped her elbows, and she was warm where their bodies had touched. She felt off balance, as if she'd started down a road new to her and didn't know whether she had the courage to see it through—or if it would ever end.

"Brad, I—you're not involved with anyone, are you?"

"No. I was married, but I'm not anymore."

"Oh."

He released her, leaving her lost, and walked to the far end of the shop before turning around. He looked too large for the crowded space, and she knew the telling wasn't going to be easy for him.

"After we'd been married about five years, we tried to have children, but Beth suffered several miscarriages," he said. "The doctor told her to let her body rest and heal before we tried again."

His voice had become robot-like, as if he were finding the only way he could through a quicksand of memories. The need to hold him again, to lessen the pain of losing those unborn children, surged through her, yet she understood he needed to get through this alone.

He sighed. "She decided to go back to college for her degree. While she was there, she fell in love with one of her professors."

Another 'oh' almost found its way out of her, but she held it in check.

"It wasn't easy for Beth to tell me that." He didn't move. "But I already knew something had changed. I didn't fight the divorce."

She'd lifted her hand to her mouth without being

aware of it and was now running her forefinger over where Brad had kissed her.

"Was he older?" she asked.

"Yes. By nearly fifteen years."

"A father figure. Something she needed then."

"Something I couldn't give her."

She couldn't tell whether he was bitter, didn't want that of him. "How long ago was that?" she asked.

"Nearly two years."

Brad's wife had left him in the winter, left him to walk alone through the silver rain. "Are you all right?" she asked.

"I am now." His chest rose and fell. "Shannon, I didn't know I was going to say what I did, but the other night you told me about yourself and I felt I owed it to you."

She closed the ground between them, taking her to him so she could absorb his body heat. But as much as she wanted to put her arms around him and offer him wordless comfort, she didn't trust herself enough. Instead she indicated the window behind him, waited for her emotional world to come back into focus.

"The rain has picked up," she said. "You might have to stay a while."

"I don't mind. Do you?"

She didn't, she thought a half hour later as rain continued to slam onto the roof, isolating and sheltering them. She'd turned on all the lights as a defense against the storm, and then because Brad had asked how she came up with her designs, she'd pulled out the pattern books she'd collected over the years. When she mentioned she had difficulty finding old quilt pictures with enough detail, he offered to look through the museum's library.

"Most people don't realize how many large items we

tore," he said. "That's what really cramps us for space and keeps me busy with fund-raising projects. There are two covered wagons, a lot of period farming equipment, and a wonderful old carriage with much of the original fringe still intact. We'll put it on display in the spring."

"By display you mean the glassed-in viewing rooms at the back of the building?"

"Yes. There's no room for it in the museum itself, even if we could get it in the door."

This was the perfect opportunity to bring up what she and Myra—mostly Myra—had discussed. Instead, she asked how the carriage had come to the museum.

"It was in a shed on the Nichols property. Apparently the former owners never took it out and really looked at it. When Carol and Cliff Jensen realized what they had, they decided to donate it."

Myra had told her about the Jensens' generosity. Without giving herself time to weigh the wisdom of what she was going to say, she brought up her conversation with Myra.

"I don't know why Mr. and Mrs. Jensen are involved with the merchants' association since they're just residents," she admitted. "but they certainly—"

"They're getting behind things because they operate a gift shop on their property."

"Oh."

"I don't mean to put a negative spin on what they're doing. I'm simply pointing out they have their own agenda."

"Everyone does."

"True. How did we get on this subject?"

"Because . . ." She sighed, then took the plunge. "The Christmas steering committee has come up with a new idea, one that, if it's implemented, will involve you."

Brad's expression didn't change while she quickly,

concisely set forth what the committee had in mind, but he folded his arms across his chest.

"I have to admit I'm uncomfortable at being put in this position," she wound up. "I'd rather Myra or one of her friends approached you, but . . ."

"But they figured you'd have a better chance of convincing me."

"They've seen us together—at least someone has. Apparently it didn't take long for the news to spread."

"Tell me about it. Shannon, what's your reaction to this proposal?"

She hadn't expected to be put on the spot. She fidgeted with a loose thread while she thought. "I see both pros and cons," she finally said. "Despite Myra's assurances that the antiques will be well protected, they'd hardly be a priority with the police department. If there's enough of a storm, the shelters she described might not provide enough protection. However . . ."

Although she wished he'd say something, anything, so she could judge his reaction, he regarded her in silence.

"It's so foggy today." She gestured toward the window. "Between that and the rain, the shortened hours of daylight, everything feels heavy. There's nothing silvery about the way it looks right now. How excited can people get about shopping if they're wet and hemmed in by fog? But if the first thing they see when they come into town are cheerfully decorated earlier means of transportation, it would lift their spirits."

"And they'd spend more money, right?"

Teeth clenched, she ground out her reply. "I have to consider the bottom line, Brad. Every woman who tries to support herself does."

FIVE

That hadn't gone well.

When Yapper charged him the moment he opened the door, Brad briefly gave himself up to the dog's enthusiasm, accompanying him into the fenced backyard and throwing a ball for several minutes while the rear porch light provided less than optimum illumination, rain pelted down on his bare head, and Yapper slipped and slid on the wet grass.

He was trying to coax the dog back inside when he noticed his neighbors on either side had put up their Christmas lights. He ought to follow suit, at least do enough that the neighborhood children didn't call him Mr. Scrooge, but the museum volunteers had been at him to allow them to go all out in decorating the nearly hundred-year-old building. He'd finally given in, their enthusiasm exhausting him.

And now Shannon and her friends—

No, that wasn't being fair to her, he admitted as he dried Yapper with an old towel. The idea hadn't been hers; she'd simply been the messenger—a messenger with a compelling argument, since there was no denying that multicolored lights strung over the coveted items would do a lot to expel December's gloom. However, it wasn't going to happen, at least not with the antiques under his care.

Shannon hadn't said anything when he turned her down, and he hadn't had to contend with an argument—the last thing he wanted from her—but she'd been unable to hide her disappointment.

Well, why shouldn't she be disappointed? She was used to clear, starlit desert nights, not fog, mist, thunderstorms and cold, drab surroundings. Besides, she was right. The whole town would look more alive if the merchants' plan were implemented. People of all ages would gain a greater understanding of the past in the process. Unfortunately, it came at too great a risk to fragile artifacts.

He could have ended his involvement by letting Shannon be the bearer of disappointing news. Instead, he picked up the phone and called Myra. The conversation took too long because Myra had never been one to take no for an answer, but he finally convinced her he wasn't going to change his mind. He also had no doubt Myra was considering taking him off her Christmas card list.

Yapper was pushing his empty dog dish around the kitchen floor in a not too subtle reminder it was dinnertime when his own stomach announced the same thing. He'd hoped he and Shannon could share a meal, but he hadn't needed to be hit over the head to realize she wasn't in the mood for more of his company.

The ringing phone startled him. He picked it up, hoping he'd hear a soft feminine voice, but it was one of the other MUTTS board members. He listened with half an ear while rummaging through the refrigerator, then gave Matthew's idea his full attention.

For a few minutes at least, he didn't think about Shannon.

* * *

"We may not be bright, but we're easy."

"You've got that right. Weak minds, strong backs. That's all we need for this job."

"Speak for yourself, Bubba. You're the one on the ladder, not me."

Shannon couldn't help laughing at the good-natured exchange between members of the fire department as they went about draping the doors and windows of every commercial building in town with evergreen boughs. Once they'd finished that, they'd string up the small white lights she had no doubt would give the town a fantasy look.

She'd had her aunt and uncle over for Thanksgiving, the two women sharing the cooking chores in the tiny kitchen. Then they'd run up her phone bill by calling various relatives. On Friday, the first official day of Christmas shopping, she'd been so busy that if it hadn't been for leftovers, she never would have had dinner.

Now it was the weekend and Oro was going into high gear. She felt excited and a little bit scared—so much of her future depended on what happened in the next month.

"I think it's their favorite thing to do." Margaret Boez joined Shannon in front of the barbershop. Margaret and her husband owned a jewelry store specializing in gold pieces they designed themselves, and Shannon so admired their work that she was planning to buy a necklace for her mother from them.

"They certainly look as if they're enjoying themselves. I just hope he doesn't look down." Shannon indicated the top of a two-story building, where a man perched on the extended fire truck ladder was stapling pine boughs to the peaked roof. "I get dizzy just thinking about doing that."

"Me, too," Margaret agreed. "It's so sweet of them to come out at the crack of dawn so they won't be in the way by the time shoppers arrive. What did you think of the coverage the newspaper is giving our tree lighting ceremony?"

"I read it twice, then made copies to send to my family. I don't see how it could get any better than the cover of the Events section."

Margaret explained it was due to Myra's diligence. Also, once again thanks to the steering committee, members of a local antique car club had agreed to park their vehicles at the entrance to town so they could be decorated.

"I don't know how Myra did it, but she managed to talk a private security firm into providing backup for the police department," Margaret added. "When that woman puts her mind to something, there's no standing in her way."

Except that Brad had held firm, Shannon thought as she slowly walked from one end of the business district to the other. It wasn't raining this morning. With any luck, the approaching storm would hold off until after tonight's ceremony. Because it was barely seven in the morning, the street was nearly deserted except for the wisecracking firemen and a few merchants out to share in the fun.

She stopped frequently to inhale the rich aroma of pine and pitch, reminded of what Brad had told her about how pioneers had celebrated their Christmases with simple decorations and heartfelt gratitude for what today would be considered paltry possessions. But he was right. What was more important than a healthy family, a roof over one's head, and enough food?

The corner toy store held her attention the longest. A large Santa Claus staring down a chimney dominated the display that sported a train chugging in endless circles around the base of the chimney, wooden toys evocative of a bygone era, a miniature Noah's Ark complete with tiny birds perched on the giraffes' necks, Raggedy Ann and Andy dolls, and a soulful stuffed dog whose glossy black eyes seemed to stare right at her.

"Takes you back to childhood, doesn't it?"

How long had it been since she'd heard Brad's voice? No more than four days, and yet it seemed much longer. Not fully trusting her reaction, she turned toward him.

"It does," she agreed, carefully keeping her tone neutral. "There's something about that dog—if he were real, I'd be taking him home with me."

As Brad studied the lifelike creature, she studied him. This morning, he wore a bleach-faded sweatshirt with a gray turtleneck under it. His old jeans had suffered the same overzealous contact with bleach.

"Is this the new dress standard at work?" she teased. "Casual is good, but this—"

"We're putting up our nativity scene today. Believe me, I don't mind an excuse to let the real me out."

"The real you?" If anyone else was close enough to hear what they were saying, she was unaware of it. "What do you want to be in your next career, a carpenter?"

"Sometimes I think I'd like nothing better." He made a sweeping motion that took in their surroundings. "What do you think?"

Smiling, she shivered in anticipation. "For once I can hardly wait for it to be dark so I can really see the lights. Everything's going to take on a fairy-tale air, I'm sure. What a wonderful idea!"

"Better than the displays at the Brabury Mall?"

"Much better. More dignified, more—more real."

"More real than draping store-bought lights over a covered wagon?"

"I'm not going to argue with you about that," she said, after a moment's deliberation. "What's done is done."

"I hoped you'd say that. Friends?" Looking into her eyes, he stuck out his hand.

"Of course." When he took her hand, he gave it a lingering squeeze before reluctantly, it seemed, releasing it.

"So," she said once she was no longer thinking about how right his fingers felt engulfing hers, "what have you been up to lately?"

"I'm glad you asked. Saves me from having to work the conversation around to that. MUTTS is taking off like gangbusters. We're going to kick off several campaigns during the holiday season, hoping to increase people's awareness of what life's like for a dog without a loving home. With people already in the spirit of giving, the timing should be right."

They'd started walking while he was talking, but she paid little attention to where they were going. Several firemen waved at Brad, and she nodded at the shopkeepers, pleased that she already felt part of the community. Still, those people were no more than a backdrop. Brad remained her only reality.

"What kind of campaigns?" She bent to pick up a few pine needles, crushed them between her fingers, then inhaled the rich aroma.

"Setting up an adoption center near the Coats For Kids drop center in Brabury, for one. Another plan we're going to implement is coming about because one of our members is a reporter for the newspaper. I'm not sure what you . . ."

"You're not sure I'm going to what?" she prompted after a moment.

Instead of answering, he took the crushed needles from her and held them to his own nose. "Wonderful. When I was a boy, my parents took my sister and me camping most summer weekends. Later I did summer trail maintenance work for the Forest Service. You'd think I'd have had so much of the woods I'd pay no attention to its sights and smells, but they've become part of me. I can't imagine being anywhere but near the woods."

She loved hearing him talk like that, revealing himself to her. If only she could take these moments when dawn was turning into morning and bottle them so she'd always have the memory of sharing the quiet scene with him.

"It's new to me," she admitted. Someone had left a pile of evergreen garlands on the sidewalk. She took one and wrapped it around her neck, letting the ends trail over her breasts. "Is this the way the forest smells in the summer? If it does, then I understand why you can't get enough of it."

Standing back, he gave her a mock-serious appraisal, his gaze holding briefly on her breasts. "You look fetching—a little overdressed, but what the heck. Actually, the aroma is much richer in summer because the tang of pitch comes out in the heat. Still, I'll take it anyway I can get it."

Maybe next summer if this—whatever—is happening between us is still alive, you'll take me camping.

Instead of risking what might be a great deal by telling him that, she removed her temporary necklace and returned it to where she'd found it. She hoped they'd start walking again, but he'd spotted something in the pile. Picking it up, he showed it to her. It was a moment before she realized he held a sprig of mistletoe.

"Are you ready for a history lesson?" he asked, his chocolate eyes sparkling. "Mistletoe hasn't always had the romantic position in our traditions it now enjoys. In the past, people used anything they could get their hands on—evergreens, apples, cloth ribbons—and hung them over doorways. Fortunately the effect was the same." He gave her a mischievous smile. "They were accepted as kissing boughs."

His hand began to move, and although he didn't say a word, she knew what he was going to do. Several more people had arrived in town and were walking up and down the street, but he didn't seem to mind their presence. After a moment, neither did she.

With his hand holding the mistletoe over her head, he was in no position to pull her into his embrace. He didn't need to. Sliding forward, feeling the magnetic pull between them, she surrendered to his warmth and strength, maybe most of all to the questioning and sensual smile that blurred as she came too close for her eyes to focus.

For the first few heartbeats, she almost believed this public show of friendship—friendship?—wouldn't take her beyond herself. Certainly she'd remain in the here and now with cold air on the back of her neck and the rain-slickened footing needing her attention and the real, everyday world surrounding her, but the thought died unmourned.

Sweatshirts were comfortable garments, practical, no-nonsense, lasting forever, and taking on the contours of the wearer. She was dimly aware of that and slightly undone by the simple fact the well-worn garment was such an intimate part of Brad that she'd be content if he never wore anything else.

Then that thought faded, too, and she was aware of nothing except the brush of his lips against hers, becoming deeper, a challenge and question, taking her beyond herself and into a world of exploration.

When she stood on tiptoe, she felt the pull in her calves, felt soft fabric over muscle and bone as she balanced herself by holding onto his arms, but those sensations were nothing compared to what his mouth was doing to her senses.

Sparks flickered to life inside her, fairy explosions that came one after another like the Fourth of July sparklers of her childhood. She danced inside the fireworks, weightless and formless, laughing with the adventure, breathless and a little afraid, mostly alive.

Had it suddenly become summer? Maybe the two of them had magically been transported on a warm wind to Arizona and the desert heat was responsible for the trickle of sunlight she felt first on her cheeks, then her neck, then into her throat and breasts and heart before flowing over her belly and lower, deeper, all consuming.

She could do this forever, surrounded by Brad, isolated from everything except him, rocking slightly with him, exploring what was nameless and alive and maybe everything she'd ever needed.

Kissing him. Holding newborn love to her.

Blending a bit.

There was no way she could have prepared herself for the sudden loss that accompanied his stepping back. Shaken, the heat he'd brought to her all too quickly fading, she tried to make sense of what had happened.

"Not here," he whispered hoarsely. "Not like this."

She only had to look around to realize that what should be a private moment was far from that. Whether the others had any inkling of what their kiss had done to her she couldn't say. She fervently hoped not. This was their exploration, their search into each other.

"You're right," she whispered back.

SIX

Shannon had been warned the day would be busy. In anticipation, she'd asked her assistant to come in early, a precaution she didn't for a minute regret. So many customers came through the door that at times her small shop felt as if it might explode. Though she was slightly disappointed in her sales, she reminded herself that people would remember she was here. That couldn't help but benefit her in the future.

A number of customers commented on how satisfying it was to shop in a town where everything for sale wasn't mass produced and where they were served by the owner, not part-time clerks. She could hardly argue with that. When she felt comfortable doing so, she asked people what had brought them to Oro. Although most knew about the town, of course, their curiosity had been piqued by the recent publicity.

"So many commented about how nice everything looks," Wendi, her assistant said as late afternoon approached. "It's hard to see the street decorations with so many people and cars out and about, but even so, there's something kind of peaceful about the area. I went to the mall with friends yesterday and the noise and congestion did me in. My senses hit overload there. Here, I can appreciate the individuality."

Shannon hadn't thought about the simple evergreen

boughs and small white lights in quite those terms, but now Wendi had pointed it out, she had to agree Oro held none of the frantic quality she'd long associated with Christmas displays.

Because the place felt stuffy, she took advantage of what she suspected would be a momentary lull in the traffic to prop open the front door. The tree lighting ceremony was set for eight o'clock tonight. Although the sun hadn't yet set, fog was already starting to roll in, bringing with it a cool dampness that licked over her heated cheeks.

Brad's grandfather had called rain a farmer's silver. Tired and hungry, all she could think was that it would be months before the trees started to bud.

"Do you mind if I say something?" Wendi asked.

"No, of course not."

"Well, I've been trying to decide what I want to do after high school. I'm not sure I'm ready for college or even if it's right for me. I talked it over with my folks and they think it might be best if I work for a few years. I love working with you and have already learned a lot about quality merchandise, but I can't . . ."

"Can't what?" she prompted.

"I don't want to make a career out of retail sales," she said, sounding apologetic. "This dealing with the public—answering the same questions over and over again, straightening up after people, making sure they don't ruin anything, having to smile all the time—"

"I agree." Shannon rubbed the sides of her mouth, momentarily distracted by memories of the way Brad had claimed it this morning. "I think it's different when the business is yours. Owners are more committed to succeeding, which makes it possible for them to put up with everything."

"Yeah, you're right. Still, that's kind of scary, isn't it?"

Because a trio of women came into the shop just then,

Shannon didn't have time to respond, but she suspected Wendi already knew the answer. Yes, always having to be aware of the bottom line was scary, but today she had something more than what was or wasn't in the till to think about.

Not long after she locked up for the day, local schoolchildren would troop through town, singing Christmas carols while their parents, relatives, and friends watched. Santa Claus would pass out candy canes and the mayor would give a speech in front of the town tree. Then the lights would be switched on for the first time.

She'd experience all that at Brad's side.

"You look as if you've run a marathon," he informed her when he came to pick her up. "Was it a rip-roaring success?"

Before she could answer, Wendi told him they hadn't had time for lunch.

"I know who you are," the girl continued. Her eyes flicked from him to Shannon, then back to Brad. A smile lifted the corners of her mouth. "Last year you spoke to my history class. It sure beat reading yet another boring chapter. I thought the old farm tools you brought in were cool."

"I call that my dog and pony show," he informed her. "However, even I'm getting tired of it. This year I hope to expand with some weaponry, show how things evolved over time. I also intend to do a lot more about the Native Americans of the area."

"Yeah, that's cool." With Brad's help, Wendi slipped into her coat. "Maybe I'll see the two of you at the lighting ceremony. I have a date."

"Youth," Shannon said once the girl was gone. "She's still bouncing, while my tongue's all but dragging."

"Hm. Let me see."

Before she could stop him—as if she wanted to—he'd tipped her head up and was pretending to study what he could see beyond her barely parted lips. Then he kissed her, but it was only a peck.

"The collective tongues are wagging," he said, after informing her he was taking her to his place for a bite of dinner before the shindig started. "I told myself no one paid attention to what we were doing out there this morning, but someone must have. Someone with a big mouth. I hope you don't mind."

"What are they saying?"

He told her, but not until he'd driven her to his place. If it had been any other time of year, she could have learned more about the neighborhood and his place, but even with the streetlights, her curiosity wasn't satisfied.

Dinner consisted of hamburgers, instant mashed potatoes, and fresh broccoli. All of it tasted wonderful to her. As they ate, he informed her he considered himself a passable cook and this was what he called his desperation meal. Then he revealed that none other than Cliff Jensen had stopped him at the post office.

"Cliff's a decent enough guy, and he's passionate about retaining Oro's historical integrity, but he's also a gossip. He stammered around for a while, then asked how long you and I'd been seeing each other. If he'd think about it, he'd realize we've just met."

They were eating at a built-in kitchen nook near a window that overlooked an extensive and overgrown garden. Brad had turned on the outside light so she could see it. His dog, a half-grown, oversized mutt with floppy ears and lively eyes, stared in at them.

"What did you tell Cliff?" she asked.

"Not nearly enough to satisfy his curiosity. Look, I'm sorry."

"For what?"

"I have to bear much of the responsibility for the position the merchants' association put you in the other day." His voice echoed slightly in the oversize kitchen with its tall blue cupboards, antique gas cooking stove, cracked vinyl flooring, and faded countertop. "I made no attempt to hide my interest in you. I'm sure that's why they pressured you to try to convince me to let them exploit—at least we have that behind us, don't we?"

She hoped so, but she had no crystal ball. Although she was curious about what else he and Cliff might have talked about, she was even more curious about his plans for the house and why a bachelor had put down roots.

He started to tell her his first priority had been to upgrade the electrical and gas service and he was now trying to work up the courage to attack the kitchen. Then he glanced at his watch.

"Darn. I was hoping for time to take you on the less than grand tour, but we have to hustle if we're going to find a place to park. If you're brave enough, I'd like you to meet Yapper."

The gangly near-pup reduced her to helpless laughter as he tore madly from one end of the yard to the other, a rubber ball clamped in his jaws. Brad stood beside her, one arm draped over her shoulder, the other out slightly to protect her from sudden doggy lunges.

"I usually have him inside with me," he explained. "But his company manners leave a lot to be desired—not that you've noticed, I'm sure. Next time we'll let him run off a little of his energy—if that's possible—and maybe the two of you can get to know each other."

"I'd like that."

"Would you?" he asked, and she knew he wasn't talking about her relationship with his dog.

"Yes," she managed.

"So would I."

Turning her toward him, he ran his fingers into her hair at the temples, then quickly, effortlessly massaged away the headache she hadn't told him about but perhaps he'd guessed had come with her day. Wondering where, if anywhere, this was heading, she covered his hands with hers, grateful for the night, yet needing to look into his eyes.

She'd been surrounded by noise from the moment she'd opened her shop this morning. The quiet and peace of his backyard with the shadow roses she ached to tend softened and settled her in a way only a ride out into the desert had ever done, but her surroundings had little to do with the way she felt.

Maybe Yapper sensed what was going on between the humans, because he silently settled onto the ground, then stared up at them. Shannon was only dimly aware of the dog, just that he was part of Brad's life, and that this man who was becoming special to her had saved the animal's life.

"I wanted the first time I brought you here to be special," he whispered, "and to fix you something memorable for dinner."

"It's all right," she whispered back. "I-I can see why you bought the place."

"Wrecked vinyl and all?"

"Beneath that is a place built with pride and workmanship, isn't it? A place that'll always remain part of the past."

"That's the way I see it," he said. "I'm glad you do, too." Then he kissed her forehead, his warm lips a gift from him to her.

Undone by the gesture and how much it meant to her, she looked around, trying to ground herself in her surroundings. "The yard and roses—I think I would have bought the place for them alone."

"That's a woman talking." There was a smile in his voice. "For me, making sure I didn't burn down the place while turning on a light had a higher priority. I can live with doing cosmetic changes a bit at a time, but not with faulty electricity."

They could debate housing priorities all evening, but that didn't interest her, and she suspected he didn't care, either. Although he lived on a hill overlooking the town, with a curtain of evergreens all around, she could hear the hum of increasing traffic below. Their time together was short. She needed to make the most of it.

"When I told my aunt and uncle I was moving here, they said they hoped I'd meet a man." She surprised herself with the admission. "All I could think about was being able to support myself. I never . . ."

"I'm glad you came here." His mouth was only inches from her forehead. When he spoke, his warm breath feathered over her flesh. "Shannon, I don't know how to play the dating game. When I was married I never once looked at another woman. Since then, I've gone on a few dates, but nothing came of them. I know we still have a lot to learn about each other, but it feels different this time."

"It feels different to me, too," she admitted. After that, she didn't have words for her emotions.

All she knew was when they embraced, when he covered her mouth with his and her breasts with his hands and she clung to his strength, it was right.

By the time they returned to town, there were so many cars about that she had no idea where they would have parked if he hadn't been able to use his slot behind the museum. Although she'd bought what she thought would be a substantial coat, he'd insisted she put on one of his sweatshirts under it. As they joined the crowd gathered around the tree, she felt surrounded by him, could smell him in the garment.

"Fortunately, the mayor isn't much of a public speaker," he told her. "I'm sure he'll let the children hold center stage with their singing."

He was right, but in truth, she remembered nothing of what the retired grocery store manager said beyond his reading of the Christmas diary entry of an early Oro miner. For that young man and his companions, the day had been one of work, homesickness, singing a few Christmas carols, and an exchange of simple foodstuffs.

Because it was dark, she could barely make out the silhouettes of those around her. Much of the crowd consisted of people with small children, and when a local miner—Brad told her he actually owned a small nearby mine—walked down the street leading several burros with bells around their necks, it was all the parents could do to contain their little ones who wanted to pet the animals. Brad told her he hoped to incorporate MUTTS into next year's event.

The parade, if it could be called one, was pretty much impromptu. A couple who raised mules had harnessed a pair to a long wagon full of senior citizens holding flashlights and calling to friends.

Someone had brought a wreath-decorated dairy cow who allowed herself to be dragged from one end of town to the other. A number of people proudly showed off their dogs, the most impressive being four magnificent Great Danes who kept trying to go into a small cafe.

"I don't know what Myra is going to think of this," Shannon told Brad as several teenage boys gave an ear-splitting rendition of "Little Drummer Boy," using drums better suited for a rock concert. "She turned much of this event over to some of the male merchants.

I think they pretty much told folks to do whatever they felt like."

"It's great." Brad practically had to yell to make himself heard. "A real hometown flavor. People being themselves instead of the whole thing being orchestrated."

"That it is," she agreed.

Once the parade was over, the mayor announced the choir from one of the local churches would lead the crowd in traditional Christmas songs. She smiled throughout "Rudolph The Red-Nosed Reindeer," turned pensive as "Silent Night" filled the crisp air, nearly cried as a woman soloist with a rich, powerful voice brought "O Holy Night" to life. She was still lost in the haunting notes when the mayor threw the switch that lit up the tree and applause broke out.

Although the rest of the town was dressed in quiet white lights, the tree, a fifty-foot-high silvertip, glittered with every color in the rainbow. It lit up the night, casting enough illumination that Shannon was first nearly blinded and then saw, between the high clouds, a few distant stars. She snuggled close against Brad's side, then pointed at the stars.

"That's what it's about, isn't it?" He spoke into her ear. "The timelessness of it all. Enduring qualities. That and sharing those things with someone special."

SEVEN

"Tonight's meeting is basically a status report," Myra said. "We're halfway into December, and the committee has decided we need to assess how well the promotional campaign has been working and what more we need to do during the last few weeks before Christmas."

One by one, her fellow merchants reported on how this year compared with last. Shannon noted no one gave actual figures, but she wouldn't want to reveal her bottom line either. She thought everyone would be satisfied because, without exception, profits were up, but she'd barely finished pointing out she had no comparisons when the conversation turned to the committee's latest brainstorm.

"It's so simple! I'm surprised we didn't think of it earlier," Myra gushed. "We've already taken care of things with the newspaper's advertising staff, and the radio stations will start running our spots as soon as we get everything to them. I don't know about TV. That's pretty expensive."

Several merchants insisted nothing had the impact of TV. Others argued an advertising budget could stretch only so far. When she heard what she'd have to cough up as her share, Shannon nearly choked.

"Ah, the radio spots—how long before they'd be ready?" she asked.

Frowning, Myra muttered everything was ready to go,

with the taping set for tonight. While local children sang carols in the background, two community theatre actors would play Mr. and Mrs. Claus and would talk about how creative their gifts would be this year thanks to what was available in Oro.

Obviously, Myra wanted to go the TV route, even if the ads wouldn't be ready to run until the week before Christmas, but when the vote was taken, the majority felt as Shannon did.

Only then did Myra play her trump card. "I don't see how anyone could object, since it's going to be handled with such taste and will be on public property, but what would have more lasting value than to have one's picture taken while wearing an authentic period costume and standing in front of the museum? The camera used would be one of those instant things, so they'll make perfect last-minute gifts. As I'm sure you all know, Carol and Cliff Jensen donated many of the clothes they found in their attic to the museum. They think the idea's perfectly wonderful."

Of course they do, especially if they get credit.

"What if someone tears the clothes?" William asked. "Knowing Brad, I can tell you that won't set well with him."

Myra snorted. "Carol and Cliff became owners of everything that was in the attic when they bought the Nichols place. Just because they turned things over to the museum for safekeeping doesn't change a thing."

Shannon wasn't sure about that, but now wasn't the time or place to bring it up. As Myra explained how the photo opportunities would be incorporated into the media blitz, she allowed her attention to wander. As before, they were meeting in the Italian restaurant, and as on the night she'd met Brad, it was raining. In fact, there'd hardly been a day in the first half of December when there hadn't been measurable precipitation.

If it hadn't been for Brad, she might be looking for the first boat out of town.

"I had the feeling things would last longer than you thought they would," Brad said when she called him much later that evening. "So things aren't winding down in the promotional department, are they?"

"Unfortunately, no. I'm sorry. I really wanted to come over this evening but—"

"I know," he interrupted. "Between the hours you're keeping and my work with MUTTS, we haven't seen enough of each other. How are we going to finish these popcorn strands for our trees? Of course, if you'd agree to spend the night . . ."

Instead of saying anything in reply to what was half tease, half invitation, she wandered from her matchbox-size kitchen into the unlit living room and sank onto the couch. She'd turned down the heat when she left this morning, and the gas furnace hadn't yet chased away the chill. Still, she was too tired to go in search of a blanket. Brad's place probably hadn't been any warmer when he got home, but if they'd entered it together, she doubted if she would have noticed.

"I just don't want to—rush things," she belatedly told him.

"I know. I'm just testing the progress I've made."

"Progress?"

"In wearing down your ladylike reserve." He laughed. "The rosebush helped, didn't it?"

When she'd gotten to work this morning, there'd been a bare-root rose waiting near the front door. Next to it was a note from Brad explaining the nursery people had assured him its aroma would be rich, and he'd plant it wherever she wanted. All he asked for was to be given the first spring flower.

"It more than helped," she told him, warming at the

memory of his sweet gesture. "What a wonderful surprise! The perfect Christmas gift, even if it's a little early. What do you know about cultivating roses?"

"Not a thing, except that whatever's done in the way of pruning should be done in the winter. You?"

"Nothing."

"Great!"

"Great?"

"We can learn together."

Together they'd work in his patiently waiting garden, how-to manual in one hand, clippers in the other, a bag of fertilizer or whatever roses and other bushes and flowers required between them. Maybe by then there'd be no question of whether she'd spend the night with him.

"Brad?"

"What?"

"I want to fix you breakfast tomorrow," she told him, her need to see him resonating in her tone. "Nothing fancy, but if you came early, I—"

"Honey, I can't."

Honey. "Why not?"

"Don't you remember? We're opening the second MUTTS adoption site then. I'm going to be busier than a one-armed paperhanger."

He had told her something about the campaign when he'd dropped by the shop yesterday afternoon, but she'd been waiting on customers while trying to talk on the phone and had barely heard him.

"Of course," she finally thought to say. "I wish you all the success in the world."

"So do I. You should have seen the dogs we picked out at the pound the other day. Talk about scruffy and scared. But the vet's given them clean bills of health and now that they're cleaned up—what do you want for Christmas?"

She yawned. "What? You gave me my gift. The rose, remember?"

"That wasn't your gift. It was just because."

"Oh."

He muttered something she couldn't hear, then, "I just realized I haven't done any Christmas shopping," he said. "Do you think my sister's family would like a dog? Another one, that is?"

"I don't know," she told him, astounded anyone could let holiday shopping slip his mind. It seemed as if she'd thought of precious little except that in forever. The only thing she hadn't done was make a dent in her own list.

"Well you're no help," he teased. "Did I just hear you yawn?"

"I wouldn't do anything like that."

"Sure you wouldn't," he said as her entire being, it seemed, wrapped itself around his words. "Look, Sleeping Beauty, I won't keep you up any longer. I just wish—I wish the whole insanity of December was over so I could properly court you."

"Court?"

"Sure. Like they did in the olden days. Do you think I should call your father and assure him of my honorable intentions? Maybe our parents should meet. I could take you to the Saturday night barn dance. If your folks disapprove because I don't have a farm or a successful gold mine, maybe I could pick you up in my carriage and drive you to church."

"You're crazy."

"No, I'm not. I'm—Yapper, get down! Sleeping Beauty?"

"What?"

"I miss you."

People traveling from Brabury to Oro had to drive past the museum before reaching the commercial district, which was why Brad had offered his place of business as the site for the second MUTTS adoption center.

Not only would people hopefully be drawn to the dignified yet catchy sandwich signs MUTTS volunteers would erect on the lawn out front, but there was plenty of nearby parking and room in the foyer for a half-dozen dogs to be displayed. He'd gone to the museum board with his proposal to make sure he wasn't breaking any regulations. As he'd suspected, they had no objections as long as he guaranteed the animals were housebroken and under control.

Still, if other people had the same reaction Myra, William, and Mr. and Mrs. Jensen were having—

"Dogs?" Carol Jensen gasped, her voice echoing off his office's high ceiling. "Of course it's admirable you're trying to find homes for those unfortunate creatures, but your timing—you can't really expect people to be thinking about taking in strays this time of the year, what with everything else they're involved in."

Would you prefer they go into hibernation until you decide the timing's right? Instead of asking what would put him in the wealthy Carol Jensen's figurative doghouse, he stared at the wall behind her where a tiny spider clung. When the foursome had showed up this morning to discuss some plans of theirs, he'd invited them into his office, which fortunately wasn't as cramped as it had been when Shannon was here. Still, he hoped it was small enough that they wouldn't stay long.

"Brad." Myra used her schoolmarm's no-nonsense voice. "It won't work. It simply won't work."

"What won't?"

That's when they laid their plan on him. Myra's words all but ran together as she explained where the merchants intended to set up for their photo opportunities. They wouldn't presume to use the museum itself, she assured him, but the grounds were for use by the public and certainly no one would object to setting up a temporary structure there. A tent and portable heaters had been donated, even makeshift dressing rooms and clothes-hanging racks.

"I'm certain you're curious about what outfits we'll be making available," Carol said. "Of course, we could rent some from a costume shop or even prevail upon a theatre group, but authenticity's important since we're tying it in with Oro's heritage. That's why we'll be using the period pieces my husband and I gave the museum."

For the better part of a minute, Brad said nothing. Then he leaned forward and fixed his gaze on Carol. "I'm sorry, but that's not possible."

"Myra, I don't want anything to do with this."

"You have to. We're going to look like fools if we can't get him to change his mind."

The merchants' association had put her in this position before, and Shannon had hoped it would never happen again. Maybe it wouldn't be so bad if she'd just had to confront Myra, but the older woman had brought along the entire steering committee. They'd crammed themselves into her shop, preventing her from locking up and heading over to Brad's, where a home-cooked meal and some much needed time with him awaited.

"Let me get this straight." She sighed. "Brad won't let you use the outfits because—"

"Something about their having been entrusted to the museum and our signing a release," Cliff Jensen grumbled.

"But the radio spots will start running tomorrow and the newspaper ad will come out at the same time," Carol Jensen finished for her husband. "If we'd had any idea he'd be so uncooperative, we certainly wouldn't have gone ahead with things."

"Not only that," Myra said, "we aren't going to have enough parking. He's commandeered the museum itself for that—that—*dog* thing he's working on."

"It's an educational and adoption program," she supplied. He was expecting her momentarily and she'd hoped to run by the bakery and pick up an apple pie for dessert. Tired to her bone marrow, all she wanted was the peace and quiet of his place—that and his presence.

"Whatever." Myra dismissed MUTTS with a wave of her hand. "He said—well, he said his group has been planning this for weeks, that it's too late to change the location, and it's perfect because of the exposure—the same exposure we're after."

"It's his timing that's the problem," Carol insisted. "This is the holiday shopping season, plain and simple."

Wasn't it also Christmas, a time of generosity and warmth? Of reaching beyond selfishness? "MUTTS is important to him," she said.

"Not more than you are, my dear." Myra smiled slightly. "I'm sure you're special to him and . . . maybe you don't understand how vital a successful season is for us. If you did, you' d realize—"

"Believe me, I do," she interrupted.

In response, Myra shook her head, her gray hair flopping. "Hmm. Tell me, can you stay open through two long months of dead time?"

"Dead time?"

"Until spring. Until the weather pulls people outside and tourists start showing up. That's why holiday shopping is vital. The financial cushion has to be built now."

"Oh." Her voice sounded weak.

"It isn't easy," William volunteered solemnly. "So many small businesses fail because they haven't adequately prepared for the down periods. We'd hate to see you have to shut your doors so soon after opening."

EIGHT

By the time Shannon pulled into Brad's long, narrow driveway, her mouth was watering from the smell of warm apple pie. She still hadn't taken the time to buy an umbrella, so she wrapped her coat around the box and hurried up the wooden steps to his front door. It opened before she could ring the bell, and she stepped into light and warmth.

"Is that what I think it is?" he asked as he took her burden. "Yes, it is. Woman, I'd follow you to the ends of the earth if you keep this up."

"The ends of the earth? Do you have any idea how far that is?" He'd shut the door behind her, but unless he moved, she'd have to remain in the entry hall. Of course, as long as he stayed here with her, this close, she didn't mind. The world? It didn't exist; there was only him.

"I'm speaking figuratively. I take it you got hung up at the shop. Lots of well-heeled customers?"

"No." She sighed. "Myra and crew."

It was his turn to sigh. After planting a kiss on her forehead, as he so often did these days, he started toward the kitchen. She followed him, focusing on her feelings for him, waiting until he'd deposited the pie box on the counter. While driving over here, she'd convinced herself she had the will and fortitude and whatever necessary to bring up the subject at hand, but, darn it, he was wearing a kelly green shirt and old jeans and had on leather slippers and his hair was slightly mussed. He'd set the table and filled a flower vase with holly and had the back light on so she could see into his garden. He pointed to a spot near the fence.

"Quail," was all he said.

Quail, their fat little bodies in constant motion, top-knots bobbing, intent on whatever they'd found to eat—probably seed he'd set out for them.

Beyond words, she buried herself in Brad's warmth. She clung to him almost desperately and breathed in his aftershave, his essence and strength, his everything. When, after a long time, she'd regained a little control over herself, she drew his head down toward her, stood on tiptoe, and kissed him.

"Look up," he said in a rough tone when, finally, they were done.

She did. Somehow he'd fastened a mistletoe sprig to the ceiling over the table.

"We're not under it," she whispered. "Maybe it doesn't work."

"Oh, it works all right," he told her, then proved himself right.

Two lingering kisses, one on top of the other, were her undoing. When she felt herself start to slide apart, she briefly told herself it was because the long days had taken their toll on her, but that wasn't right. Brad was always doing something that touched her. Tonight, with the table and view he'd provided of the backyard, the enticements he'd provided for the quail, the mistletoe, the little bit of love she felt for him burst into flame. That quickly, that simply, whatever concerns she had for her financial future evaporated.

He'd prepared a Cornish pasty. While they ate, he explained that the dish, which consisted of meat, potatoes, and vegetables wrapped inside a pastry shell, had gone down into the mines with generations of Cornish miners.

"Their wives and mothers made the pasties up in the morning and the miners would leave them beside their lanterns to slow cook while they worked. I've experimented with some refinements, such as cutting down on the fat, but I think we should pretend we're miners."

She felt more like a fairy princess with a handsome prince waiting on her. Christmas carols played softly on the stereo in the living room. She felt in love and loved, complete when it couldn't possibly have happened that fast. And, yes, ready to take that next and exciting step in their relationship.

Tonight. After dinner.

"So," he said much later as she was cutting into the pie, "have you put the office behind you?"

"What office?"

"Good girl." Coming up behind her, he wrapped his arms around her. "I'll be glad when this insanity is over so you and I can have some time together. I've been thinking, planning, fantasizing—about a lot of things." He winked. "Even if you aren't ready to become a ski bum, we can go up to the ski resort and watch. I also want to take you to the coast. Have you ever seen the ocean?"

She shook her head and tried to concentrate on his body against hers, refused to ask herself how she could afford to get away.

"Poor thing. No ocean sand between your toes or spray in your hair. That's certainly something we're going to have to remedy, isn't it? How about if we take a week and slowly wind our way up into Washington? I have vacation time coming and you can get someone to man the shop. Besides, this time of the year it's often warmer at the coast than inland. As long as we both have umbrellas—"

"Brad."

"What?"

She was going to tell him she didn't have the money to hire someone to take over, but he'd slipped his hands under her sweater and was running his fingers over her naked flesh.

More aware than she'd felt in a long, long time, she let the pie server slip out of her hand and rested the back of her head against his shoulder. His hands moved this way and that, over the top of her bra, under her waistband, around to the sides, then back to her bra—or, more specifically, her breasts. When she offered no resistance, when her breath came fast and ragged, he pushed her away from him, but only long enough to unfasten the confining garment.

His hands were like liquid silver on her newly freed flesh, fluid warmth and exploring fingertips, test and challenge and—please—promise. He'd become quicksand and she a butterfly hovering dangerously, excitingly close.

"Brad?"

"I love the way you say my name." His breath danced across the back of her neck.

And I love the things you do to me.

"I also love the feel of your skin," he said when she remained silent. "The way your breasts respond to my touch."

There was no denying her nipples had tightened. He had to know what he was doing to the rest of her, the melting down of muscle and bone. Maybe if she faced him—touched him in return—maybe a little of the control could be hers.

But she didn't care. She wanted him.

Eyes closed, she turned inward. Her breasts were fully covered by his hands now, his to play with, to command and ignite and caress. Her legs trembled, and she couldn't stop her hips from moving. No curtains covered his rear windows, but why should he cut out the world when no one could look inside? Whatever the two of them did tonight would—

"Shannon. Shannon."

"Wh—at?"

"The phone."

Why hadn't she heard it? When he walked into the living room, he took her with him, one hand wrapped around her wrist while his left lifted the receiver to his ear. Whoever it was wasn't her concern. Brad would deal with the intrusion and then—

"It's for you." He handed the phone to her.

At first nothing registered, but slowly, irrevocably she understood Myra was talking to her.

Something was going to be delivered to the museum grounds tomorrow. In order to ensure no customers missed whatever it was, all merchants would fasten some kind of notice to their front doors and hand out fliers.

"We're burning the midnight oil here, Shannon." Myra spoke in a clipped tone. "I take it you haven't tried to persuade Brad to put our concerns first."

"No. I—"

"That's what I thought. Having to change our plans at this late date is most disturbing and more than a little unnerving, but we're determined. After everything we've done so far, we can hardly give up, can we? I trust you'll come on board."

"Why do you think I wouldn't?"

Myra snorted. "You're with *him* instead of here."

There was certainly no denying that. Nor, as Myra's tirade continued, did Shannon need to ask why Brad was considered the enemy. Thanks to Myra's habit of repeating herself, she soon understood the picture taking event was being moved to the Nichols place. In order to ensure that no one would miss the change of location, a sign would be set up in front of the museum to alert people. In addition, the merchants would do everything they could to pass on the information and work up enthusiasm.

"I can't pretend I'm not disappointed with Brad's stand on this," Myra wound up. "He has to understand we have a limited window of opportunity here. Why he can't put off this dog thing until after the holidays or move it to another location I'll never understand."

"MUTTS is trying to ensure as many dogs as possible have homes through the winter." She looked at Brad. as she spoke.

"What happened to those animals before MUTTS was formed?" Myra snapped back. "I don't mean to sound unsympathetic, but holiday shopping is more than an exciting time for folks. It can also mean the difference between success or failure for merchants, you included. Certainly you won't let what you feel for Brad make you forget that."

I don't dare.

"What did she want?" Brad asked after she'd hung up.

Shannon told him, eliminating only Myra's anger. "There's more. The fliers they want us to give our customers—they need my help."

"When?"

"Now."

"Are you going?"

Two pieces of apple pie waited on the kitchen counter. She'd wanted nothing more than to sit next to Brad while they ate dessert—that and allowing their relationship to take the next step, one that would culminate with their offering their bodies to each other and her staying the night. But if she gave in to her heart and body's need, maybe by spring she'd be out of business. Her throat aching, she told him that.

"How is helping direct traffic to the Nichols place going to benefit you financially?" he asked.

"It-it's not just that. The whole holiday season—it has to be successful. If potential customers think we're small potatoes and can't deliver on an advertising campaign, they won't come back."

"Shannon, the fate of the free world doesn't hinge on whether or not people have their pictures taken before Christmas."

He was right, of course. Still, did he have to sound and act as if her concerns were unimportant? If only she weren't so confused.

"We wouldn't be having this discussion if you'd agreed to let the merchants use the museum," she blurted.

"And throw the dogs out? Is that what you're saying?"

No! No! "I don't care how you interpret my words." Feeling as if she might fly apart, she started toward the entryway where her coat waited, then faced him. His face was precious to her and she felt lost in his eyes. Still—

"Brad, if you're sick someday, you'll still have a job. It isn't the same for me. Everything's on my shoulders, everything."

"I realize that."

"Do you?" In a moment she'd start crying. "You mentioned our going to the coast. I'd love to do that, but I can't simply hire someone to take care of business for me. I don't have the money. Maybe—maybe I will before much longer, but right now I have to do everything I possibly can to keep my doors open and my bills paid. And if that means spending the night designing a flier instead—instead of with you . . ."

* * *

"You look awful."

Wendi's cheeks flamed. The girl stammered, trying to find a way to blunt the impact of what she'd just said, but Shannon knew she was right.

"No sleep will do that to a person," she admitted.

"No sleep?" Wendi slipped out of her rain jacket, careful not to get any drops on the quilts. "Are you telling me you and Brad spent—"

"No, we didn't," she interrupted, then unnecessarily explained that designing, copying, and distributing fliers had taken a massive chunk out of her night. What she didn't tell the teenager was when she'd finally crawled into bed, sleep had remained a world away.

Insane as it was, even though she had no idea what she'd say to Brad, she'd spent the day hoping he'd call. He hadn't.

"So how has business been?" Wendi asked, her features registering concern.

"Okay, I guess." Grateful Wendi hadn't prodded, she walked over to the window and looked out. The blasted rain had started at dawn and still showed no sign of letting up. Fortunately, the little white lights were left on all the time, and they cast a welcome if weak glow over everything. "Do you know what the forecast is for the weekend?" she asked. "If it pours . . ."

"It depends on which forecaster you're listening to," Wendi said. "You look like a kid who's been told she can't go out at recess. Why don't you take advantage of the lull and take a walk?"

"In this?" She indicated the rain.

"Sure. If I can swim over here, you can do the same. Besides, there's nothing like getting away for a little bit to put things into perspective."

Wendi was right. She'd been cooped up inside her

shop all day, trapped with the echoes of last night's argument with Brad. She needed to clear her head, try to decide what to get her father for Christmas, try to remember all the words to "Joy To The World," try to stop wondering whether Brad had eaten the pie she'd cut for him, try to answer the question of where she'd spend Christmas morning now she and Brad wouldn't be together. Try to find a way to stop hurting.

It wouldn't take long to walk over to the museum and see what the last-minute sign the merchants had put up looked like. She certainly wouldn't go inside. She had no reason to see *him*.

NINE

Thanks to Wendi's umbrella, Shannon was still relatively dry when she reached the museum grounds. She'd heard business often picked up in early evening as people did some shopping on their way home. It looked as if, despite the rain, that was starting. She couldn't remember what the statistics for last-minute shopping were, but with any kind of luck, she'd do some decent business right before Christmas—maybe enough that she could afford to hire Wendi to run things while she and Brad . . .

There wasn't going to be a getaway for her and Brad, not after the way they'd parted last night. Why couldn't she get her heart to understand that simple fact?

Caught in the dark cloud cast by the fatal words they'd spoken to each other, she didn't notice the massive new sign until she nearly bumped into it. It had been fastened to metal stakes driven into the ground and angled so no one could drive into town without seeing it—without feeling overwhelmed by it.

The wooden monstrosity had been painted on both sides, the two-foot-high red and green block letters urging everyone to begin or end their trip to Oro by having their picture taken outside an authentic historic house. The printing was anything but historic, and the proclamation included a grinning Santa Claus surrounded by garishly costumed elves. Someone had hung several strands of conventional Christmas lights over the sign's edge. They blinked relentlessly, reds, greens, blues, yellows, purples turning the raindrops into a light show.

Behind the display, all but hidden by it, was the simple black and white sign the MUTTS people had set out.

Feeling sick, Shannon could only stand and stare at what had been done. She tried to tell herself whoever had erected the commercial advertisement had been concerned with little except maximizing exposure. In today's material climate, that was normal operating procedure. Surely there hadn't been a blatant attempt to undermine what Brad and the other members of MUTTS were trying to accomplish. And yet maybe . . .

Brad had to have seen it. He was entirely within his rights to take down the abomination, yet he'd allowed it to remain, to jeopardize his hopes of finding homes for . . .

"Well, what do you think?"

Startled, she stared at Cliff Jensen, who she now realized had been there all along.

"It's huge," she blurted. "I had no idea it was going to be this big."

"Neither did anyone else when we started." Cliff wiped at the rain running down the freshly painted sheet of wood. "But the more we thought about it, the more sense it made to have it as large as possible."

"The lights." She managed. "They're—they're so different from what's been done throughout the town."

"You've got that right." He sounded pleased. "There's no way anyone can fail to notice."

Be overwhelmed is more like it, she thought. She indicated the small MUTTS announcement. "Was that deliberate? People are at odds with Brad, so they've decided to undermine his venture?"

"Of course not." Cliff looked hurt. "Shannon, there's

an article on the front page of today's paper about MUTTS. Didn't you see it?"

She shook her head.

"I knew it was coming out," Cliff explained. "That's why I took charge of designing this." He again tried to wipe rain off Santa's face. "Brad and MUTTS got the newspaper. The merchants get a sign."

"Has—has he said anything to you?"

"Nope. Shannon, the way I see it, he knows you're involved and he's not going to do anything to mess up his relationship with you. That's working to our advantage, so thank you."

Their 'relationship,' as Cliff put it, was more than messed up. It no longer existed.

Her teeth clenched against the pain in her heart, she nodded. She didn't trust herself to speak. What she was going through emotionally was none of Cliff's business, but maybe, just maybe, Brad still had enough compassion for her that he was concerned about her ability to financially support herself. That's why he hadn't objected to the outrage she was staring at.

"Look, I've got to be going," Cliff said. "I saw the flier you threw together last night. Not a bad job. Not bad at all."

Whether it was good or not meant nothing to her. Numb and yet alive with emotions she had no control over, she stood on the wet and leaf-strewn grass while raindrops relentlessly thudded onto the umbrella. She felt alone, isolated, trapped by the storm and yet needing it. What was it the mayor had said during the tree lighting ceremony? That the miners' Christmases had been much like this, a day defined by the weather.

After a moment, she turned away from the headache-producing flashing lights and focused on the town with its subtle and peaceful decorations. She loved Oro. It was part of both today and yesterday, ageless and yet part of this world. Hopefully most of its visitors would sense and touch base with the past during their time here. Beyond that, when they walked into her shop, they'd realize history's traditions held true and had a place in the future.

That's what she wanted Oro and her part in it to be about, not some makeshift and garish sign exhorting people to spend even more money.

Money. Christmas wasn't about that—neither was life. The town's first residents had gifted each other with songs and companionship, nothing more.

Looking around, she spotted the electrical cord in the grass and pulled apart the connection. Her headache faded the moment the lights stopped their demented blinking. Political or any other kind of opposition wasn't in her nature, but this was so out of character with what Oro should be, so wrong. She couldn't do anything about the sign itself, short of ripping it out of the ground, but . . .

The sodden soil under her feet made her wonder if she was going to lose her boots in the mud, but it didn't matter. What did was pulling up the MUTTS sign and then replanting it on the narrow strip of grass between the street and sidewalk. Standing back, she surveyed what she'd done. Better. Much better. Dignified and simple. There was nothing left for her to do except go back to work.

Instead, she studied what Brad had had a hand in creating. The uncluttered sketch showed a trio of dogs huddled together. The words said everything:

ALL THEY WANT FOR CHRISTMAS IS A HOME.

Eyes burning, she looked over at the museum. A man was standing on the covered cement porch, watching her. *Brad.*

"I tried to call the shop," he said when their respective steps had brought them together, his voice surrounded by and yet separate from the storm. "Wendi said you'd gone for a walk. I was going to look for you when I spotted you."

Her legs trembled a little, but it wasn't from the cold. She didn't speak until they'd walked to the museum and she stood on the porch near him but not touching.

"Why didn't you do what I just did?" she asked. "You would have been within your rights."

"It was your call."

Was it? At the moment, she was only sure how much she needed his arms around her, needed to spend Christmas with him and Yapper and the quail.

"I want MUTTS to succeed," she told him.

"And I want the same for your business."

Not yet ready to risk looking into his eyes, she studied her handiwork. Because neither sign was lighted, the gray drizzle nearly hid them. Maybe she and Brad could come up with a solution for that, some clear, clean lighting, but she couldn't concentrate on anything except him and the long, long hours they'd spent apart.

"Why didn't you call?" It might be the hardest question she'd ever asked, but it had to be done.

His sigh rumbled through her. "Both of us needed space. Time to think."

What decisions had he come to? That their priorities were too many worlds apart?

"Yes," she managed. "We did."

She heard him suck in a breath. "I have to hear it, Shannon. Last night, after you left, how did it feel to you?"

"Feel?"

"Did you believe you'd done the right thing?"

He was asking too much of her, needing words when she didn't go beyond emotion.

"Maybe," she managed. "I—I thought a lot about what we said to each other."

"Did you?"

She opened her mouth to tell him of the thoughts that had bombarded her, but someone had strung tiny pale lights around the museum porch and "Silent Night" played faintly from inside the building. The dogs up for adoption must already be in there; she heard one and then another yip playfully.

A steady stream of cars drove past, and yet the rain muted most of the sound. The stars, ageless and mysterious, waited far beyond the clouds. Those stars had witnessed Oro's first days, been there when Brad's grandfather had talked about rain being a farmer's silver. They'd still be there when she and Brad no longer existed.

"You're right. You have to care about your financial future. I don't want you to think I'm downplaying that."

"I know you aren't. But my success shouldn't come at the expense of what the past's lessons are about, what's really important in life."

"What is important? What are you thinking?" Brad asked. He was so close, warmth and life.

"That this is what it's all about." She held out her hand to capture the rain dripping off the roof. "The larger picture."

"More important than what concerns you and me?"

"Oh, yes."

"Shannon, that's why I was looking for you. To tell you that something special has started between us, and I don't want it to be jeopardized by—by . . ." He pointed at the competing signs. "I want to spend Christmas Eve with you, just you. Everything else is secondary. Everything else can be put into perspective."

"Yes, it can."

It didn't matter which of them reached for the other.

Now, nestled within the warmth and safety and right-ness of Brad's embrace, her heart began to sing.

"It can't be just the two of us," she whispered. "You have Yapper, and I don't want him to be alone."

He started to say something, but the yips and barks increased in volume. Laughing, they stood together with the rain falling all around. The drops landing on the shake roof overhead made their own music and turned silver in the muted light. When he leaned down and she rose up and their mouths met, his heartbeat became part of the music.

"Shannon," he whispered, his lips still against hers.

"What?"

"I want more than Christmas Eve. Tonight . . . will you come to my place?"

"Yes."

He didn't say anything, only held her closer so she no longer knew where she left off and he began. Not that it mattered. She was crying a little, tears warm with happiness and the wonder of falling in love.

"Brad," she whispered with the last of her sanity, "I need a Christmas gift from you. Just one."

He waited.

"A dog so I can give it the gift of a home."

COMING IN DECEMBER FROM
ZEBRA BOUQUET ROMANCES

#25 SEDUCING TONY by Jona Jaffrey
___(0-8217-6439-X, $3.99) Caught in the juiciest scandal to hit New York City in years, maverick newspaperman Tony Ross finds his life in ruins— until he meets Eden, a beautiful, mysterious woman who offers solace and nights of sensuous abandon.

#26 MOUNTAIN MOONLIGHT by Jane Anderson
___(0-8217-6440-3, $3.99) Vala Channing can't decide which is more dangerous—the fact that she's about to take her troubled young son trekking in Arizona's Superstition Mountains or that the guide who will lead them is the one man from her past she's never managed to forget.

#27 EVERY BREATH YOU TAKE by Suzanne McMinn
___(0-8217-6441-1, $3.99) When harrassing phone calls turn more menacing, Natalie Buchanan makes a desperate call to the police, never expecting Officer Miller Brannigan to show up at her door. Years ago, she'd broken their engagement. But Natalie underestimated the depth of Miller's love . . . and the persistence of her own feeling for him.

#28 FIREWORKS by Cindy Hillyer
___(0-8217-6442-X, $3.99) Assuming responsibility for a five-year-old niece has softened New Orleans divorce attorney Bullock Stockwell in ways he could've never imagined. For when beautiful pediatrician M. K. Channing arrives in his office to give a deposition in his latest case, he finds himself considering a partnership . . . of the romantic kind.

Call toll free **1-888-345-BOOK** to order by phone or use this coupon to order by mail.
Name _____
Address _____
City _____ State _____ Zip _____
Please send me the books I have checked above.
I am enclosing $_____
Plus postage and handling* $_____
Sales tax (in Ny and TN) $_____
Total amount enclosed $_____
*Add $2.50 for the first book and $.50 for each additional book.
Send check or money order (no cash or CODs) to:
Kensington Publishing Corp., 850 Third Avenue, New York, NY 10022
Prices and numbers subject to change without notice. Valid only in the U.S.
All books will be available 10/1/99. All orders subject to availability.
Visit our website at **www.kensingtonbooks.com**